THE FIVE TURNS OF THE WHEEL

THE FIVE TURNS OF THE WHEEL

by
Stephanie Ellis

The Five Turns of the Wheel
Copyright 2020 © Stephanie Ellis

Edited by Kenneth W. Cain

Cover illustration and design by Elizabeth Leggett.
www.archwayportico.com

First Brigids Gate Press Edition: May 2022
First Edition printed by Silver Shamrock Press: October 2020.

ISBN (paperback): 978-1-957537-21-4
ISBN (Kindle ebook): 978-1-957537-20-7
Library of Congress Control Number: 2022937445

BRIGIDS GATE PRESS
Bucyrus, Kansas
www.brigidsgatepress.com

Printed in the United States of America

With much love to my parents, Alan and Elsie Brooks. Without our years at The Cider House, The Five Turns would never have been born.

Content warnings are provided at the end of this book.

ACKNOWLEDGEMENTS

The Five Turns of the Wheel holds a special place in my heart. The world I created derived from the country pub where I lived for a number of years. Without The Cider House and its regulars, this book wouldn't have come into being – one day I might even reveal the customer on whom Betty was based! It is also a book that I have watched Steve Ventura from Brigids Gate Press promote regularly and tirelessly when it was first published by Silver Shamrock and when his own publishing company was no more than a twinkle in his and his wife Heather's, eye. For that support alone, above everything else they have done for me, I would like to thank both Heather and Steve. In a way, it feels as though Five Turns has found its natural home.

There are also friends and writers who have offered their support for Five Turns – Laurel Hightower, T.C. Parker, Kev Harrison, Alyson Faye – in its first publication and whose opinions I value highly. It helps keep the old imposter syndrome at bay – as did the knowledge that Jonathan Maberry himself, rated the book. The gang on Discord – Steve, Heather, Max, Laurie, Cindy and Kim – have also continued to offer words of encouragement. To them, thank you for giving me the confidence to continue, thanks I would also like to extend to those who offered advice and support during the recent turmoil in the publication world.

As always, my family play a big part in my writing life. With the children grown, they are all supportive of my decision to make writing the career I have long wanted. To my husband Geraint and our children, Bethan, Dylan and Rhonwen, thank you for giving me the space and time to write my words.

And to everyone who's ever read my work, thank you. It means the world.

FROM THE WEALD HERALD
21ST DECEMBER, 2021

Extract from *A Weald Miscellany*, a collection of folk songs rediscovered in the home of Megan Cooper née Wheelborn, late of The Five Turns Inn in Cropsoe. Very little remains of the former village. Recent storms destroyed many buildings, and the whereabouts of the previous inhabitants are unknown. This particular song has piqued the interest of folklorist, Edward Redman with its mention of Tommy, Fiddler, and Betty. The three form an unholy trinity about whom many grim and dark tales have been written. Whether they really existed is something he hopes to discover. He is currently researching the villages of the Weald, and we will be publishing the first of his articles in the near future.

Readers will find this song follows the melody of the famous hymn, *Lord of the Dance.*

The Dance

They danced in the night
As the world was begun.
They danced for Hweol,
Nature's only son.
They played their music
And they took sacrifice
From Man's blood and bones
To turn the Wheel of Life.

Dance, then, wherever you may be.
I'll lead you all in the Dance, said he,
Five times, five turns of the Wheel, said he.
This is a Dance for eternity

Tommy called the tune

While Fiddler struck the bow.
Betty was the monster
No maid should ever know.
They came in the Winter
And they took Five Turns,
Five nights in all
So that humans learned.

To

Dance, then, wherever they may be.
Dance to the tune of the Unholy Three.
Five times, Five Turns of the Wheel, said he.
This is a Dance for eternity

On one last night
From beyond the human veil,
The Umbrans came,
Let their spirits unfurl.
They gorged on the flesh
Of myriad murdered souls,
All for the Mother
They had never really owned.

Dance, then …

At last the Mother woke,
Saw the sky was black
And the Son's corruption.
A devil on Man's back,
She stopped the Wheel;
Made the Umbrans learn
That Hweol's will
Was no longer hers.

Dance, dance …

The Mother sent them back
To the OtherWorld.
Though the Three would live,
The Wheel no longer turned.
Her sons and daughters
Were finally free,
And the land once more
Was left in peace

CHAPTER ONE
THE RETURN

Across the cave's floor, two other shapes moved. The darkness did not hide them from one another. It was their natural habitat. He could see Betty, huge and bearlike in appearance but with the eyes of a wolf. Small in comparison was their other brother, Fiddler. A creature no less dangerous, despite his more diminutive size.

"It's time," said Tommy, stretching out limbs stiff from hibernation. His stomach growled. He was hungry.

He stood and walked slowly to the entrance. Across the clearing was another dwelling. The House of Hweol, their father. Its entrance was edged in bone, the jaws of some ancient monster. Hweol would sleep for a while longer. It was for Tommy and his brothers to lead the return.

He breathed in, the air cold and crisp. It told him of lengthening nights and the change of the seasons. The villages that lay beyond the border of their Umbran home were waiting.

"Will we Dance?" asked Fiddler.

"Yes," said Tommy. "We will need your music to lead us and Betty to bring laughter."

Betty grinned. "I have a wardrobe ready and a new dress was made for me before we slept."

"Then we are ready," said Tommy. "Time to visit our Wheelborn family, see what mischief they've been up to in our absence. I hope they haven't been getting any ideas."

"We'll soon find out," said Fiddler. "They can't hide anything from us. Not when they share our blood."

"Some can," said Betty. "The mothers."

Tommy sighed. That state was a continued annoyance. It meant the women could keep secrets from him. The people of Umbra worshipped Mother Nature, and one of Her commandments was the reverence of the status of all who became mothers themselves. It was a nuisance. Hweol and his Umbran family demanded blood and would not let such a nicety get in their way. Their father had developed their rituals in apparent reverence of the Mother whilst subverting it to their own needs. The three had never been stopped or punished by Her. Tommy regarded this as the same as receiving Her blessing. The Mother loved her sons. "Time for a little reconnaissance."

"A rehearsal?" asked Fiddler, picking up his instrument case.

The fiddle had been newly strung before they closed their eyes, and his brother was itching to play it as much as Betty wanted to wear his new dress. It wouldn't harm anything to let them off the leash for a while before they returned to the village of Cropsoe. He would go with them a little way, listen in on the gossip, and then he would leave to walk his own path. It was for Tommy to lead their return and begin the rituals of the Dance. The Five Nights. The Five Turns.

They walked overgrown tracks, their route imprinted on memory, to the edge of the forest. Ahead lay the path that would take them to whichever one of the six villages in the Weald they wished to visit. A way hidden from the human eye unless the Umbrans pulled the veil aside.

As they walked the path, Tommy sent his mind out across the landscape. He could see into every village, every house, every heart.

Not far ahead of the three, they saw a small group heading towards Fleshing. Two had fishing rods and their friends carried blankets and a picnic basket. *All we need to round off a beautiful autumnal day*, thought Tommy, *is a bit of entertainment.*

"Fancy a dry run?" he asked his brothers, nodding his head in the direction of the party.

"Why not," said Fiddler. "Doesn't do to get rusty."

Tommy thought of the swords waiting for him in Cropsoe. Their blades never rusted. That particular Dance would have to wait.

"Put your dress on, Betty," he said. "We've a performance to give."

Betty gave a yelp of delight and pulled his dress from the bag. The three walked innocently toward the group. Nothing more than a traditional mummers troupe. The teller of tales, the player of songs, and the comedian in the woman's dress with a woman's name. For centuries, such travelling bands had performed across the British Isles in this manner. These three could recount their histories with accuracy. They had been there.

It didn't take long. Tommy kept to the three-act structure for their show. A quick run-through before the main events of the coming days. He was pleased with the result. Fiddler's bow had been sharp, Betty's punchlines a knockout, and Tommy's stories had ended well.

They walked back up the road to the river from which their audience had come. It didn't take long to wash the blood off. The taste had heightened their hunger, increased their need to get back to the villages of the Weald.

They returned to their original route. Tommy could see Cropsoe in the distance, waiting for him.

"High Ridge farm," said Fiddler, nodding towards a nearby hill. "Shall we take a look?"

Tommy nodded. "Always worth checking in. Make sure the lesson learned holds."

It was late afternoon and the sun still shone, although it was a cold light. Summer was becoming a distant memory. Trees added a splash of colour, their leaves having turned. They had gone from green to that last glorious palette of reds and golds, yellows and browns. Hedgerows were revealing empty nests and skeletal branches. The three tramped across fields bristling with stubble, the crops long harvested. The soil needed ploughing. Nourishing. Tommy could do something about that when the occasion demanded. The Weald was beautiful. This little pocket of England was theirs and Tommy intended it would remain so. Their visits ensured the modern world was kept clearly at arm's length.

The trio found themselves a position overlooking the farmhouse. They made no attempt to hide themselves as they could only be seen when they wished it.

Three men stood outside the house, or rather a man and two youths. A father and his sons. There was no mother. Not anymore. She had become part of the land.

Betty started to sway, and Fiddler was humming.

"I can hear her," said Betty. "She's still singing."

Tommy looked at the nearby hedge. The interwoven branches were not wood, but bone. She protected the land, held it in a maternal embrace. She had died because of the mistakes of her children. They could never forget.

He could see by the way anxiety had etched itself on their faces. No doubt they were casting about in their minds for anything they had done wrong this time. Their father steadied them with an arm around each shoulder.

"Will we choose him?" asked Betty. "I would like to see him Dance."

Tommy threw his brother a quick look. The man had no compassion. He was a monster. This father had already given much—or rather, his wife had. If any of them were chosen, there would be nothing they could do and his sons would have to accept it. This time, however, it would be an honour, not a punishment. It was all a dance, and the Dance was only just beginning.

Tommy smiled. The memories remained, and the lesson had been learned. A hard lesson, but necessary.

The three tramped on, using their path to take them from Ashburn to Scythington and Soulsbury, Reaper's Hill and Fleshing.

At the latter settlement, they saw a group of youths gathering for a 'pre-Dance' party, clutching beers and old bottles of spirits probably raided from parents' cupboards. They had forgotten those who Danced before. One of the tricks Tommy played on them in the guise of a blessing.

"Spare a drink for an old man," said Fiddler, wandering up to the group.

"Only if you play us a tune," said one.

They hadn't recognised him. Tommy would lift the curtain of memory soon enough. In the meantime, he would let Fiddler have his bit of fun.

"I thought you'd never ask," said Fiddler, pulling his fiddle from its case and plucking its strings.

His notes took control of their minds, and soon they were all laughing and dancing to Fiddler's tune.

Tommy nodded to his brother and walked on with Betty, leaving the sound of the music behind. They would meet up again later.

Through the village they rambled and Tommy saw old women sitting motionless at their windows. In a back garden, one woman sat seemingly oblivious to the grandchildren who tugged excitedly at her skirt. He knew where her mind had gone. To that night of the Dance which celebrated not the Maid or the Mother, but the Crone. All ages of woman were venerated in their celebrations.

"Have you chosen?" asked Betty, as they continued on their way.

"Yes," said Tommy. "Want to see? Or would you rather it be kept as a surprise?"

He didn't wait for an answer. Betty was too impatient. Whenever he'd planned a surprise for his brother, Betty discovered it early. Sometimes with disastrous results, despite the planned end result usually being the same. Blood was never wasted in their family.

He led the way to Reaper's Hill. To Anne Slattery's house. He could see her in the garden with her friend Rose, hear their quiet chatter. That one had a few years left in her yet, unlike Anne.

Anne had poured them a sherry each. They sat quietly, watching the path he walked. The old saw and understood so much. They could sense the change, feel the turn of the land.

"Not long," said Rose, sipping her drink.

"No," said Anne.

"Who do you think will be chosen?" asked Rose.

"Can't you tell," said Anne. "Can't you smell the taint on me?"

"No," said Rose. "We won't know until the actual day."

Tommy knew Rose was lying, as did Anne. That was what friends were for. They would lie to keep dark thoughts away for a little longer. Across the Weald it would be the same. Grandmothers gathered together or sat alone, all focused on the one night when the Crone was celebrated.

"It is an honour," said Anne.

She was right. It was the privilege of the chosen Crone to know it was their time.

"Yes," said Rose.

This time they were both lying and so was Tommy. It wasn't an honour. It was an extra layer of suffering he inflicted on the women. An additional enjoyment.

Betty was pacing up and down behind him. Fidgeting. "I'm bored."

"Soulsbury," said Tommy. "Playtime."

Betty perked up and started skipping ahead of him. He was a child at heart.

In Soulsbury, the children were outside. It was a time of playing before the final summons indoors. They could hear the shrieks as the youngsters played hide and seek, darting in and out of hedgerows, jumping out of ditches. The atmosphere was charged on the night of the return and the children could sense it. It sent their spirits soaring higher. As it did to Betty. Tommy could see their parents shaking their heads. They would have a difficult job getting them off to sleep tonight. A feeling he knew well, as he regarded his brother fondly.

They found themselves outside the last house on the road out of the village. Could see and hear the husband and wife inside. They had successfully called in their offspring and were now talking in the front room.

"Tell them the story," said the man.

Good, thought Tommy. *This is as it should be.*

"You tell them," said his wife. "They're children. No need to open their eyes so soon."

She was angry. She didn't want them to learn the ways. Not good. Women. They should know better. Should be obedient.

"They're old enough," continued the father.

"Then tell them," said his wife, and walked out of the room. Left her husband gazing out the window straight at Tommy, although he could not see the man his wife hated so much.

Tommy smiled. Time to change all that. Get things moving. He showed himself to the father, watched his eyes darken as he was claimed by the spell Tommy cast on the land.

When his wife returned, Tommy watched her back away from her husband, understanding the expression on her partner's face. She could do nothing except keep her distance.

He could tell her she was safe. He had already chosen each for the Five Turns, and also for the Sixth Turn, when all his Umbran brethren would join in the Dance. Nobody in the Weald mentioned the Sixth Turn if they could help it. It was perfectly understandable.

The Wheel of Life turned faster, it was pulling him on, back to Cropsoe.

"Do you want to stay, Betty?" he asked.

The giant stood beneath the children's bedroom window.

"Yes, I'd like to hear the story," he said. "Make sure they get it right." He grinned.

Tommy nodded. "I'll see you at The Five Turns, then."

"Will you be going straight there?"

"No," said Tommy. "Something tells me I have to make another call first."

Betty nodded and settled himself down beneath the bedroom window. He loved bedtime stories. Especially when they were about him. About monsters.

Tommy left him there. He was thinking about the Fifth Turn. The Night of the Unborn. There was a woman, a new mother. He could smell her on the air, the closer he got to Cropsoe.

Catherine. He could always smell a mother. He walked the back lanes of Cropsoe and made his way to her house. It was as if a thread pulled him toward her. He wove the web, and she was the fly. He gazed up at a lighted window. Used his third eye to see into the room, a nursery. A baby slept peacefully in her cot. A daughter. Small. She was one born too early. As soon as he detected that, Tommy's anger grew.

This was a child who should not be here, should have remained in the womb. She was to have been the offering of the Fifth Turn, but her mother had thwarted them.

Catherine looked anxious, tense.

And so you should, my dear, thought Tommy. *You do not take what is not yours.*

The child should've been their gift to Hweol. Her sacrifice would've allowed the Weald to continue to prosper and, in so doing, give life to Umbra.

The Weald. He looked back along his path. Saw the landscape darken, charcoal hills hiding the red claw of nature—a weapon gloved in velvet that tore flesh from bone during the daylight hours. Pitch forests and woods wove their own canopy of black over other crimes. Every little death camouflaged so that only the rural idyll remained in view. The Weald was Mother Nature's cradle, her cycle of life driving everything from birth to death.

"Thought you could escape from me?" asked Tommy.

He saw her start. Peer nervously out the window. He would let her hear him but not see him, not yet.

"Remember Mary?"

She continued to stare in his direction, trying to seek him out.

"She was to have had a child. Decided to escape. You watched her walk out of Cropsoe, didn't you? Shall I tell you where she went? Do you want to know where she is lying? Her final resting place?"

Catherine moved back from the window.

"She didn't go beyond the Weald. Her body is feeding Nature as intended. All of you are expected to return to the soil, one way or another."

He heard Emily whimper slightly behind her mother. The child was sleeping, dreaming. He knew those dreams, was creating them for her.

Catherine rushed over and scooped her up into her arms, held her close. Small and soft and so helpless. He would visit soon. Hold the baby, give her his blessing. The father was no problem. He knew his place, what he was required to offer up.

Tommy's stomach growled a little louder. He sniffed the air. It carried a tang of something earthy, something from beyond. It was the smell of his family.

He set off again along the lane, pushed aside the veil between the modern world and Umbra, allowing those creatures to step through the curtain, into the light.

"I beat you," she cried, through the window, holding her child tight. "I won."

"Did you?" he called back, turning to see her reach for another of those bottles that gave her the strength to speak so to him. Her defiance would be punished.

They both knew the answer. She staggered, spilled the drink, dropped it. Glass and wine went everywhere. Emily was crying.

The nursery door burst open and her husband appeared on the scene. Tommy had known he was coming. Wanted to see the explosion. He wasn't disappointed.

CHAPTER TWO
TOMMY

When the season changes, the Wheel turns. That's what the locals say. When the Wheel turns, the Dance begins. Tommy looked down the meandering lane leading into Cropsoe, sensed the itch both in himself and the land. *Soon*, he thought, *soon*. First, he had to get the swords. Their blades had a song to sing, and they'd been silent too long.

He walked toward the village, continuing to enjoy the sharp tang of late autumn, the vibrant colours on trees soon to be stripped of their remaining foliage. Only Tommy walked this road on the return. His coat, a patchwork of animal skins, hung loosely on his frame. His hair, wild and unkempt, snaked down his back. A peacock feather dangled from the top hat clamped on his head. His boots crunched satisfyingly amongst fallen crimson and gold leaves. Nature had rolled out her carpet for him

He paused and reached down to pick up some of the castoffs. Brittle and dry, they turned to dust in his desiccated hands. There was still flesh there, as gnarled and rough as the trees which so thoughtfully provided this welcome. How many years had he walked this way? He couldn't remember, nor could he recall how it had begun, how *he* began.

The wind was stirring, lifting the leaves into swirling shapes, rainbow fingers dancing, as he would soon. It urged him on, back into the world which lay waiting for him as it did this time every year. He fixed his bright grey eyes on the road ahead. Alert and eager, they sought the soft curves of the landscape, the open fields and woodland borders.

As he walked, the setting sun burnished the sky with a final blaze of gold. This was his time. The moment between day and night, light and dark, when shadows moved and wanderers stirred. This was when things that should not be—the monstrous and the grotesque—returned. Like Tommy and his family. It sharpened his appetite further. With each step, the road widened, and he soon found himself on the edge of the village. A settlement of thirty families, never more, never less. His visits ensured its stability. The entertainment he provided ensured its continuation—and his own.

It was the same in the surrounding villages of the Weald—the five he had passed through on his way here. Census returns showed no deviation from this figure. Nobody from the outside ever queried it or asked how such a thing could be in times of rising population. Cropsoe was the hub sat in the middle of the wheel containing the other villages. A road led from each directly to its centre.

Down the darkening lane he walked. A silent thoroughfare, it was always empty on the night of his arrival. Ahead, lay his destination. Well-lit and inviting. Warmth and laughter danced behind those windows. Oh, the Dance. No one could escape its call. Tonight was only the beginning.

Above, the pub sign swung gently, and Tommy doffed his hat to The Five Turns as he always did. The painting showed the Five Turns that man would make for him when they joined Tommy in his Dance. In the image, one man held five swords aloft in a pentacle. These were the swords Tommy carried on each Turn. Their razor-edged steel a warning to the villagers. Here, was where they rested. This was their home. Simon Wheelborn, the landlord would have them ready, but first they would drink the Dance in.

As always, Simon opened the door to him, and Tommy stepped fully back into the world. He inhaled the aroma of beer and cider, welcomed the warmth of the fire in the old Victorian range. Without saying a word, the landlord handed him a pewter tankard, a peacock feather etched into its side. This was his own pot. Nobody but he ever drank from this jar. Two others occupied hooks on either side of where his own had hung. Betty's and Fiddler's. They would appear in their own time. He was always the first to arrive, it allowed him to renew old acquaintances, remind them of their place.

Tommy sipped his cider, enjoyed the scent of apple and earth, the slight tartness giving it bite. He stretched his legs out, felt the life return, the blood flowing easier in his body. He flexed the fingers of his right hand. The deep grooves carved into his flesh disappeared as his skin plumped out, becoming smooth and pink as the years fell away.

Sheltered by the stone arch containing the range, Tommy could enjoy its comfort and warmth whilst being able to take in the rest of the bar; a sight as warming as the flames. An old oak bench ran around the edge of the room with tables and stools scattered in between. Across from where he sat, some farmers were playing quoits. Burly, weathered men throwing small rubber hoops over a steel nail. He smiled. It was a game he was fond of, but he didn't use hoops. He preferred things on a somewhat larger scale.

Now and again, the other customers would shoot glances in his direction, but on the whole, they ignored him. They hadn't been summoned and could pursue their own amusements free from his influence for the time being. He emptied his pint and placed his tankard on the nearby table. It was the signal for Simon Wheelborn to come over and join him.

Tommy had known many Wheelborns. They had lived in the pub for generations, been part of the Dance since time immemorial. All knew their blood intermingled but, by mutual agreement, no one spoke of it. Theirs was a tangled family tree, branches interweaving and looping back, a never-ending forest of tortuous and almost incestuous connections. They only needed to look in the mirror. He wondered if Simon ever considered it, valued its privilege. The man lowered himself carefully onto the bench next to him. He refilled Tommy's empty tankard from the jug he carried over, and took a drink from his own glass.

"Welcome," said Simon, his grey eyes regarding Tommy steadily.

Tommy raised his pint, and they toasted each other. "Trade good then, Simon?"

"Can't complain, can't complain," said the landlord. "A lot of pubs have gone out of business in recent times, but we've kept going. We've kept Turning."

The comment was an acknowledgement of Tommy's own role in the continued success of the establishment. Without his patronage, they both knew the inn would have gone under long ago.

"Time to Turn again," said Tommy.

"Time to Turn," agreed Simon, as he always did. "I have everything ready. I've put them up in your room."

Tommy nodded and held out his once-more, empty tankard. The next few days would be busy, so he always claimed this first evening as his. Simon refilled it and then headed back to the bar. An old Labrador wandered over to sniff at Tommy's worn, battered boots, at the ancient rabbit skins hanging from the edges of his coat. Tommy took its head in his hands and held it firmly. Obediently, the dog sat down, but it didn't wag its tail. Its owner watched on nervously. He did not interfere.

"Think I smell good, do you, old boy?" Tommy crooned, although nobody would've understood what he was saying, speaking as he did, in the language of the Wheel. The dog whimpered slightly and tried to pull back. Tommy tightened his grip around the animal's head. This time the owner made as if to step forward but a look from Tommy halted him.

"I have a treat for you," he continued, reaching into his pocket and pulling out something dried and dead. He held it up to his own nose and sniffed at the object. "This smells good," he said, and offered it to the dog. Again, the animal tried to turn his head away. Once more, Tommy's grip tightened. "Smell this boy. Go on. This is good. You know it is. Sniff it, breathe it in, eat. You're hungry, aren't you? Go on, there's a good boy."

He forced the dog's jaws apart, pushed the object, shrivelled as it was, into his mouth. Then he snapped the jaws shut and forced the dog's head to point upwards, making it swallow, unwilling as it was. Once or twice the animal convulsed, tried to free itself, open its jaws, but Tommy held on. "There you go, boy. All done."

He moved further forward, continued crooning in his strange tongue. Then he held the animal's face to his own, a final embrace before he released the dog and leaned back once more. The dog bolted for the open door, choking and hacking as he went. Its owner ran after him, casting a quick, frightened look at Tommy as he did so. The pub stopped its chatter at the animal's desperate exit. It was an unwelcome silence which Tommy disliked. No, that would not do. He raised his pint to the room and said something again in the old language. Immediately, everyone relaxed and good humour was restored.

Tommy's stomach growled more urgently. He thought of the dog outside. Damned animal had taken the last of his snacks. Yet he would eat soon. Simon always greeted him with both a drink and a meal, ready and waiting for him at his table. A great big juicy bloody steak. Rare. He liked his meat rare. The juices were the best part.

"Looks like you could do with a bite to eat," said Simon. "Liza reckons you could do with some fattening up."

"And how is your lovely wife?" asked Tommy.

"You'll see for yourself soon enough," said Simon.

And he would. She was something else on the menu in The Five Turns, offered freely by the landlord. Liza had no say in the matter.

"Maybe," said Tommy, thinking of their last time together. Age was beginning to tell on her. "Any other news?" There was something. He could sense Simon holding back, reluctant, fearful. "Your lovely daughter, perhaps?"

Now he saw guilt.

Simon swallowed. "Megan married old Cooper's lad a few months back." It came out in a rush, his tongue tripping over his words, terror evident.

Megan. Ah yes. Simon's only child, the apple of his eye. He'd deliberately kept her away from Tommy. The man's one small act of defiance. Did Simon think he did not know? Tommy allowed it because it suited him. He would say nothing yet. One day, she would have to join him in the Dance. *Blood will out*, he thought. *Blood will always out.*

He smiled. "Congratulations. I will have to get Fiddler to play for the happy couple. Give them our *blessing*."

He noticed with satisfaction how Simon squirmed. It never did any harm to remind him where the balance of power really lay, regardless of how he treated him almost as an equal in front of everybody else.

There was a cheer in the background as the winner of the quoits match was announced. Simon glanced in their direction.

"Go on," said Tommy. "Go and give the winner a drink, on the house."

"You don't need…"

"No," said Tommy, smiling. "You've given me plenty to get my teeth into here." He stabbed the beef with his knife, watched the blood ooze out onto the plate. A beautiful sight. "You've outdone yourself as always with your welcome," he said. "Go, look after your customers. Pretend I'm not here."

Simon rose and made his way back amongst the farmers. All present were sons of the soil, some more so than others, thought Tommy as he speared a piece of meat into his mouth. The first bite was not to be rushed. Taste was one of his favourite senses and had to be indulged. You could detect a lot by taste alone, a piece of meat, a jug of cider, a person's fear. Emotions were the greatest delicacy of all, and there would be a feast to indulge in over the next few days.

Alongside his steak he could taste the men around him. The sweat from the day's work, the animals they husbanded, the soil they turned, their humour and their pain, their petty jealousies and rivalries. His stomach stopped growling as it took its fill. Tonight would not sate his hunger. Only the Dance could do that, but it was serving up the perfect appetizer.

He chewed with deliberation, allowed his teeth to shape themselves once more to the task in hand. He discarded the knife and fork, picked up the slab of meat with one hand, and bit into it. A piece came away as easily as if he'd carved it with a cleaver. Blood ran down his chin, and he chewed with relish, deliberately keeping his mouth open so those around him would see his teeth at work. So they would notice their sharpness, see how they guillotined their way so easily through the meat. It would remind them of his task, of the swords. Eventually, his plate was empty.

"Time, gentlemen, please," called Liza, ringing the small brass bell over the counter.

Tommy grinned. With the end of business, she could avoid him no longer. She greeted him reluctantly, asked to speak to him privately about Megan. She showed more guts than her husband. He would enjoy their conversation. He invited her to sit down. Reminisce.

And then it was just him and Simon sitting on either side of the fireplace. Drinking, not talking, allowing the turn of the Wheel to absorb their mood, pull them into the parts it required them to play. Empty glasses and bits of rubbish remained on the tables around them, small spillages dried into sticky patches on the quarry-tiled floor. The aftermath of a happy gathering.

Simon's customers would have gone home and told their families of his arrival. They would start preparing. In a way, they were the lucky ones. Yes, Cropsoe was always his starting point on his return to the Wheel, but only insofar he had to collect the tools of his trade - the rapper swords currently sleeping upstairs. The other villages came first. They would Dance and he would gather their tithes of blood. Cropsoe itself, was the final Turn. This was the Sixth Turn of the Wheel which nobody ever talked about. The night when the creatures of Umbra took whatever they could find and Danced for themselves. From his arrival to that final night, Cropsoe was the alpha and omega.

"Will you walk with me?" he asked Simon.

The landlord nodded. There was no real choice. This was part of the ritual.

The two men finished their pints and walked out of the pub. Tommy noticed the quick glance between husband and wife—he spotted Liza hiding around the corner—but said nothing. How they felt was not his concern. He was here to turn the Wheel. Once outside, he breathed in deeply. He inhaled everything from the village and the surrounding countryside. His hunger subsided a little more.

Across the road from the pub was the old village green. The site where they would Dance on his last night in the village. Beyond was the church of St Catherine's. Abandoned by the priests who once tried to stand up to him with their useless prayers and irrelevant Bibles.

It amused him the church was named for that particular saint, a woman martyred on the wheel. St. Catherine-by-the-Wheel. She must surely approve of what he did. He thought of Catherine on the hill, the daughter she'd birthed, the unborn denied him. Their paths would cross again soon, but she could wait.

The sky was a perfect pitch lit with gently twinkling lights. There were no clouds to mar its beauty. Cold and clear, the air rejuvenated him further. He passed through the lych gate and entered the church. Tommy had no real business there, but he took pleasure in entering the once hallowed sanctuary, to prove to Simon, if nothing else, God could not stop him. If God could not stop him, didn't that tell Simon how powerful he really was? The Mother had ordained him to follow this path. He was the child of Mother Nature. She demanded the Wheel be turned and that he was the one who would turn it.

Inside was colder than the world beyond. Most would think this was caused by the property of the stone from which it was built. Tommy knew the real reason. Others were gathered here. They always rose when he visited. Left their world of shadow to see what he would do next. All had once performed for him, taken part in his Dance. Some even lent their voices to his swords. One day he would allow them to meet with those they left behind, but not yet. That would only happen when the Dance was well and truly done. Nor did he feel threatened by their presence, despite the violence of their endings. They had known, expected nothing less, and there was no justice to be sought.

"You keep the altar clean, I see," he said.

"Thought it was the right thing to do," said Simon, slightly nervous. "Seemed the respectful thing to do."

"Respectful? I suppose. You are not a religious man yourself, so why bother?"

Simon didn't answer. Tommy knew Simon was playing *just in case*, hedging his bets. You couldn't blame him. Yet, whilst the altar was spotless, the roof was falling in. Nature was extending Her realm into the building. The Mother reclaiming what man declared as theirs.

Tommy walked back down the aisle.

Simon followed mutely, allowed himself to be led outside and into the village.

The walk Tommy took that night was one of a returning squire examining his property. Down Rose Lane they strolled, stopping every so often for Tommy to enquire about the inhabitants before they passed on to the next. Then they turned into Ivy Dene, Turnabout Close, Maiden's Lane before circling back onto the Green.

Tommy sat down on a bench outside the pub. Simon remained standing. The questions Tommy asked were superfluous. He had tasted the answers as he entered the village, as he dined in the pub. They were part of tradition, made Simon feel as if he had a part to play. Which he did, although one not as major as he'd probably like to think. Unlike his daughter.

"I think the Dance this year will be a good one," said Tommy, looking directly across at St. Catherine's once more.

"And the Wheel will turn," said Simon.

"The Wheel will turn," agreed Tommy.

They continued in silence for some time. Simon no doubt wanted to be inside, but Tommy kept him standing there, a deliberate little ploy. They'd known each other for so long, it would have been easy to allow too much familiarity. Tommy guarded against that. Even the Wheelborn of the Weald had to know their place.

It wasn't long before Tommy sensed the change he'd been waiting for. Not in the village, but in the air around him. Something else was coming. Along the lane he'd walked earlier he could hear their footsteps, eager and expectant, striding toward him. He felt the weight of their presence as they sucked new life into themselves, almost pulling Tommy and Simon from their positions.

Tommy smiled. Betty and Fiddler had arrived.

CHAPTER THREE
WYVED

Liza watched Tommy eat his steak, blood running freely down his chin. When he returned, he was always hungry—and not just for food. Tonight, her revulsion rose stronger than ever. All those years forced to share his bed, the offering coming from both her husband and her father. *Their* gift to Mother Nature. Always, they claimed the women in the Mother's name, but that was a lie. A lie which grew bigger every year. Tommy hid his evil behind the Mother, as did Hweol, Lord of Umbra, of the OtherWorld, the Son of the Mother.

After she'd Danced all those years ago and her unborn child had been offered—no, stolen—Tommy had taken her to Hweol to be Wyved. Then, when he was done, she was given back not just to Simon, but also to Tommy. A pure Wheelborn twice-husbanded, Hweol had said, a true honour. It ensured the bloodline and it had given her Megan. This child she was allowed to keep—with a proviso. Now, she had broken her promise. Megan had married another and not the one she was promised to at birth.

"So," said Tommy. "How is my lovely Wyve?"

"As well as always," said Liza.

"Simon has told me of Megan's marriage. I must offer congratulations." He smiled at her. Blood continued to drip from his chin onto the plate. "Whenever I hear of weddings, my mind often turns to our own. It gives me joy to recall such happy memories. I would like to hear you talk of them. Good cider, good food, good conversation. It's all I ask."

Liza felt sick. He had returned as cruel as ever.

"Tell me," said Tommy, "does Simon ask about Hweol and the Wyving?"

She shook her head. "Never. He prefers to pretend it didn't happen." *Like my nights with you don't happen*, she thought.

Her answer seemed to please him.

"Your father took a different view from what I remember," said Tommy.

That was true. Her father had regarded it as an 'arranged' marriage. A practice not much different to those of the well-to-do families of times gone by, who bound themselves together in order to gain wealth and status. The woman remained, in this so-called enlightened age, no more than a bargaining chip. It had shored up the family's position as the foremost amongst the Wheelborn in Cropsoe. Wheelborn married to Wheelborn. Not quite cousins, but not far off.

"We could call Simon over and get him to listen. If you would like," said Tommy. He was grinning.

Liza glanced over at her husband, busy at the bar.

"No." She might want Simon to know exactly what she had had to endure but she did not want to indulge Tommy.

She had tried to talk to her husband in the past, but he'd always been too busy. Found excuse after excuse to avoid it. The bond between them had become a tenuous thread. But that thread, which appeared so fragile, was the steel of her Wheelborn heritage. It bound her to Umbra and Hweol and somewhere, almost lost beneath its skein, the Mother. It had wrapped itself around her so tightly that night, she knew it would never let her go. A foreshadowing soon to come true.

But the memory remained.

"Then tell me," said Tommy. "I tend to get nostalgic. I enjoy the stories of our past. It ties us closer together. Don't you think?"

If only she could escape, but he was right. They were tied too closely. A spark of anger flared up.

"You want to hear it? You want to hear it all?"

"That's my girl," said Tommy, unoffended at her sudden change in mood. "You've still got spirit. Tell me everything. It was the Fifth Night, wasn't it? The Fifth Turn?"

He knew exactly what night it had been. He wanted to torture her. Her suffering was as much meat to him as the steak on his plate.

"Yes," she said, feeling her rage build. "You stole my child, ripped it from my womb."

Tommy looked offended. "I didn't lay a hand on you! At least not then." Then he laughed.

Liza glared at him. "You were in the field. You directed everything."

"The Wyves looked after you though, didn't they?" said Tommy.

"If you could call it that."

Those old Crones, the Wyves of Umbra, had raised her from the field and wrapped her in a velvet cloak as crimson as the blood she'd spilled. They'd offered no comforting words.

"And the Lords led quite a procession. A real occasion." Tommy sounded almost wistful.

She remembered the Lord who'd lifted her onto his horse and held her tightly in front of him. They had taken her to Umbra, leaving the villagers of the Weald behind them on the other side of the veil. They had not been invited. Along that shadow path they had ridden, hooves muffled, horses snorting quietly. Even the imps had walked in a subdued manner. Those horrible little creatures had stopped laughing for a change.

"I don't think I was in a fit state to notice much," she snapped at Tommy.

Her vision had been blurred by exhaustion and pain. Her stomach had continued to cramp and she had felt the blood trickle warm down her leg. She had wondered how she could still bleed. Hadn't they emptied her in that field?

"Oh, it was quite something," said Tommy. "The Wyves were there to greet you. You were given to them by the Lords and they carried you to the readying chamber."

Chamber. It had been a cave buried in rock and within had been a pool, as clear as glass. The Crones had stripped her without comment and plunged her into the water, and she had felt none of it. Emotion had fled and it seemed as if she would never feel anything again.

"I suffered," she said. "Did that never mean anything to you?"

Tommy looked at her. "Of course," he said. "Your suffering meant everything to us. It was as much a part of your offering as any flesh and blood. Although you nearly escaped us. The Wyves were a bit upset."

The Wyves. They hadn't been merely upset, they'd been furious. The water had suggested another way out. A final exit. Its chill had swept through her, numbed her body to match her feelings. A blissful oblivion had called. Then clawed hands had grabbed at her shoulders, stabbed her arms as they jerked her back and upwards, out of the pool.

"They beat me. Said I'd dishonoured Hweol."

"He is the Lord of this land," said Tommy. "He turns the Wheel, and he chose you. You needed to show obedience."

"I've been nothing but obedient," said Liza. "I've been passed over like a commodity by both my father and my husband. I have given everything."

Renewed waves of loss washed over her. She had never forgotten the baby she had lost. Never would. The child had existed to her, if not to anyone else.

"Tell me," said Tommy.

"They clothed me. I still bled but they did not staunch the flow."

"Blood is prized by Hweol and the Wheelborn of Umbra," said Tommy. "Your blood honoured him. I remember your garments. You looked like a queen with the ivy braided in your hair and the crown of antlers on your head." He sounded almost wistful. "The imps gathered the train of your robe and we all followed you."

She had been swept toward the House of Hweol. A house that was no house. She'd been there before, as a child, had played with the imps in the garden, but never entered its bone-carved walls. The entrance had always made her shudder. Skeletal jaws erupting from the ground, the bones of some long-forgotten monster framing the doorway into the darkness of Hweol's heart.

Words had been spoken and chanted by those gathered. Her hand had been given both to Tommy and to Hweol. Only then had she started to wonder at the nature of the event, what lay ahead.

"Do you remember the sacrament?" asked Tommy.

"No." A lie. She had never forgotten no matter how hard she tried.

"The words were beautiful," said Tommy. "Such an occasion should be burned on the memory. Perhaps you should hear them again."

He did not wait for her answer. Started to recite. "In this world, you will be Wyved to Hweol. You will always be forever his. In the Weald, you will be Wyved to Tommy. You will always be forever his. Double-Wyved is an honour, pure Wheelborn and true. The Mother claims you for her

Son."

Double-Wyved. The words had formed her prison.

After the vows, Fiddler had struck his bow and the folk of Umbra had danced, but Hweol had not stayed. Instead, he'd led her through those jaws and into the void.

"You will not speak of the rest, I know," said Tommy. "But you see it."

Like the words, she recalled every little detail. These she hid from Tommy, buried the memories in the part of her that was the Mother. A small rebellion, denying Tommy access to the heart of this age-old pain. She couldn't stop herself though. He had set her thoughts in motion and it was all there before her, refusing to go away.

The walls of Hweol's dwelling had been carved from bone and oak. The hangings were of flayed skin and pelts, the decorations skulls and dead foliage. Along these corridors he'd walked, pulling her easily along behind him, not talking, giving away nothing of himself.

He'd stopped. Beyond the ivory of bone had lain only darkness. As they stepped into the pitch, braziers had flamed to life, casting long shadows around the chamber. Demonic shapes had crawled at her feet, slunk up over the side of the bed. A bed unlike any she had ever seen before. More like a cage, a rib cage, it had bones crossing the base and then rising up and curling over. There had been no silk sheets or deep pillows. None of the trappings you would expect of a ruler in any realm. It had been covered with leaves and foliage, clumps of moss piling up around the edges, heaping up into pillows at the head.

He'd pushed her forward, commanding her to lie on the bed. She'd had no choice, crawled onto the cradled cage, held onto the bones to steady herself. Reluctant to grasp them, she'd had a greater fear of slipping through and being lost forever. Shafts of darkness between the bars had risen up around her. The torches of the room hadn't reached that far. Liza had felt sick and unsteady. Heat had crawled its way across her skin. A fever had poked at her.

She had moved further back, looked for Hweol. His shape had moved at the bottom of the bed. He'd murmured something in the old Umbran language, scattered something, something dead on the bed at her feet. He'd stood tall, an antler-crowned giant, a monster, red eyes glowed at her. Then he'd gone. Vanished.

Liza had crept forward a little, tried to see where he'd disappeared to, tried to prepare herself for whatever cruelty he was about to inflict upon her. She'd edged forward a little more, tried to see into the room, but the bones curving up around the bed had somehow moved, built up a barrier to prevent her escape. It had become the cage it resembled.

The dark had deepened and she'd realised the ribs were moving down, interlocking around her, weaving out the light. Tendrils of ivy had slithered across her body, wrapped themselves around her, probed, pushed inside so she'd felt them invading every aspect of her. At first, she'd fought against their assault, but it had only increased the pain, made the journey of vine and leaf rip and burn. She'd became a statue, found herself observing the scene as if she were someone else, a mere spectator. The darkness had grown, became a void in which she'd hung suspended, floating, embryonic in the womb of Umbra.

As she'd looked down at this other self, she'd seen how her gown had ripped away, the ivory bones had pushed foliage aside to examine her more closely, sliding into those channels opened by the creeping vines. They had been fingers exploring her, a violation of everything that had made her a mother for such a short time. How long this invasion had lasted, she couldn't say, preferred to close the eyes and ears of her other self so she neither saw nor heard her own suffering.

And then it had stopped. She'd sensed a change in the air around her, something digging down into her subconscious, forcing her to open her eyes. Reluctantly, she'd allowed herself to look, took in the strange bed whose ribs had opened up to the chamber, held her prisoner no more. Weak and traumatised, she'd barely been able to raise herself from the mossy mattress beneath her. She'd preferred to lie motionless, until she'd seen the creatures wriggling through the foliage, now dead and decomposing with none of the sheen she'd first observed. Scuttling legs and searching antennae, worms wriggling through the mulch, maggots increasing in number. White and pink, their bodies were plump, moving sluggishly as if recently sated. They had fed on this bed of pain.

"The Wedding Night always feeds Hweol," said Tommy, interrupting her thoughts. "And the Wyves cared for you afterwards."

He knew. He couldn't see into those thoughts of hers but he had witnessed others.

They'd given her a woollen robe to wrap herself in, but had not tended to the cuts across her body, the abrasions on her legs, her thighs.

"They gave you a choice, an honour," said Tommy. "You could have followed a different path, avoided all… this." He waved his hand around the pub, at Simon, towards the ceiling where Megan lay.

An honour bought by subjugation and violation, although not in the sense she'd assumed. Her body had been taken from her by a spirit she hadn't understood. Hweol. Where had he been?

"That night, you saw my father as he truly is," said Tommy. "The Son of Nature. It was on Nature's bed you lay, where you became one with our world."

All because of the Fifth Night. She should have fought for her child in the field, refused to allow them to take her baby. She should have fought against the Lords when they'd lifted her up and carried her into Umbra. She should have refused to enter Hweol's home. Should have… So many things she should have done, none of them possible.

"If you had stayed, you could have become a mother to the imps," said Tommy. "Worked in the Hollow Fields with the Wyves. He only claims you once and he could never have touched you again, for anything. None of us could. You would have become Crone, the third age of woman, an age venerated by the Mother."

"Mother to those blood-sucking horrors? I don't think so."

"You used to play with the imps quite happily," said Tommy, his tone slightly offended. An act.

"Because you never let me see them as they really were. Did you?"

He shrugged and smiled. "That night brought us here though, didn't it? You and me. With the blessing of the Mother."

"You're not going all sentimental on me, are you Tommy?"

He burst out laughing. Slapped his hand on his thigh with mirth. "Got me there, Liza. You really do know me so well."

She wished she didn't. She wished he'd go away and never come back. An impossible dream. She wished she could escape. That too, was impossible.

The only good thing that had come out of all this was Megan. Regardless of her daughter's true parentage, her baby had saved her. She had become a mother and would do anything to protect her child.

She had remained amazed at Simon's acquiescence to Megan's marriage to John. A small step taken to prevent the fulfilment of the promise Tommy had given to Betty. Always subservient, she had supposed Simon had been kept in ignorance of the Umbran betrothal. Or was it his attempt at belated revenge for the loss of that first child all those years ago? Without talking, she would never truly know—and they no longer talked of much, of anything.

How many years had passed caught up in this strange triangle of Hweol, herself, and Tommy? Too many. Too many nights of lying with the animal wearing the peacock feather in his hat and carrying the dead in his pockets and in his soul. Too many nights of lying with him knowing Simon was in the next room and would do nothing to stop it. Because it was an honour. She thought of her own mother. The woman had vanished from her life when she was a young girl. She'd never queried it, and her father had never discussed it. What honour had she denied?

Tommy mopped up the juices from his plate, sucked them from his fingers.

"Ah, Liza. What good times we had, eh? And more to come I expect. I must thank you for the meal and the conversation. Both were extremely satisfactory."

He took her hand and raised it to his lips. She didn't flinch.

"You can go now," he said. "Tonight, I'll be taking the air. Don't wait up."

With this dismissal, Liza made her way back to the kitchen. She walked calmly although her heart was racing. She felt some relief at not being required to sleep with him that night but he had not let her off lightly. The evening had been a deliberate torment.

The Fifth Turn of the Wheel. Liza couldn't shake it from her thoughts.

Her mind drifted over to Catherine and her baby. She knew what Catherine had done, a dangerous mutiny against Hweol and the Dance. Liza had rebelled by allowing Megan and John's marriage to go ahead without seeking Hweol's permission.

Two small challenges to the accepted order of things. Were things changing? What else would this Dance bring? Liza continued through those last minutes of drinking-up time to act the part of convivial landlady. Laughing and joking with the customers, listening and commiserating on their woes. She maintained the façade until the pub had emptied, then she took herself away.

She did not walk with the men as they toured the village, nor did she sit with them to welcome Betty and Fiddler. She went up to her own room and sat by the open window to watch and wait and listen. She heard Betty's anger at the promise broken so near to his claim on it. Tommy's placatory words. They froze her. Made her realise Megan had not yet escaped.

The Dance had started with Tommy's arrival. Would history repeat itself? Would her own daughter be twice-Wyved? *She* was not pregnant, was she?

Fear snatched at Liza and the dark doors she had kept closed for so long threatened to burst open. With effort, she locked herself down again and rushed out into the corridor.

CHAPTER FOUR
EAVESDROPPING

From her window, Megan could see her father and Tommy walk across to the church, disappearing into the black-handed night. Tommy the ghoul, the puppet-master of proceedings, pulling her father's strings. He always became wooden at this time, showed nothing of his feelings toward the newly-arrived Wheelborn. No doubt he thought he was protecting her, yet she would have preferred to know his mind, his heart. Even knowing his fear would be preferable to his emotional withdrawal from not just herself, but her mother.

Behind her, John slept deeply. He never really asked about her Wheelborn heritage, so much purer than his own. It allowed him to sleep easier. A fact which made her both envious and angry in equal measure. They had hidden themselves away at her mother's instruction. Her parents did not want her to cross Tommy's path if she could help it. John had been told it was a little family 'misunderstanding' which would soon be remedied, something he accepted quite readily. Yet, in a village this size, they were bound to see each other sooner or later. What then?

She had known Tommy all her life. Had sat on his knee as a child, allowed him to run his bony hands through her hair, be petted. Always it was under the watchful eye of her parents. Sometimes she had not felt safe, had sensed a disturbance about the man. At those times she had looked across to her father and seen her concern reflected, with something else, a look in time she came to recognise as helplessness, before he caught her eye and became wood once more.

The pub, her home, her haven, no longer felt safe. Things changed when the Wheel turned. She knew. Had had to accept it. This time, she felt the change creep inexorably toward her.

Megan felt an urgent need to get out of the village. Her eyes followed the two men as they reappeared on the green and then headed off around the village. Once, she had regarded Simon Wheelborn as a giant of a man, bear-sized, sturdily built. She had felt safe in his arms. He had always stood tall, straight-backed, grey eyes twinkling in good humour as he shared a joke with the customers, soft and tender when talking to her. The pub was well run with no barroom brawls, no lock-ins or other shenanigans.

In recent years, her father seemed to shrink as age caught up with him. He even hinted that she and John should become more involved in running the place. It had always been in the Wheelborn family and, as their only child, it would go to her and her children. Her children, her child, a secret as yet untold, even to John.

Her husband would jump at the chance to become landlord. A reluctant farmer, he had always wanted something different. They had even discussed moving beyond the villages, beyond the scope of the Wheel. Surprisingly, John had been all for it, until the prospect of taking over The Five Turns emerged, then that conversation died, her hopes evaporating. She wondered if her parents had sensed their intentions, used the pub as a hook on which to catch them. It had snared John, but she was still wriggling. Tomorrow, she would raise the issue again. Once he knew about the baby, he would want to get out—wouldn't he?

Only now she was to be a mother herself did she realise how few children there were in Cropsoe and the surrounding villages. It seemed carrying a child to term was a rare occurrence and not for the first time, Megan wondered at Tommy's involvement in this. Briefly, she thought of Catherine. So lucky to have given birth before Tommy's arrival. *Her* baby was beyond his reach, for the moment.

Lucky. Megan remembered the talk about her, the comments about how far along she really was. When Megan had asked her directly about her due date, Catherine could barely look her in the eye. She knew then, Catherine had cheated Tommy and, in doing so, had made her own position even more precarious. It was Megan's child in danger.

She drew back from the window as the men returned to the pub. It was slightly ajar, and in the silence that reigned throughout the building and across the village, their voices floated up to her.

"We will sharpen the blades tomorrow," said Tommy.

"They're waiting for you in your room," said her father.

"And the whetting stone is ready?"

"*Everything* is ready."

It was the way in which her father said 'everything' that scared her. She felt so much more aware of the undercurrents swirling around the village, the barely perceptible change in people's behaviour as the day of Tommy's arrival neared. Eyes not quite meeting another's, the reluctance to talk, especially to her, as a Wheelborn. She'd even overheard someone question her parentage. That was something she had pushed swiftly to the back of her mind. How could the creature, dressed in dead animals, an inhuman monster be her father?

She had slipped out of her room earlier and hidden, watching events below with a more appraising eye. Once, Tommy had raised his eyes toward her and she had shrunk back, but it would not have been possible for him to spot her from his vantage point. Yet there was something that told her he could see through walls if he had to, through brick, into hearts and minds. She had seen her mother, also hiding behind the bar, watching Tommy. She had never seen her mother so disgusted or so scared. The comments came back.

"She's got the same eyes."

"The shape of the jaw."

"She looks right through you, exactly like he does. She's Wheelborn, all right. But which one?"

They had spoken of Tommy and Simon as being family. Megan wanted to ask, wanted to know, but then her mother would ask why and she knew she would tell her what the villagers had hinted at. Those comments would hurt her mother. Or was that really the truth of it? Was she trying to protect herself from something which increasingly appeared to have a seed of truth in it?

This made her even more concerned for her child. The monster would claim it in one way or another. Even worse, if the rumours were true, how would she feel toward the baby? Would something of Tommy be evident in its face? It? Only a little while ago, she had started mentally referring to it as 'she,' had given her some humanity. Tommy had taken that away and a little spark of fear took hold she would birth some kind of monster.

The men outside had fallen quiet, and she realised it was because of the approach of others. Peering out, she saw two shapes walking down the lane toward the pub. One a creature of slight build, the other a true giant, his footsteps drowning out all other sound. Tommy's companions, his troupe as he called them, Fiddler and Betty. As they passed the few streetlights glowing at this hour, the lamps sputtered and went out. The men had brought the darkness with them and it swallowed the village. Only in their little bubble was there any light, as if the spotlight had already determined it should shine on the main actors in the play about to be performed in each of the nearby settlements.

Fiddler came into view first. Clad in green as always, he carried a battered case. This contained the instrument to which they would all dance. During the daytime, she had often passed him without realising it. When he stood still, he would merge into the countryside around him, and the eyes of the villagers would wander over the space he had occupied without registering his presence. Every so often, he would notice her watching him—how could she see him when others couldn't?—and he would raise a finger to his lips in a shushing motion, as if they were playing a game together. He was a quiet man, until he played those wild tunes on his fiddle, then he was at his most dangerous. His music could make you do so much.

But he was dwarfed by Betty. At present, he wore tattered grey trousers and a jacket whose sleeves failed to reach his wrists. He wore no shirt. As the pub's light shone down on the shaggy-maned creature, she could see the nest of hair matting his chest, his beard tumbling down to meet it so that it was hard to see where one ended and the other began. His trousers, were on the short side leaving a clear gap between hem and the top of unlaced boots. When he danced, wearing his mummer's dress, more of his hirsute legs would be on show. A sight which always made her shudder even as fascination kept her eyes firmly fixed on him.

Tommy stood up and embraced the two men. Her father stood but merely nodded his head. They responded in similar fashion.

"Cousin," said Fiddler.

Megan thought he was addressing Tommy at first and then realised he was turned toward her father.

"Cousin," said Simon.

And she wanted to know, needed to know. Quickly, Megan dressed, pulled on her shoes. John did not stir. As she crossed the hallway to the stairs, she found her way blocked.

"Where are you going?" asked her mother.

"They're...they're all here. I heard them. Dad called them cousin. People say I look like Tommy, I'm his daughter."

Her mother grabbed her by the arm and put her hand across her mouth. "Never say that. Don't *ever* say that."

"You can't protect me forever," said Megan, pushing her off. She felt like an out-of-control juggernaut. Not wanting to, but needing to ask. Not wanting to know, but obeying an impulse driving her onwards. Forcing her to ask questions whose truth would probably destroy her life forever. "I've always wondered about them, where they come from, but you never told me." Oh, she knew about Umbra. Had visited it even, but only a small part, the rest forbidden. She did not know its extent or even its origins.

"We told you only what you needed to know," said her mother. "It was safer that way. Now that you're married, they can have no claim over you."

"Claim?"

"You have nothing of theirs. Nothing they can take anymore." The implication was clear and Megan felt revolted. Yet there was also something in Liza's voice which told her there was still something they could take from Megan, her emotion contradicting her words.

"I need to know." Again, she tried to push past her mother. The pub remained settled in its shadow world, the ghost of the day giving it a quiet atmosphere. The smell of beer and spirits drifted lazily up from the bar, a perfume which tomorrow would be temporarily dispersed as windows opened to air the rooms and her parents polished and buffed fittings and surfaces.

"Why?" asked Liza. "What on earth can you hope to gain apart from putting yourself in the spotlight. They notice you and you'll become part of the entertainment."

A wave of nausea washed over Megan, and she staggered back against the wall. She pushed her mother's concern away. "I'm okay, been feeling a little sick lately."

Liza stared at her daughter for a moment. "I've noticed you seem a bit off colour, you…" And then she stopped as realisation dawned. "Don't," she said, almost fearfully, "don't tell me you're pregnant."

Megan smiled, relieved she could at last share her secret with her mother. But in place of the traditional embrace, of joyful congratulations, her mother shrank back.

"Who else knows?"

"No one," said Megan. "Not even John. I'm going to tell him tomorrow."

"No!"

"What d'you mean, no? He's my husband, the father of my child." This was not the reaction she had expected. Then again, she could never remember her mother discussing having grandchildren or indeed showing any longing to have them.

"Please," said her mother. "Don't tell him yet, I need to speak to your father about this. Above all, if you see Tommy or Fiddler or Betty, do *not* tell them."

"Believe me, they'd be the last people I'd tell," said Megan with feeling. She didn't want them anywhere her baby.

"I mean it," said her mother. "For your own safety, and the child's."

As she spoke, her mother was turning her, pushing her back toward the bedroom, casting anxious glances over her shoulder as she did so.

"What's going on?" asked Megan, beginning to feel frightened.

But her mother shook her head. "Tomorrow," she said. "Tomorrow, we'll sit down and talk. You, me, and your father."

"And John."

"No, not yet."

Liza had manoeuvred her daughter back to the bedroom door and had pushed it open, almost dragging Megan inside in her desperation. Behind them, John slept.

"How can he sleep?" asked Megan, resentful at his undisturbed slumber. Her husband. He should be awake, supporting her, protecting her.

"On the night of the return, only the purest Wheelborns are awake, or those gifted that status," said her mother as if that answered everything.

"Get back to bed and get some rest. You're going to need it. We'll talk in the morning. And remember, not a word to anyone." The door closed, and Megan found herself staring at its tired blue wood. Regardless of her mother's words, she could not go back to bed. She returned to her listening post by the window.

The group were not talking. They seemed to be waiting for something. The gentle glow of the streetlight held them in its bubble, had softened from orange to a gentle gold. Fiddler had pulled out his violin and was tuning it up on a scale unlike any other she had ever heard, each thrum of the string triggering a corresponding vibration in herself. John slept on, merely turned over as a particularly discordant note was struck. Then Fiddler started to play. Low and haunting, this was a tune she did not recognise from the gatherings. This was melodic, almost beautiful, and she felt herself drawn to the tune. It was as if he was playing a love song.

Betty danced, swaying gently under the one light, arms out as if holding an unseen partner. He waltzed and circled, pulling the invisible woman closer, turned, turned again a little quicker, around and around he spun so Megan felt dizzy and had to lean against the windowsill for support. The world was turning, the pub was turning, the Wheel was moving. The pace slackened, became a gentler presence, and as Fiddler stroked the strings, she could have cried.

"Perhaps we should ask Megan down to dance," said Tommy. "Celebrate her marriage."

The mention of her name jolted her out of her trance. She shrank back from the window, although this meant the conversation became more disjointed and indistinct. She couldn't fail to hear the roar of anger coming from Betty.

"No. You promised her to *me*."

Promised to Betty? Waves of nausea swept over her at the horror of it. Since when was she something to be given to somebody as if a mere object. The thought of those huge arms, those hands touching her. This time she fled to the toilet, found herself heaving into its bowl, muscles spasming as ugly images chased themselves through her mind. It subsided as she realised how close her escape had been. She was married and had a husband. Unless something happened to John during the Dance. Had they chosen their star for each performance already? Had they chosen *him*?

There was a scuffle and then Tommy's voice, soothing. Loud enough to reach her through the small bathroom window, almost as if he wanted her to hear. "When a Wheelborn makes a promise, it is kept. Isn't that so, Simon?"

There was a mumbled answer, but it did nothing to stop the waves of nausea once more rising up to claim her. Her empty stomach clenched, spasmed continually even though she had nothing left to give. The violence of her body's response shocked her and she worried about her baby, fear at loss of another kind making itself felt.

John slept on, so deeply and so peacefully whilst the world she had known for so long unravelled itself around her. She felt the stirring of anger rise toward him. Outside, strange men, monsters, were threatening his wife, and he slept on oblivious. She remembered what her mother had said about this first night. Only the pure Wheelborns remained awake, everyone else slept. He couldn't help it, and she hadn't told him her secret, but she felt that was no excuse.

When she returned to the bedroom, the voices outside had vanished. Peering out of the window, there was nothing but darkness, the last remaining light having been turned off to hide Cropsoe completely. Megan disliked those hours. Other places beyond the Weald kept the lights on to keep the night at bay but in the six villages of the Wheel, there was a certain point, when the moon shone at its fullest, the lights went off. Nobody went outside at that time. Except for occasions like this when you had the company of a Wheelborn from Umbra.

She had grown up knowing this curfew, occasionally wondered what would happen should there be a fire or an emergency of some sort. But this never occurred, and the curfew remained one of simple acceptance. It was a curfew which the Weald broke freely once the Dance began. They would walk that night. Everybody would walk—and Dance. Tonight, the curfew maintained its usual menace, albeit one which felt deeper than normal, seemed more solid, a creature alive and prowling the lanes.

Megan wanted to run to her father, ask what Tommy had meant about the promise, what was intended for her? But she was too weak and nauseous to do anything more and night was stalking her village. Safer to stay indoors. Like everything else, it would have to wait until morning, although she had a strong feeling time was running out. Not just for her. Instinctively, her hand dropped to her belly and she rested it there, tried to convey to her child she would do anything to protect her. At the same time, she had the horrible feeling that when it came down to it, she could do nothing. Like her husband. Like her father.

CHAPTER FIVE
TOMMY KNOWS

Tommy watched Simon retreat to the sanctuary of his pub. He grinned. The man had no safe haven, nowhere to run. The Wheel had been turning for centuries and he was Wheelborn. There was no escape. A scuffling of stones behind him drew his attention back to Betty. The big man's breathing was heavy. He was snorting like a bull, almost ready to charge something, anything, in his rage; Megan's marriage, the red rag.

"She was promised," said Betty, his petulant expression showing him for the child he remained within this beast's body.

"And don't I always keep my promises?" soothed Tommy.

Discovering the girl—no, the woman she now was—had married without his permission was an irritation. No more than that. Such things could be resolved at this thinly-veiled time. Besides, he sensed something else. He knew she watched, eavesdropping from the window above. She thought brick walls would hide her from him. Another misconception. He could see through *everything*.

Misconception. Oh, what a word to be played with. He knew. He knew what was living inside her. Blood called to blood. A child of the Wheelborn. Something that didn't happen very often these days. *Girl or boy?* he wondered. He would speak to her in the morning. She would walk with him, like it or not. It was so much easier when she was younger. Children trusted so easily. Her hand had been so small in his.

Betty continued to sulk, stomping up and down the road, making enough noise to wake the dead—if they hadn't already been awake. Let him sulk. He'd calm down. Fiddler came over and sat beside him.

"Been a while," he said, pulling out a long-stemmed ivory pipe and lighting it. Allowed himself to puff contentedly in marked contrast to Betty's tantrum.

"No more than usual," said Tommy. "No more than usual."

"Are you sure? It doesn't feel…"

The man struggled to put his thoughts into words, but Tommy understood what he meant. The Wheel was turning, but it would need something special this year to feed it. He glanced back up at Megan's window. Perhaps the marriage would prove a godsend. Well, for *his* god, anyway. He pulled his own pipe from his pocket and filled it with ancient tobacco, sitting back to mirror Fiddler as Betty's childish pacing came to a stop.

Around them, the village slept. An owl screeched, became a ghost flying across the night sky. He allowed himself to fly with it, saw the small creature scurrying below in the undergrowth, not yet aware it was prey. Then he was diving, adrenaline coursing through his body, eyes fixed only on the prize. Tommy did not stay to taste the predator's victory. His own would come soon enough. At present, he was enjoying the build-up, savouring the feeling of change, the spice of expectancy, the spike of adrenaline. This moment was a glorious moment, fully restored to the Weald, all lay before him. It was his to take and set in readiness for Hweol's return.

All it needed was music and Fiddler was ahead of him, opening his case and once more taking out the violin that had served him so well. He raised the instrument to his shoulder and rested his chin in its groove. Watching Betty, he plucked the strings. Tommy nodded his head in approval. This was not the time for the bow. Tonight was a night for calm and for rest. The notes swirled toward Betty, silvery little notes dancing beneath the lamplight, taking form as they drifted. So by the time they reached the giant, they had turned into butterflies.

Betty loved anything that glittered. He was a magpie in that respect. A collector. It was why he had wanted Megan. As a child, she had glittered. She'd never seen it, the strange aura coating her slight frame, but they had. Such an aura was only ever found in the true Wheelborn, in those of his line. That was how he had determined she was his daughter, and not Simon's.

Liza had protested this fiercely, ashamed at being forced into this annual betrayal, not just by him but by her husband. She did not want the added shame of birthing the child of a monster. To see Megan develop normally was to further deny her fears. To allow her to indulge in the fantasy that something, one thing, in her life in the prison of The Five Turns, was normal. Tommy never argued over it. He had always known and was satisfied he would claim her one day. He could tell Simon had no inkling of the truth, unless he was closing his eyes to the unpalatable fact as a form of self-protection. The only problem was that Simon expected him to claim Megan as a replacement for Liza. No. Even *that*, for him, was beyond the pale. He had mellowed somewhat over the centuries.

Tommy continued to pull at his pipe, smiling as Betty laughed and clapped as he danced between the musical fireflies, good humour restored. Dancing. The Dance. That was what they lived—and died—for. Already the notes were beginning to fade away as Fiddler lessened the tempo, the fireflies and butterflies fluttering down to the ground to coat it in a shimmering glitter. Fiddler had brought the frosts with him. Always a good sign. He was preparing the ground. That was what they were all here for anyway, preparing the ground for the Wheel to continue.

Betty ambled over to the bench, sat on the other side of Tommy. "You promise?"

"I promise," said Tommy.

This time, the man was happy with the answer. He could wait for a few days. The Dance was exerting its pull on him.

Fiddler packed away his violin, satisfied with this little bit of practice. Beneath them, they could all feel it, the shifting of the soil, the stirring of the elements. It was around them, in the air, in the trees. Such excitement, such expectation. This was Nature returning.

"Soon," murmured Fiddler, "soon."

They sat in agreeable silence to wait until the sun rose. Only then did they head indoors to the rooms prepared for them. These rooms were never occupied by anyone else. The chambers had always been reserved for their visits, at one time more frequent than now. Once someone else had foolishly spent the night in Fiddler's room. In response, Fiddler had played them a tune they would never forget, nor did anyone else in the village when they saw the madness descend on the unfortunate creature.

Tommy's room was empty. Liza had not warmed his bed whilst he attended to business with her husband. It did not worry him. He had allowed her to stay away. The first night, he never slept, he always stayed up, waited for the sun. To see the golden orb rise after spending so many months in the darkness of Umbra was another tradition. It warmed him, fed his heart as much as the Dance. When the sun rose, he knew all was well and his troupe had been blessed.

He threw himself down, fully-clothed, on the quilted bed. Tired as he was, as he always was, after the first day, he did not close his eyes immediately. Instead, he sent his senses out into the rooms of The Five Turns. The dreams of the sleepers were troubled tonight. Simon was concerned at what might happen to his daughter. Liza fretted over the revelation of Megan's true parentage—Megan and her child, the one as yet unannounced to the world.

Only the man lying next to Megan, her husband, slept soundly. He knew nothing of this thread running through the Wheelborn, the unsevered umbilicus binding them with its Gordian knot. He was unaware of his child. He did not sense the distress in his wife. He was a man of no imagination, and as such, he would be easy to break. The child, what was that creature dreaming? What did it see in the darkness of the womb? Tommy sent his voice through the dark, into the sea in which the child swam, anchored in safety to his mother, blood pulsing strong and healthy between the two.

"Can you hear me, little one?" he crooned. "Would you like me to sing you the lullabies I sang to your mother?"

He felt the child retreat from him in that darkling cavern. His voice was a strange voice. It only knew its mother.

"Soon you will know more than her," whispered Tommy. "Soon you will know me."

The baby kicked sharply and Megan groaned in her sleep. The movement, no more than a tickle showed the bond between mother and child was already strong. That could be broken. Especially when the troupe needed new blood. Tommy let out a happy sigh. He could sleep. He would rest through the day whilst the village returned to life, allow his body to settle to the new pattern. Then he would gather up the swords and he and Fiddler and Betty would perform the first Dance of the cycle.

Which village would have the honour? The dice, as always, would decide. Fiddler and Betty were dead to the world. It had been a long journey, and it was time for them to rest. Tommy closed his eyes and slept.

*****

As the sun rose, its warmth touched Tommy's skin, woke his mind although his body needed rest. At times like these, he would claim the bodies of others. This time he summoned a hawk. Sent it across the fields. Watching a day which dawned sharp and clear. The frosts brought by Fiddler crusted the ground, made it hard and slippery in some places, but the villagers did not complain. Winter was the season of cleansing.

Through the windows of The Five Turns, the hawk watched as the windows were opened to blast the air through the bar. Saw everything polished so it sparkled as brightly as the frost outside.

Across the valley, the five other villages also stirred, mirroring Cropsoe's activities, homes opening up to the elements, and their own cleansing beginning. None of them knew who would be first, but they would all be prepared. To have done nothing, to have welcomed the three into slovenly homes and along unkempt roads, would have been disrespectful. No one wanted to disrespect those who turned the Wheel.

In each house, the lanterns were prepared. Carved with the face of the Wheel, they were placed in windows, ready to be lit at the end of the day, should they be summoned. The women baked the Wheelcakes which would be passed around when the villagers gathered, whilst their husbands worked together to prepare barns and grounds. The only work done that day was related to the planned events of the evening.

In the fields, foxes poked out inquisitive noses, mice scurried a bit nearer to dwellings than normal, birds congregated in the trees. Everyone, everything, waited. Across the unclouded sky, the hawk flew, returning to The Five Turns.

He settled himself on the top of the pub sign and observed, feeding every sight and sound back to Tommy.

The day wore on, and the sun rose. The locals attended the pub as always and business was brisk. Tommy roused himself, released his feathered spy, and took a seat at the window to watch the world go by. Betty and Fiddler continued to sleep on, as did Megan. Her husband was helping his father-in-law in the cellar, tapping the barrels for the night ahead. As Tommy had noted, he had little imagination and no doubt put Megan's unresponsiveness down to 'women's problems.' In all this time, nobody directly referred to the recent arrivals.

Looking across the fields, he saw old Fairbrother, the man whose dog he had fed the previous night. That dog had been his shadow and now the shadow was gone. He watched as Fairbrother appeared to be looking around for something. Tommy had taken from him the thing he cared about the most. It was the way of the Wheel.

CHAPTER SIX
A SPEAKING OF SECRETS

Megan woke to an empty bed and the dull glow of the drawing down of dusk. She'd missed most of the day and the world was shutting down, as she had done. Her hand stretched over to John's side of the bed. He had pulled up the covers neatly, plumped the pillow, almost as if eradicating himself from her presence. The sheets where he had lain were long cold, and a chill crept through her. She withdrew her hand quickly; it had made her feel unbearably alone. Carefully, she stretched out her body, noticing as she did so a slight ache deep inside. That feeling was unbearably familiar, coming as it had done, regular as clockwork, month in, month out.

She pushed the thought to the back of her mind. Her reading on the subject had told her such twinges were common as the body adjusted to its new state, threw off its old way of behaving. Yet there had also been other articles warning of those dangerous early months, the signs to watch out for. *No*, she thought. That was not happening. She eased herself hesitantly out of bed examined herself and the sheets for any sign her child was in danger. Nothing.

Megan allowed herself a small sigh of relief and headed into the bathroom. A warm shower would relax her, disperse her worries, ease mind and body. She kept the window slightly ajar to allow the steam to disperse, so heard the comings and goings of the pub's early evening trade. She was supposed to be working tonight, but they had let her sleep in regardless she had yet to share her secret with them. That was unusual. Voices wafted in and out, words merging, unintelligible, but she didn't need to hear them to feel the excitement flowing beneath. The water washed her aches away. A twinge, that was all, nothing to worry about. Soon she would have to tell people, see the doctor, the midwife.

The thought of allowing Dr. Hayes to examine her made her cringe. He had a way of looking at women, proprietorial, owning. She'd seen him that time in the bar when he'd let slip Catherine's condition to her husband, effectively announced what was private in the most public of ways. He had broken the bounds of confidentiality, and she had witnessed the result, the closing in of the village as it circled Catherine over the following months, smothering her. The doctor always appeared to pop up near the poor woman whenever she was out and about, watching, guiding, stalking.

From the gossip (when safely away from his waiting room) she understood some had suffered at his hands. She had felt at risk when younger, his attentions a little too close. Tommy must've also noticed something amiss because a summons was sent for the doctor to appear before him. Never again did he bother her, and any subsequent visits were chaperoned by her mother. Tommy had insisted. As did the doctor. Whatever Tommy had threatened, frightened him beyond measure.

That was back in the day when Tommy felt safe to her, the favourite uncle who returned after wondrous journeys to tell tall-tales and then disappear again. A man who dressed as he chose, knew the ways of the animals and the countryside. Like a snake-charmer, he could hypnotise.

She thought him magical then. He still was in a way. Except the magic she felt coming off him was darker than anything she had ever seen, *black as the Devil*, she often thought. And after last night? She needed to talk to John, start planning her—their—escape.

At the top of the broad oak stairs she could see down into the pub. There was a small gallery running off to her left. It was where they would sometimes allow musicians to play to those gathered below, when chairs and tables would be pushed back and everyone danced. Those dances were safe and good-humoured, there was no purpose to them beyond having a good time.

As she recalled those occasions, Megan realised they normally occurred after Tommy, Betty, and Fiddler had taken their leave for another year. An annual event only then, yet they fixed themselves in her mind. She came to think of them as happening more frequently than they had done in reality. The excitement of those celebrations seemed different to the tension she could feel building around her in the present. The sensation after the Dance was akin to a prisoner throwing off their shackles, the thought of freedom, of relief from danger.

Danger again. A word she could no longer separate from Tommy. She looked down from the gallery and saw him directly below, her father laying out the swords before him on a cloth-covered table. Simon arranged them like the spokes of a wheel. Everything that night spoke of the Wheel and the Wheelborn in this village. The weight of it pressed down on her. She was part of this.

Tommy looked up at her.

She held his gaze, pushed her guilty thoughts of escape to the back of her mind, hoped he could not read her heart. The look was a summons. Tommy demanding she sit with him. His eyes and his easy smile commanded it, and she had no choice except to obey. Another sudden pulse deep inside, an ache in her womb that was harder to dismiss this time yet somehow, she did. She fixed a broad smile on her face and made her way down to Tommy, taking the seat he offered her.

"I hope you're well-rested," he said.

She retained her mask. "Must be coming down with something. I don't normally sleep so long."

"It's not unusual," said Tommy looking at her.

She forced herself to return his gaze, hold his eyes with her own, see the knowing gleam spark in the depths of those grey pools, a glint which carried with it a brush of cruelty.

"How long?"

She wasn't surprised at the question, and there was no point denying it. "Ten weeks."

Her father had moved away for the moment and heard nothing of their conversation. She wondered if her mother had mentioned anything to him.

"Early yet then," he said. "I take it you've not told anyone?"

"Only my mother," she said.

"Not your husband?"

Again, no response. To form words was proving difficult. She could feel him *inside* her, roaming the corridors of her mind, reading her thoughts, understanding and knowing everything.

"I'm sorry I missed your wedding. I would have brought you a gift."

She had not invited him. A deliberate snub. Something else they both knew.

"Perhaps tonight I can make a suitable offering to the Wheel," he said, picking up a rag and starting to burnish one of the blades in front of him.

Images formed unbidden of flesh carved and torn, of pain and blood. Another pulse. Nausea washed over her.

"No," she said. "No. I want to tell my family first, privately." She did not want her news announced to all and sundry on this first night. To do so made her feel as if she was inviting bad luck. She did not want to become another Catherine. The young mother was already under the microscope, waiting for whatever punishment Tommy deemed fit for her crime.

Her mother came over and hovered anxiously at Megan's shoulder.

"Please, join us," said Tommy, as if he was the owner of the pub and not Liza or Simon. "It does my heart good to see the family together again."

Megan caught the look exchanged between the two, his sharp and cruel, Liza's anxious and fearful. There was something here of which she was unaware. The three sat in silence. Tommy smiling, whistling softly as he gently stroked the blade's edge. The women, statues.

"Families have so many secrets," he said. "So many families have been destroyed by secrets." He held up the sword he was cleaning, twisted the weapon around so its metal reflected off the lights, sent a dozen glowing rays across the room. "Do *you* have any secrets?"

For one moment, Megan thought he was directing his comment at her until she realised it was her mother he was addressing. The woman's lips tightened and her skin paled. Her mother was scared. *What had she done?* At this she realised how little she knew about her mother, what she had undergone. Reading the expression on the woman's face, she understood without a doubt that she *had* suffered. Soon, she would get her to talk. She was a grown woman, after all.

"I have secrets, you know," he told Megan. "They travel with me on my journeys, but sometimes I allow them their freedom." He had picked up another sword, dabbed a little oil on a cloth.

Megan glanced across to the bar, saw her father busy serving the customers, caught him looking across in their direction, his expression of fear mirroring her mother's.

"Don't," said Liza, reaching across and putting her hand on Tommy's arm.

Tommy stared at the hand and then raised his eyes to her mother's face. The smile was gone. She swiftly removed her hand. He continued to polish the sword.

"You must've wondered at my relationship to your family," he said to Megan.

She nodded. Kept silent. Something was coming and she didn't trust herself to speak. Saying the wrong thing to any of the troupe was dangerous. She kept her face fixed on his, she did not want to look at her mother.

"Simon!" The order was barked across the room.

Simon muttered something to one of the customers who promptly took his place behind the bar. He came over to the group and sat on the other side of Megan so the family of three were all facing Tommy. Yet there was no safety in numbers.

"Perhaps you should sit by me," said Tommy, finally looking up from the swords. This was not a request.

Simon moved immediately.

"Now then," Tommy said to Megan, "tell me what you see."

She shook her head. On occasion she had noticed the likeness and then dismissed it. In an area like Wheelborn, you could guarantee you were related to everyone else—one way or another. Tommy, whilst appearing a visitor, had clearly originated from these parts.

"Tell me," he repeated.

She could no longer ignore his command and for the first time allowed herself to take a long hard look at her father and Tommy.

"Come on," he urged. "Tell me."

"You've both got grey eyes, same shape," she said. "Same jaw, nose. Same height." As she continued her observation, they appeared more and more alike. Until it became hard to tell them apart. Only the difference in build remained. An impossible thought came to her. "Brothers?"

Tommy laughed. "No, I'm too old."

"His father?" Megan had never met her grandfather. Simon never mentioned him, refused to discuss him.

"No. I am older still. But we do share the same blood."

Simon didn't speak. Liza continued to look nervously between them, plucked at the edge of the cloth covering the table.

"The sharing of blood," said Tommy, resuming his cleaning of the swords. "So important, don't you think? And supremely relevant on a night like tonight."

"Where are you going to first?" asked Megan, jumping at the chance to turn the conversation away from a direction she did not want to go.

"Can't say until the dice has been thrown," said Tommy, putting his sword down, apparently happy to allow this diversion. "This really makes for thirsty work," he said.

Simon immediately made his way to the bar to get him a pint.

"The father of a child is important," said Tommy watching the man's back as Simon wove a path between his customers.

Megan heard her mother gasp, felt her own pulse start to race. Was he going to say something to John before she even had a chance to do so privately? She looked for her husband. So far, he had not been invited to sit at their table. He was nowhere to be seen.

"I often wonder how you feel about yours," Tommy continued.

Megan looked toward Simon, heading back their way. "He's my dad. I love him, of course."

"Your dad," said Tommy, taking his pint from Simon as the landlord rejoined them. He didn't drink. He merely stared down into the pint for a long time as if contemplating something.

Megan felt as if they were on a knife-edge, an apt metaphor considering the weapons arrayed in front of them. Idly, she wondered what it would be like to lift up such a sword, allow it to slice into flesh. Orbs of light danced across its surface, a beautiful glitter, mesmerising.

It's easy, whispered a voice, *the blades are blessed, they cut like butter. They have a power beyond imagining. Why not take the sword and cut?* An image flashed through her mind, of her picking up a weapon and stabbing her father with it. She saw his blood flow, and she was smiling. The nausea which had remained in abeyance, returned with full force. Her hand flew to her mouth and she pushed her chair back, looking up into Tommy's eyes as she did so. She read his message there. *See,* they said, *it's in your nature. You could kill even those closest to you.*

"No," she choked, causing her father to look at her with surprised concern. She couldn't bear it any longer. The nausea continued, bile rising, that pulse again, the swords, the vision. "You'll have to ..." But she couldn't say any more, turned and fled back up the stairs. She felt as if all eyes were on her. She didn't care. Just wanted to get to the safety of her room, get in there and lock the door, keep them all out.

"But you can't, can you?" said Tommy's voice, floating through the ether as she turned the key. "You can't keep any of us out because we're already part of you. I'm already part of you. You are my —"

She knew what he was going to say before he even said it. If she didn't hear him utter that word, it meant it couldn't be true, it wasn't true. She sang, gabbled nonsense, put the radio on, opened the window wider. Anything to add more noise and drown him out.

CHAPTER SEVEN
THE FIRST TURN OF THE WHEEL

Tommy was enjoying himself. The terrified expression on Liza's face was one he could feed off. It was the perfect aperitif to the evening ahead. He would keep them in suspense a little longer, a delicious delay. He was hungry but not for anything Simon's kitchen could provide. The knives were almost ready, their edges as sharp as his own appetite.

He picked up the last remaining sword and spat on its steel. This was his blessing, this was to be the sword of the chosen one. Smearing the saliva across its face, he continued to work at the metal. As he looked into its surface, he could see Megan's shadow reflected, her eyes drawn to the rediscovery of light in the dulled blade. The connection was being made, the thread woven between them. It was time for her to discover her true heritage, an apprenticeship that would begin tonight. With the child growing inside her, her heritage was secure.

Eventually, he was finished and the swords were wrapped up once more in their shroud and placed in Betty's pack. The giant would appear soon. Only when Fiddler played could they begin the Dance. Simon placed an old dice on the table before him. Immediately, the pub silenced as if in response to some unspoken command. The locals rose as one and brought their drinks over to gather around him. All eyes were on the dice, waiting for the roll that would tell them where the First Turn's festivities would be. All the villages were ready, and each would take part in the five events, but the order had not been determined.

A single note sounded at the top of the stairs. Bow scraped on string, a discordant knife piercing the good-natured atmosphere, floating out through the open door and along the village lanes, summoning any who remained within, calling to them to prepare themselves. Inside, backs straightened and eyes hardened.

Silence reigned as Fiddler made his way down to them. Then it was Betty's turn. Tommy gazed up at him. In spring, the giant wore a crimson dress, slashed with silver and gold. In the autumn, this changed to black scattered with a starscape of silver and with orange tongues flaming along its hem. Betty brought fire when the Wheel turned, a bonfire which destroyed the rotten and the useless, cleared the way for the new. His beard was plaited and trimmed with ribbons as fiery as the flames on his dress which fell only as far as his knees. His legs remained exposed to the evening air. His hirsute covering meant anyone looking at him would not be able to imagine him feeling the cold, his animal pelt would keep him warm. Tommy saw the golden glint in Betty's eye, the wolf in the pack was ready.

The dice lay heavy in Tommy's hand. Carved long ago from the bone of his ancestors, each face carried a rune carving, one for each village including Cropsoe. If it had landed on the latter, he would roll again, but it never did, its inclusion a mere courtesy. Cropsoe, the centre of the hub knew its place in the order of things. It was where the Umbrans took their own turn, on the Sixth Night so rarely spoken of, at least aloud. On that night, the villagers would remain indoors and those who looked outside never did so again.

Tommy rolled the dice.

"Ashburn," he announced to the company. "Make way, gentlemen. Let Fiddler play the tune. It is time to Turn and turnabout."

Out they went into the newly born night. Ashburn, like the other villages, was a good three miles away. The sky was clear, early clouds had dispersed and there was no sign of the rain that threatened. It was always this way. Nature understood what was to happen, this was for her. She made sure things went smoothly.

Betty raised his face to the heavens and let out a long, unearthly howl. Somewhere in the distance came a response. Wolf calling to wolf.

It was a sound that in other places would cause nervous glances to be exchanged, worried looks, the locking of doors. Here, it meant doors opened and the village's inhabitants poured out onto the streets.

The three men, Tommy, Fiddler, and Betty, took their place at the front of the procession and headed along the lane leading to Ashburn. Fiddler played the tune he had performed beneath Megan's window. Again, the silvery moths and fireflies came into being, sparkling in front of Betty, so he clapped his hands and moved in a strange rhythmic manner that caught amongst their followers.

Hypnotically, they swayed and moved along the narrow country lanes, not noticing how the path they followed was not one they normally saw on the map. It was a road between worlds, a wide dirt track lined with sentinel yews, their needled leaves almost black in the half-light. Other trees also lined their progress. Bare limbs twisted into grotesque shapes, their bark gnarled into contorted faces.

Behind the trunks and from perches on high, bright eyes watched the villagers with eager anticipation. Like Tommy, they were hungry. The next five nights, the Five Turns of the Wheel, were their feast. The chance to eat their fill before they slept. Tommy could see them, felt their presence, but those from Cropsoe danced on with blind eyes. For that was what the music did. It closed their eyes and opened this pathway, allowed them to travel the path of the Wheelborn.

Tommy turned. Megan was behind him. He reached out his hand and she took it. As she had always done as a child. There was no reluctance despite the fear he sensed growing inside her toward himself. Did she remember the times he had brought her to play in this land? He had introduced her to its inhabitants, and they had accepted her. She was known and should she wander off the path, she was safe. But anyone else who was not Wheelborn, they were not protected.

He could see that although the music was making her move, she remained aware of her surroundings, was looking around with a dawning realisation, a smiling remembrance. He skipped forward and Megan moved with him. The resistance ended. The Wheelborn within her was on the ascendant, muffling her protesting inner voice. Simon looked from side to side, but his searching gaze was more wary. Tommy had revealed what lurked in the fields and woods beyond. The warning kept Simon in check.

Along the straight and unwavering path, they walked until the tree-lined passage gave way to the emptiness of tilled cornfields, occupied only by stubble. This would be burnt tonight as the villagers made their way back. These fields were not subject to government directives and clean air laws. The burning had to be done.

Across the fields they danced, one or two stumbling, their movements caught by unseen hands drawing them down into the soil. This was the other side of Nature's reach, the taking of life to feed the soil, continue the cycle of death and rebirth. These creatures, blind and beyond time, crawled along dark passages, scavenged and fed where they could, turning the earth as if worms. Nothing was wasted. Those who were taken remained in the Weald, helping to feed future generations. The nutrients from their bodies were richer than any fertiliser. In this way, the Wheelborn unwittingly fed upon themselves.

Nobody saw their disappearance. All responded only to Fiddler's music. Then the darkness around them drew back and they were once more beneath the star-laden canopy of the Wheel, feet turned onto the road leading into Ashburn. A scarecrow stood guard at the sign proclaiming its boundary, a small pile of twigs and kindling built up around its legs. Tommy stepped forward and lit a match, set fire to the scarecrow. Fiddler played, but his notes had changed to orange embers, merging with those from the fire and swirling up into the sky. Occasionally, an ember would drift down again and take up position on Betty's clothing, adding to its decoration.

"Pretty," he cried, as they sparked and glittered. "Pretty, pretty dress."

One or two landed on Tommy's unclad hand. They warmed his skin, but did not burn. Fire was a friend tonight. The First Turn of the Wheel was The Burning. He doffed his hat to the blazing effigy, and those who followed did likewise, raising their caps if they had one, or bowing their heads. They were here to serve the fires. To walk past those who gave themselves to the flames, even those who were not animate, was disrespectful. Swift punishment was always meted out for disrespect.

Fiddler moved further ahead, carrying his music into the village, summoning its inhabitants to the square. The bonfire stood ready. The villages mingled together around the edge of the arena, leaving a clear space between themselves and the bonfire. Into this area moved Fiddler. He continued to play, his notes moving legs and arms until they were all arranged as he desired. Tommy stood to one side of him. Betty danced his wild and manic dance around the dead wood, hair and beard flying out in all directions, booted feet thudding heavily on the ground, his dress lifting up to reveal thighs as hairy as his calves. Nobody laughed.

The whirling dervish slowed. He waltzed near to the crowd, looking deep into the faces of those who watched. Tommy followed his progress. Who would he pick for the Maid tonight? Tommy knew of course. Had already instructed Betty. It didn't mean he always did as he was told. Tommy had to keep an eye on his brother in case he should go off script.

Betty paused in front of Megan. He had not forgotten his upset of the previous night, but he moved on when Tommy gave him a look. After another circuit, he stopped and thrust his hand into the crowd, pulling it back to bring a young woman with it. Blonde and blue-eyed, elfin build, she was a stark contrast to her partner for the Dance. Tommy knew her. Another child he had walked with along the paths of the OtherWorld. He had found her blood to be poisoned, like more and more youngsters these days as the modern world encroached on their little corner. This poison was something which needed to be lanced in order for the villages to survive.

The woman, no more than a girl really, stepped out willingly. Amy. She smiled broadly, pleased at this public exhibition of his approval. At this age, many aspects of the Dance were revealed, but some remained veiled in order to remove any possible unpleasantness. She did not know she had broken the rules of the Weald, spending too much time in the nearest town, promising herself to a man there, one not of Tommy's choosing. It wasn't just Amy at fault. Her parents carried some blame, allowing her beyond the bounds without his approval.

He would visit them at some point during the Dance, remind them of the error of their ways. They had a son, one who would inherit the family farm, probably quite a bit sooner than expected—depending on the decision of the jury—and he would not presume the verdict was a foregone conclusion. He watched her momentarily preening on Betty's arm. The chosen one. The Maid.

Tommy stepped forward and Fiddler's music finished at last.

"Greetings, people of Ashburn. The Wheelborn thank you for your welcome on this, the First Turn of the Five Turns. You have sustained the land for centuries with your devotion and your sacrifice. Tonight, you continue the tradition. Tell me, what is the First Turn?"

"The First Turn is the Wheel that burns, the Maid who is wed to the land of the dead. The Dance claims us all."

"We bow to the Maid who will show her love," said Tommy.

"We bow to the Maid," came the response, and the crowd kneeled to the girl standing by Betty. Amy smirked in response. Her pride knew no bounds. He would allow her that. It was a small thing in comparison to what she would be giving.

"What is the Second Turn?"

"The Second Turn is the Wheel that crushes. When the son of the soil is ploughed into the land. The Dance claims us all."

"What is the Third Turn?"

"The Third Turn is the Wheel that flies. When the crone rides the night and old bones are crumbled. The Dance claims us all."

The chant and response were music to his ears. The words filled Tommy, took the edge off his hunger. The winter would be a good one.

"What is the Fourth Turn?"

"The Fourth Turn is the Wheel that freezes. When the Whelp walks in the forest. The Dance claims us all."

"My friends, tell me. What is the Fifth Turn?"

"The Fifth Turn is the Wheel that bleeds. When the unborn are taken into the womb of Nature, their blood the right of the OtherWorld. The Fifth Night is the night of the Wheelborn. The Dance claims us all."

Betty took to the centre of the circle then and roared into the night, "The Dance claims us all." It was the roar of a bull and it went deep into the soil beneath their feet, echoing through unseen chambers, waking those who slept.

Tommy could feel them stirring. Soon the crowd would swell in numbers, but the people of Ashburn would not notice.

"The Maid," cried Tommy, striding over to Betty and taking his prize from him. "The Maid requires a husband. Who will wed her tonight?"

Fiddler played a mournful tune, one more suitable to a funeral than a wedding. It had its desired effect, drawing out a young man from the mass of bodies.

Nearby, Simon, who had hauled a small handcart from Cropsoe, reached into its depth and pulled out an antlered skull. At a nod from Tommy, he walked over and placed the skull on the man's head. Then he returned to the cart and took out a smaller skull, without antlers. This he placed on the head of the Maid. Betty pulled some ribbon from his pocket and draped it over the Maid's head.

"The happy couple need a horse," called Tommy. "Who will carry them away on this night?"

Simon stepped forward. He always did. He performed the same role, year in, year out. Again, he leant into the cart and pulled out the Hobby, sliding the grinning horse face over his own. He pulled a small piece of string and its jaws snapped open and shut in a satisfying manner.

There was no need to summon a priest to tell the couple their vows. That was his own role in this little play. All they needed was the script and Fiddler's music would provide their words. Fiddler played again and Tommy watched with satisfaction as the antlered suitor raised his head to the sky, sniffed audibly as if searching for something. Then he cocked his head to one side, his eyes glittering in the dark beneath. He had caught the scent. The Maid had stood motionless until the music started once more. Then she had turned to the youth and laughed before skipping lightly around the slumbering bonfire. The youth chased after her, his wooing a comic ungainly leaping around the square.

As the Maid was pursued and the crowd laughed at their antics, Tommy walked over to the pyre. It was time to prepare his church. Carefully he removed a few upright posts aside revealing a hollow within the wooden frame. Inside was a table and two chairs. Such things would have been prepared in all the villages but only here would they be used.

The bridegroom-to-be caught his intended and swung her up in his arms, lifting her above his head to roars of approval and much laughter. Even the Maid was giggling. The slapstick wedding was always a crowd pleaser and proved the perfect opening for the events to come.

Tommy raised his hand and the people hushed. From the corner of his eye, he saw Simon hand out blazing faggots to some of the onlookers. They stepped forward to form a circle within a circle. Their light dancing and glowing on their faces bringing warmth and an air of security.

"Will the Maid and the Suitor kneel before me?" he asked.

The couple laughed together as they walked up to Tommy and lowered themselves before him.

"In the dead are the living remembered," he said, stroking the smooth ivory of the skulls in front of him. "From bone are we made and as bone are we returned." He bent down and took the couple's hands, placed them in each other and his own on top, raised them up.

"Tonight, they take each other in good health, in life and in death. As man and wife they have a new hearth. Their floor has been swept and the threshold awaits." As he spoke, he walked backwards toward the entrance into the bonfire, stopping just before it. Then he stepped aside, gestured for the two to enter. A woman appeared carrying a tray of food. She followed them in and placed it on the table in front of them together with a flagon of wine.

Tommy turned to Megan who stood a little way from him. "Daughter, will you pour their wine?"

She gave no reaction to the title he bestowed on her. At such times all in the villages were his children and he called them all Son or Daughter. Nor did Simon notice as he stood there with his wedding carriage.

"Eat, drink, and be merry," cried Betty.

As if by magic, food and drink were soon in circulation around the square. People ate and drank their fill, the night coming alive with the sheer goodwill shared amongst those below. Some would drift into the happy couple's chamber and they would share a toast or a joke and they would drift out again. The lights burned and gradually the people gravitated toward each one, feeling at last the cold of the night. They needed a fire. Inside the chamber, the couple appeared to shiver.

"We are cold," called the Maid. "We need a fire."

"Fire," came the response. "Turn the Wheel and light the fire."

On cue, those who carried the torches circled the bonfire, a wheel of light in motion. As they walked on, they dipped their fires into the base of the mass, the kindling there catching almost immediately. After each had completed a full circuit, they all stepped back. Watched as the fire took hold, flaming up the side of the heap of wood.

Tommy took out the sword for the first night, handed it to Megan. "You must wash the flames with the blood of the Wheelborn," he said softly. "A small cut will suffice."

It was an action normally performed by Simon but it was time to hand over to the next generation, and the land needed to be reminded of who she was.

Megan slit a cut on the palm of her hand and approached to the fire, holding it up over the edge of the flames so her blood dripped down. In front of them he could see the Maid and her bridegroom sitting at their table. The fire had not yet reached them, but already the heat was causing their skin to blister. Neither moved, it was as if they were unaware of everything going on around them. They appeared to feel no pain.

As Megan performed this action, Tommy spoke again, "The Wheel has turned and the Maid has burned. Let fire dance at the wedding. Let the people Dance!"

And at those words, Fiddler was off. His strings played violently, exuberantly amongst the crowd. He spun as his bow brushed over the bridge, fingers nimble and frantic. The melody was hypnotic. It sent people spinning, took their senses to another place. His music had brought madness, and only then did anyone hear the Maid as she sat in the midst of the flames. Her voice, her song, added to Fiddler's music. Pitch perfect agony roared out from the fire but her suffering was ignored, all caught up in the physical frenzy produced by Fiddler, too busy leaping into Betty's arms to be spun aloft and then tossed back into the crowd. Only three remained separate. Tommy, Simon, and Megan.

Tommy took the sword from Megan and returned it to its case. He did not want to risk harm to her this night and so restrained her from joining in even though he could see her body sway to the music.

Simon had positioned himself in front of the cart, wearing his horse's head. Flowers garlanded the bridal carriage.

"You will walk with your father tonight," said Tommy to Megan. "He will show you the bridal bed, and you will learn its path."

He did not attempt to read her thoughts on this. When the music played, all were under his complete control. That would wane with the dawn, and then she would question and fight her destiny. Tommy would be ready.

CHAPTER EIGHT
BECOMING WHEELBORN

Megan felt the heat from the bonfire scorch her face as she danced close to it, yet she revelled in its touch. Something was claiming her, turning her into another being, and she did not even feel the urge to fight it. She felt no threat, only a sense of recognition. Considering her earlier fears, the worries over her child, perhaps she should have been more concerned. But it was as if something, or someone, had waved a magic wand and dispelled all her anxieties. Tonight, was a night to dance.

The movement of the crowd, the turning of the Wheel, forced her to weave in and out between friends and neighbours. At regular intervals she found herself opposite the entrance to the chamber where the Maid and the bridegroom were seated. The couple rose and joined in the dance. A desperate puppetry as they despairingly fought the flames. Their screams went unregarded beneath the roar of the fire, and it wasn't long before even that small effort was quashed. Their shapes were visible through the cage of wood, become torches, contorted, twisted. Despite their agony, she could not turn her face away from them, again felt the strange fascination for those inside.

The music continued around her, the pitch of the fiddle rising, the pace increasing faster and faster. She stood there, an isolated point of calm in the midst of the storm.

Tommy came and stood at her shoulder, watched with her as the wood caved in, hiding the two unfortunate prisoners. It was a horrific end, yet she felt her lips curve in a smile. There was a beauty in this cleansing, this offering of fire. Could she ever condemn anyone to such an end? Something told her that maybe, away from the influence of Fiddler and Tommy, she might have felt disgust and loathing. But now? She was continuing to change, and her child felt it to. She could feel it inside her womb, dancing to the music with as much abandon as those she could see. At a few weeks, such movement should not be detectable, but *she* felt it. She felt its delight.

Megan and Tommy continued to stand there, playing their part as the

Watcher and Witness. Waiting for the fire to die down and the Wheel to be sated. Exhaustion filtered throughout the revellers, the food and drink consumed, hunger satisfied. The sacrifice had been chosen, and the others celebrated as much from relief as anything else. They gave no further thought to those who paid the village's tithe. To consider them would be to expose their consciences to something beyond comprehension. Forgetfulness and denial, these were the way of things.

As the dark of night gave way to the grey of dawn, the villagers made their way home. Simon brought the small cart over and took his place behind Tommy. Fiddler continued to play, a dreamier sound, languid and melodic, in harmony with the hope and promise of a new day. Betty stood and swayed, his trance deep and beyond anything Megan could understand. Where did his mind go when the wildness took him?

"Where does he go?" asked Tommy, reading her mind, the fact strangely undisturbing. "He goes to the between place, to the path we walked. He is there, bringing the two worlds together."

Her father moved forward with the cart, took a rake to push the remnants of the fire to one side so he could get to the bridal chamber. When a small flame flicked back into life and threatened to claim the rest, Tommy raised a hand and it stopped. The fire as much a servant to him as was everything else in their valley. From amongst the debris, Simon pulled up charred remains. The flesh had gone, bone stripped, and these warm remnants were tossed into the little wagon. Only the skull crowns which they had worn at the start remained whole. Simon picked them up with reverence and placed them at Tommy's feet. How he handled those items without burning his hands she did not know.

It was strange after witnessing such ceremonies for twenty-one years, that only now was she really seeing them as the veil lifted, sensing what was happening, wondering.

"Go with your father," said Tommy. "It is time for you to return to the OtherWorld, to Umbra, to walk the path between and enter the woods. It is time to renew old friendships. You have the offering, and you will be welcomed."

Obediently, Megan set off after her father who was already heading out of the village, pulling the small cart effortlessly behind him. Across the stripped field and onto the path, they walked. The sky, dark and full of bat-like stars. The moon, rusted, bleeding. Beneath their feet, the ground was like ash, warm, as if it had come from the bonfire. They stopped at a crossroads. They had passed this before on their outward journey but kept straight on. Simon turned left and led them down a narrower path. Beneath the stark and daggered trees, he wove. The leaves had long gone from their empty branches, nor could she have said whether they bore any foliage in the first place.

Strange memories were filtering back, images of a previous time when she had been a child. A small part of her was trying to process the deaths she had witnessed, the complicity of the villagers in the murder, but it was such a tiny bit of her conscience it went ignored. She knew it was the Wheelborn within her rising to dominance and preferred to travel that consciousness, to try and understand. And yes, possibly to absolve herself. It was the easy option.

"Come and play, Wheelborn." An imp's voice broke the silence, startled her out of her reverie. "Come on, Wheelborn. It's been a long time, too long."

"They're calling to you," said Simon. "Why don't you go and renew old friendships?"

A part of her was tempted. Those voices had delivered laughter and fun. Her eyes fell on the newly-minted bones. They were a tribute. Megan needed to see who ruled over everything. Who commanded even Tommy and his cronies. She shook her head, and she saw a glint of something in her father's eyes. Disappointment? *Fear?* He did not want her with him.

He dropped the handles of the cart, turned to face her. "If you come, you will learn everything, of what has been, what is, and what will be. The Wheel will make you part of it, and you will be Turning with the land for the rest of your life."

"I know," she said, and she did.

"I thought you wanted nothing more to do with the Wheel?"

How did he know?

"I've heard you and John talking. I know you want to leave. Although, that was before the child."

Again, how did he know?

"On the First Turn of the Wheel, all is known to those of the Wheelborn. We are one mind. Can reach into each other, into the very depths. I've always known what you were thinking. Your child has not yet learned to guard its thoughts. On such nights as this, no one can hide."

Her hand reached down to her belly. Thoughts? Too young, surely.

"The Wheelborn carry the ancestral memory," said Simon. "Already it knows, wants to see, to feel, to taste. What you do will be as much a result of your child's desires as your own. Your child also gives you protection, has created a part of you which no one can infiltrate."

She stared at him, glanced over her shoulder to see if Tommy was close by. She had a feeling he would not be happy with what her father was about to tell her.

"When you become a mother—and I mean when a child is in the womb, not just when it is born—there is a part of your spirit which can be closed off from all. A mother is *the* Mother and no one, not even Wheelborn, can read what is written in that part of your heart. Keep your hopes and fears, your plans, locked in there. Then you will be safe. At the moment, you are too open."

Already she knew the truth of his statement. She was no longer her own person. Both curiosity and heritage were claiming her.

"You wish to accompany me?" His face begged her to say no.

Megan glanced back. Two shapes were coming toward her, shrouded figures wearing the skull and antlers so recently borne by the dead in the wagon. From their shape she could tell it was Betty and Tommy. Fiddler walked behind them, his instrument strangely silent. Even if she'd wanted to return home, not go any further, she would have been unable to. Her control was eroded.

"I wish to see my daughter," said a voice. Disembodied and as ancient as time, the utterance washed over her. It was not her father who had spoken, nor was it Tommy. "It is time we looked upon each other, became family. With new life, our line has hope. The land will become refreshed, given a sustenance much missed. We have waited a long time for this."

The look Simon gave her was despairing. He had given her a chance, but she had refused. All they could do was go on. He picked up the shafts of the cart again and headed further into the forest, she following and the little troupe bringing up the rear.

She noticed her surroundings change. They were deep in the forest, but the greys and browns gave way to dark and emerald greens. Vines of ivy crawled across the surface of the earth like an army of worms, climbed the bark and swept across to the next tree to form a curtain of jade. Old wood wore new green. The foliage muffled the rumble of the cart, the sound of their footsteps, hushed even Betty's chatter. Absolute silence hung over everything as something waited for them. Waited for her.

"You've come home, Daughter," said the voice. "It is time."

The path narrowed even further, seemed to head into a wall of rock, a startling structure in the middle of these ancient trees. As they neared, she realised it was a cliff-face, and the path led through giant bones arcing over a small entrance at its base. Simon had to bow to enter, as did she. All who entered had to show respect. Inside, the cave widened, hollowed out into a roofed dome, curving high over them. In the middle of the circle was a pit, a hollow which, when you peered over the edge, led down into a void beyond all comprehension. Her father walked up to it and prepared to cast the bones into it. Tommy stood at his side.

"Tonight, the Wheel turned for the first time, and we offer you the Maid and her husband." He picked out a bone from the cart's bed and cast it into the pit. Then Simon, Betty, and Fiddler did the same. Tommy gestured to Megan. She picked out a femur and stood at the edge of the pit, wondering how far it went down. She dropped the bone, watched its glimmer of white disappear into the darkness. How many bones lay down there?

"It doesn't matter," said the voice. "It is simply returning life to where it came. They will be born again."

Simon took the remainder of the bodies and tossed them into the same gap, this time a touch more disrespectfully, as if he wanted nothing more than to be rid of them.

Then he moved ahead into another chamber. A small fire burned in the middle sending a golden glow around the vault. A long oak table was laden for a feast and chairs, enough for each of them, stood ready. At the head of the table sat a figure. Crowned with the skull of a wolf, the antlers of a deer, robed with the pelt of a bear and gloved with ivy, the creature gestured to them to approach. Each bowed as they neared, even Tommy.

Steel eyes, as grey as her own, bore into Megan. They commanded her, summoned her forward. She knew this was the source of the voice. How could it call her daughter? The thread between them, she could feel it, the connection. She waited for him to explain.

"We are of the land and of the Wheel. My blood flows through your veins as it has done for centuries, gifted to my followers who take it out into the world and choose those who will continue to feed Nature with what she desires. Satisfy her cravings when needed."

She stepped closer, and it held out a hand to her. Beneath ivy, was cold, cold bone as bare and unclad as those tossed down the pit in the previous chamber. What life could this dead thing give? And those grey eyes drank her in, reflected her back at herself.

"I am the Wheel, the beginning and the end, Mother and Father, to those of this valley. I have been here since before time and its petty Gods and foolish saints. I have withstood false idols and bigoted gospels. I have not murdered or tortured, imprisoned or sold."

Megan thought of the couple who had died that night.

"They gave themselves. I did not take or steal. They have always known of this night. Blood of blood is freely given."

It raised its hand to her face, stroked her cheek. Raised the other hand, took her head in them both. Held her tight. A vice but a gentle vice. "You bring life, and you will give life," it said.

She nodded. Uncertain as to his meaning, knowing only she was part of this picture. It was time to play her role.

"I have prepared a feast for you all," said the skull. "You stood vigil tonight, delivered what was mine. You have done well, Wheelborn. You may eat and then rest. The Second Turn will demand much of your energy."

CHAPTER NINE
THE HUNTING OF A TRAITOR

They took their seats at the table. Tommy was starving. The day's exertions had drained him. So much of his own life force had been expended in the preparation and delivery of events, he needed time to replenish. Hweol did not join in with the eating. He watched from behind the mask of his bone casing. Tommy sensed him reading their hearts as he did every year, seeking out their faults, determining their futures—measuring them. Tommy's troupe had once been a larger size but, through failure or irreverence, greed or conceit, its members had been picked off until only the three of them remained. Their hearts had remained black. They were truly Hweol's sons.

Simon had never sat at this table before. He'd had to serve them, much as he had back in Cropsoe. Tommy understood it rankled, but the man carried out his duties with care. Tonight, Hweol regarded him more so than usual. Did Simon understand why he'd been invited to eat with them? He was smiling. Did he consider himself risen to their ranks? Betty was heaping Simon's plate with meat, filling his tankard with ale. Roles reversed.

Hweol watched as they ate. Unlike the others, Megan only picked at her food. Normally Tommy would be concerned such a thing would be regarded as a sign of disrespect, but he understood her lack of appetite, and Hweol, father of the cycle understood also. He was watching her with approval. The mother in their midst was to be venerated, nourished.

No one talked as they ate. Each took in a life returned. Tommy pushed his plate away, sated. He had no more need to eat or drink until the Fifth Turn. But from the unusual invitation for Simon to sit with them, he knew tonight he would be called on to provide an extra task. Hweol nodded at him.

"Betty, Fiddler. I trust you to entertain Hweol and the Daughter."

His brothers smiled and nodded. Fiddler pulled out his violin once more to play the melodies that would soothe both the Daughter and her child. When he returned, he would dance with her. Not the Dance of the

Weald, the one of family reunited. Megan's expression was distant, dreamy, following the song Fiddler played. He had taken her mind elsewhere. Nothing could be allowed to interfere with what had to be done.

"Simon," he said, turning to the landlord, "we have work to do in the woods."

Simon nodded, smiled amiably. The man swayed slightly as he stood, the ale he had drunk was Hweol's own brew. One not for those beyond this shadow world, even those Wheelborn of the Weald. It dulled the senses and shifted perceptions.

"Come, cousin," said Tommy.

He took the man's arm, leading him out of the protective shell of the cavern. Simon followed obediently, smiling and nodding at everything around him. Megan looked up as they left the gathering, but Fiddler's music soon pulled her back. Should he have allowed them more time together? Father and daughter? Simon had played his part well for many years, but he had erred. His was not to be a trial in front of the villagers. His subterfuge was not widely known in those parts and to reveal his faults might serve to undermine Hweol. Best this was dealt with in Umbra, in the traditional way.

The light shifted around Tommy, moved beyond the grey to subtle silver. It was a world that glittered and shone. Rime ran its alchemist's finger along the edges of branch and trunk, outlining shapes in a pearled border. Soft flakes drifted and sparkled around them. The temperature had dropped.

Simon shivered slightly. "Hope this is going to be warm work."

Tommy laughed out loud. "Of course, cousin. Isn't our work always *warm*. Come."

He slapped the man on the back and put his arm round his shoulder, guided him into the glowing forest. Their breath frosted on the cold air and the brittle-leaved carpet crunched beneath them. It was silent except for a giggle, first from beyond, among the trees, then behind. Like a child playing hide and seek, an impish game, a jingling laughter drifting around them. Both men smiled.

"You've never met the Folk, the whole Folk, have you?" he asked

Simon.

"No, wasn't my place to walk these deeper paths was it?"

"No, it wasn't," said Tommy. Simon had met a few of the inhabitants of Umbra. Enough to make him feel he held a special place in their world, that the name Wheelborn meant something. "And that is such a regret of mine. That we didn't walk these paths together, that you didn't enjoy our games. We are cousins after all, family."

Their blood link was real. Hweol had ensured those from Umbra bred with those from the human world, created a bond which would tie them permanently together. It simplified so much. Yet the Wheelborn did not see or hear how they were truly regarded in the OtherWorld. Mere servants and playthings, to be discarded once no longer any use. Tommy looked around him. Nearly there. They were in a clearing very few ever saw. For those that did, those that walked there with Tommy, it was the first and last time they saw it.

Silver-barked trees, bare limbed and slender stood like classical statues at regular intervals around its perimeter. An elegant border to delight the eye. Here the frost was heavier, a silk mist which drifted over and around them, gave the air a weight it had previously lacked. It was like walking through milk, heavy and liquid. The giggling started again, and this time its owner emerged from behind the tree.

"You will play with me?" it asked, huge trusting eyes turned up to Simon.

The spell of the Wheelborn worked its way into the man's mind. He could speak its language, so it teased him, lulled him. Small and childlike, there was nothing for Simon to fear in its presence.

"Yes, I'll play," said Simon.

"Then you must run," said Tommy. "Time to play Catch-as-Catch-Can. Remember how you and I used to play this with Megan?"

The reminder of an old memory drew a smile across Simon's face.

"Ah, and who will chase?" asked Simon.

"I will," said Tommy. "We all will."

Others had gathered between the statues, their shapes indistinct, obscured by the mist. Simon appeared not to notice their numbers.

"I take it I get a head start," said Simon, laughing.

"I'll count to one hundred," said Tommy, grinning, feeling a thrum rise up from the soil, into his body.

The land was waiting for the chase to begin. The mist moved closer to the men, ran its drifting fingers over Simon's so it left a sheen of moisture behind. It was a lover's kiss and one of farewell.

"Never thought I'd feel like a kid again," said Simon. "I want to run and jump and..."

He looked a little more alert, the excitement had brought a flush to his face, a gleam to his eye. It was time.

"One," said Tommy.

"Oh, right, better get going."

Simon jogged deeper into the mist. He was in no hurry. Tonight was the First Night, a time of family and feasting and fun. He was among friends.

"Two."

"Three." Other voices joined in, a chorus of counting, a jingling scale of numbers rising into the waiting arms of the trees, their silvery edge turning to steel, gaining a sharpened edge. Razor numbers cutting, slicing into the mist, until ...

"One Hundred. Ready or not, we're coming!"

Tommy moved forward with small folk at his heels, a Master of the Hounds with his pack eager and ready for the off. Behind him, he heard the hoofbeats of the Hunt itself, the low snorting, the chomping at the bit. He raised his fingers to his mouth and let out a piercing whistle. A horn sounded behind him, and the mass surged forward. He ran, light and fleet of foot. Refreshed by the rebirth of the Wheel, he ran as if fifty years younger, a hundred years younger—no, more than that, but it didn't matter. His blood roared through his veins and his heart pounded in time with the thunder of the hooves. He did not need a mount. He had always been able to keep pace with the Hunt.

As he ran, he sniffed the air, picked up Simon's scent. It was as clear as if he'd left a trail of breadcrumbs to lead them to him. Occasionally, the horses would close him in, block out the forest. All he could see was the muscle working beneath the ebony flanks. Not a sweat was broken. He could smell the must of their coats, the leather of the saddles, the musk of their riders. He did not look up at these creatures. They were all the sons of Hweol and rode at their father's direction.

Tommy thought briefly he could have become one of these, if he had remained in the shadows. But he had been allowed to walk in the world, had seen the people of the Wheel, experienced the life of humans, and it had entertained him. They had amused him, fascinated him with their petty rivalries, their little rituals, their blind faith in so many gods. He had decided he wanted to give them a god, build up his father's church, and he had succeeded to a certain extent.

Times were changing, however. The old ways were being forgotten as thoughts and ideas flew invisibly through the sky, entered homes along wires or via satellite. This magic was something beyond him—for the present. One day he would master it. In the meantime, he would block it as best he could. Hweol had allowed him to remain beneath the blue skies even though it cost Tommy so much in terms of energy. He wanted to stay and he needed the Wheel to turn to renew him.

"Brother, you run well tonight."

The voice above him was well-remembered, and this time he did glance up. Saw the blazing red eyes and the ivory antlers crowning the creature's head. Its pelt could almost be mistaken for a cloak as it hung on the rider's frame, sat easily on the galloping stallion.

"Always," laughed Tommy joyfully, "this is a night to be reborn."

"And a night to race, little brother," said the rider. "Let's see which of us is the fastest." And he urged his steed on, Tommy responding by sprinting even faster.

Simon's scent was closer. He was hiding up for the moment, thinking this was a game, not knowing on the First Turn, sacrifice was demanded also of the Wheelborn. As they closed in on him, the riders deliberately eased their pace, called out to each other expressing pretend dismay at not finding their quarry, for surely he was a clever rogue?

The imps added to the general chatter with their silvery tongues, and the horses stamped and snorted with impatience. Their expectation heightened as they savoured the approaching moment, the time when their prey would reveal themselves, laughing at the hunt's inability to capture him and then the exquisite moment of realisation. Tommy once more gave the signal.

Tommy had returned to his position at the head of the hunt. Stood there, staring into the glistening mist. He could see Simon's shape. It had become a shroud, a winding sheet. An apt analogy. Simon stepped toward him, unaware. The hunt took a sharp intake of breath, soon. Tommy winked at them then turned back to Simon.

"Cousin, we are not done," he said.

Simon smiled. Bent over and placed his hands on his thighs, breathing deeply to recover himself. "I think I am," he said.

There was a roar of laughter. Simon looked up, puzzlement on his face at the tone beneath the merriment there. He had detected the cruelty in their humour, understood how those in the shadows worked. He frowned.

"When I said run," said Tommy. "I meant run—and don't stop."

He stepped toward Simon, pulled the sword for the First Night out of its sheath. It was dazzling even in the sheen of the half-light.

"It's a game," said Simon.

Tommy nodded sympathetically. "Yes, it is a game, and we must play it to its end. I suggest you run. I cannot answer for what will happen if you are caught. We have fed well tonight, but there are others," here he gestured to the riders and the imps, "who have not dined as well. I am a fair man, and you have a chance. If you get back to the path, you are safe."

"But the path is only over there," said Simon, jerking his head in its direction but backing away as he did so, obviously aware the mood toward him had changed.

"True," said Tommy. "Then it will be easy. My brothers are getting impatient."

"Wait," said Simon, confused by the change of tone. "I am Wheelborn. What right do you have to do this? I have lived and served here all my life. I have done nothing, *nothing*, to warrant this."

Tommy stared at him. Did he really not understand he could keep no secrets from him?

"I know," said Tommy. "We know, Hweol knows. The Daughter. We know what you intend."

Simon paled under his grim stare.

"You would have denied us the Daughter and the child. She is to become the reborn Mother, and you would have sent her away."

Hweol had decided Umbra and the Weald needed to see the Mother made flesh, Mother Nature incarnate. Who better than Megan, a pure Wheelborn?

The look on Simon's face showed realisation dawn. The man had said nothing to anyone, had only told Liza as they set out for this First Turn. He had made preparations for Megan to leave the village, to break the Wheel. And Liza had told him her secret, of the strangers she had invited. Both intended Megan would leave with their visitors. If the blood of Hweol did not claim their daughter before then.

Simon could never hide his secrets from Tommy and Liza had made a mistake confiding in her husband. His mind was always open to Tommy. The strangers would be allowed to come, allow the illusion of escape to continue for Liza. Give the woman some hope. Add to the fun. It also gave Tommy greater scope, should the Dance require extra bodies.

In this world, for the present, Megan was listening, but Hweol's influence was not yet total. Once the Five Turns had been performed, she would be theirs, but the next few days…time was critical.

The visitors would soon be on their way. Not complete strangers, a couple who had visited from time to time. One of those intrusions permitted into the Weald to create the appearance of normality to outside minds. Beyond their borders, the villages of the Weald were considered a rural backwater with nothing of any interest to warrant a visit. Their blood, so different from those who lived in the realm of the Wheelborn, was tainted by the modern world. Perhaps he could induce them to Dance. Hweol would let them enter the land, but he would not let them leave.

He had given Simon enough time to rest.

"Run," barked Tommy.

The man, at last, turned and ran. There was a howl, a solitary cry at first, before it was taken up by others. A host of sharper *yip, yip, yips* from the imps forming a terrifying chorus. Tommy kept his hand raised. Only when he dropped it would they surge forward.

The seconds passed, turned into minutes. Impatience and desire grew behind him. He could feel it building, becoming solid, tangible. Something he could mould and hurl forward as a battering ram against the puny human running away from them. He no longer saw Simon as his cousin, family. The man had a traitor's heart. He was no longer Wheelborn. Higher and higher rose the excitement. They scented blood, real blood, blood on which they could gorge themselves.

Tommy dropped his hand, and the hunt set off in pursuit.

CHAPTER TEN
OF HWEOL

Across the gentle countryside, night gazed down on scenes hidden from the modern world. To those in their high-rises, their townhouses and terraces, rural Britain was a quaint and tranquil place. It occupied a corner of every Briton's heart as being part of an idyll most dreamed of, but when faced with the reality, they sought to escape. All those empty fields, the interminability of Nature, it *was* pretty. But after a while it got pretty boring. Its urban visitors soon scuttled back to the civilisation of fast broadband and reliable mobile coverage, the anonymity of crowds. Boring? Gentle? The idea would often make Hweol laugh. More blood was spilt in the fields and hedgerows than in the cities. The rural idyll was mere illusion.

In Hweol's valley, with its wheel of villages and Cropsoe at its hub, the truth of Nature emerged. It raked its red claws across the landscape, turning the soil and the Wheel. It buried those who walked its surface. It paved the way for monsters living below ground to come up into the light. This tiny part of Britain, untainted by the little yellow man from Google Earth, hid itself very cleverly. It allowed only a few into its boundaries, allowed even less to leave. Life here operated at a different pace to the outside world. It was out of kilter with progress but completely in step with the desires of those who lived beyond the sight. Gentle Nature was a fallacy.

This Weald, camouflaged behind hills very few sought to climb, was the place where the veil was thin. It was here the shadow world and the twenty-first century co-existed, placed under the rule of he whose influence had once stretched far to the north and south of the country, claimed these islands as his own. Yet, whilst the realm of Hweol shrank, he harboured dreams of being restored to his rightful place. Already he noticed the disillusionment of some with technology, the turning–not toward religion—but to the spiritualism of the land and the earth mother. These were encouraging signs.

Hweol. Son of the Mother. The Wheel. The beginning and the end, the Alpha and the Omega. *He*—not the man on the cross who had come centuries after him—*he*, was the one to whom all would kneel and offer their prayers and their sacrifices. Hweol was ageless. He had seen his children live and die. They were ruled by the cycle of life, their span beyond anything most could imagine, yet still finite. Centuries were their lot, a blessing to some, a curse to others. Now was the time for renewal, when he would rebuild his family once more.

Through Tommy he had a daughter and, through her, another child. His sons, Tommy, Betty, and Fiddler had many years left, but it was time to start preparing the ground before he gave them their rest. They accepted this, in fact were looking forward to the moment when they could return to the soil, lay down their weary bones. They had no fear for this end of their time. They knew what lay beyond the veil, had visited it often enough. It would be a mere change of existence.

In the shadow world of Hweol, other creatures also lived. They were his subjects, and he took his duty of care toward them seriously. Fed them. Clothed them. Entertained them. It was through the music of the Dance he exerted his greatest influence. They were, after all, children of the Mother.

Here in Umbra, the Land of Shadow, lived those whose form could not survive for long beyond the veil. The silvery imps who scurried about in the leavings of the Forest of the Dead, fed on the rotting and the decayed. Their own bodies would fertilise the soil when their time ended. These imps would feast on the leavings of any hunt, would scavenge beneath Hweol's table. Nothing was wasted in this world. Androgynous beings, they were born from the bones of others. The skeletons reduced to pellets and sown in the Hollow Fields. There, they were tended by the Wyves; Crones who crooned over the little ones, called them to the surface, gave them their song of silver.

Nobody ever saw a Wyves's face. These, they hid, even from Hweol who had no wish to look upon them once he had taken them. It was said should anyone ever see them as they truly were, they would turn to dust in a second. Hweol, however had seen them. The Mother had shown them to him as he grew. He had to know all his subjects. Had to venerate and respect all for the role they played in the circle of life. He had crawled with the worms and flown with the Corvus.

Hweol was everything, and everything was Hweol. He was the many-faced god, although most saw him only as the Horned One. And the Hunt? The horses lived in stables tended by Ostlers. They took solid form only when a Hunt was called and the Lords demanded it.

The Lords were the aristocracy of Umbra. They termed themselves brother to Hweol, regardless they had none of his power, were given no special privilege by the Mother. She had decreed her son should have companions who would serve him. The Hunt served its purpose, feeding not just the Umbra but forging the link between that world and the life beyond. Sometimes one would assume they could overthrow him. This Lord was allowed to plan and plot, was fooled into thinking such a thing was possible. Then Hweol would expose them and reassert his supremacy.

He fed the Lords well, and they were allowed out amongst the Wheelborn to feed, to breed and forge the bonds between the worlds. Their children populated the Weald as the outside called it. Those belonging to Hweol were fewer in number but their place was secure.

And in Umbra there were other places, some forbidden even to him. Places where only his Mother went.

The pit into which the bone offerings were flung was one such place. If he looked into its eternal darkness, he would have seen creatures blind and limbless. Monsters who crawled in the tunnels carved by their ancestors, eating earth and changing its face unknown and unseen by those above. These crawlers had once extended out beyond the Weald, appeared in books of myth and legend, been dismissed by those who sought them out as pure fantasy. They had burrowed deeper than any human had searched, carved out the abyss into which many fell, unaware of what lay below them. All their tunnels led to the void from which none could escape.

One day perhaps the void would grow to encompass Hweol, suck him in and destroy him. But at a time determined by his Mother. In the void, all came to an end, in Umbra and in the Weald, across continents and oceans. All would fall into the pit.

The time of ending, the event carved into Hweol's heart, nothing could change that which was written. Not even the Mother. Provided all served her as she had decreed, kept the balance of things.

And what lay above the Umbra? What formed their sky, their coverlet of light? They shared the same constellations as their human counterparts, saw the same stars, the same sun. Only they saw more, saw further. Glinting at them in the darkness were those who visited Earth, the sons of other Mothers. These travellers were sent out, as Hweol had once been, to establish Her rule in different worlds. Sometimes Hweol would speak to them, but mostly he just allowed them to watch. His was the oldest rule, and they had come to learn. This fed his pride.

In Umbra there were also rivers and streams flowing from north to south. They contained fast currents, forced their channel through the land. The water was undrinkable, but the Umbra folk did not need to drink. Not water, anyway.

There was one road into Umbra, and it appeared only when needed. The same highway along which the villagers had walked from Cropsoe to Ashburn. A grey, twilit route lined with shadowed trees and cloaked in silence. It hid its true nature well. The Umbra chose its sacrifice from the feet who trod the ashen path. It could tell those who walked falsely, had detected the truth buried in Simon even before he himself had realised it.

It too, joined in the Hunt, appearing so as to give hope to the prey, always there, almost reachable, but in reality, forever beyond the quarry. It straddled the landscape as the Hunt galloped toward it, Simon ahead. There were watchers on the path, grinning and laughing, urging him on, holding out their hands in mock sympathy.

Hweol could see it all as they surged over his land, for he was part of it. Simon's face, white, bathed in sweat, terror stamped firmly on him. His body was failing, even with his Wheelborn blood. He had grown soft and lazy in the Weald, had not understood fully Tommy's warnings. Hweol felt Simon's erratic pulse, the ache in his muscles, the flagging of his heart. The vice exerted its grip on him, an invisible hand clamping down on that vital organ, squeezing and squeezing, forcing him to his knees.

The Hunt had reached him, the horses strolling leisurely toward their quarry whilst the imps danced excitedly around him. He did not see them. Hweol understood at times like this, a man's eyes turned inwards, became unaware of all around them. Only the pain, the slowing of the blood, the dying impulse, had any effect on them. On this they focused, their awareness of death increasing tenfold, their acceptance by as much. Sometimes he allowed them this little death, but when the mood took him, he stepped in to prevent such an early demise. It did not do to cheat the Hunt, to show sympathy for any, especially one who some might consider a traitor.

Hweol reached out to Simon, mind to mind, forced the man to open his eyes and look around him, take in those who waited to launch their final attack. This was his gift to the Hunt. He gave them the man's pain and suffering. He gave them his death and his blood. It would make it all the more sweeter.

The imps moved a little closer, prodding and jabbing, leaping in and poking Simon before darting back. Stabbing him with tiny little knives, a thousand needles pricking his skin. He swatted at them ineffectually. The more he waved his hands at them, the more they laughed. Blood dotted his shirt, ran down his face. Then one imp leapt onto his shoulder, clambered to his face, and began to carve around the eye socket. Another followed suit on the other side, peeling back the eyelid, scooping the eyeball out. Simon's screams made them laugh all the more.

At last he had fallen, was writhing in agony on the floor as the monsters stabbed and hacked. Although the blood flowed, the damage done by their weapons was minimal. Then there came a guttural command from the Lords, and the imps dropped back. It was time to divide the spoils. The leader of the Lords stood directly above Simon. The man could not see him for he had passed into a world of blindness and pain.

"Finish it," begged Simon. "Finish it now."

They understood his words but desired to extend their fun a little longer. To enjoy another's torment was delicious. The Lords circled him, cut at him as the imps had done. They allowed their blades to sink in a little deeper, avoiding vital organs or arteries—a temporary respite. Hweol watched them and despised them for their cruelty, much as he despised himself. Yet the Mother had created him, had made him this way, and it was not for him to change himself. This was the natural order of things.

*****

The rest of the village had ambled back to Cropsoe through the emerging dawn. Their chatter was hushed, in stark contrast to their outbound journey. They were satisfied. Nature gave them a gentle morning; she was pleased with what had been done in Her honour on the First Turn.

Liza walked arm-in-arm with her son-in-law, both more subdued than the others. Out of the throng, only these two failed to ease their faces into a smile. Liza saw her cousin Susan over to the left, suddenly stop and twirl gaily. Her eyes were sparkling and her face was flushed. The lines of worry she normally wore day to day, soundly erased. She looked ten years younger. It was the same with all of them. As if their minds had been wiped clean of any anxieties, prevented from dwelling on any of the horrors they had witnessed. Not that they would have called them horrors. No, these were traditions. Events that happened as regular as clockwork. Part of the villages' calendar of life. Nobody questioned where the Triumvirate had gone to, nor did they ask after Simon or Megan.

But Liza and John were worried. They had sensed a change in attitude between Tommy and Simon, an air of possessiveness developing toward Megan. Liza in particular, forced to serve the son of Hweol for so long, felt that for her, too, the Wheel had changed its rhythm. That soon it would stop spinning, and she would cease to exist.

Had Simon already gone? The looks Tommy had given him had not boded well. She could've asked if she'd gone to Tommy's bed. He might have answered her, given her the chance to warn her husband. Then what? Even if she'd known what was to happen, she would not have told him because neither of them would've been able to do anything. There was no escape from the Weald. None that they had been able to discover so far. The land had a way of trapping those which belonged to Her, and Liza had no influence over Tommy.

No. It was better she didn't know. That way she could pretend. Avoid imagining what was happening to her husband. She was coming round to the view their lives would change soon. Her season, and her husband's, were almost over. Her main concern was Megan and the child she carried.

She looked at John from the corner of her eye. From what he had said that evening, he had no idea Megan was pregnant. Liza was unsure as to what to tell him. Knowing the rituals of the Weald, it might be as well not to let him know—in case the child was to be used for something else. She recalled her own suffering. Better no attachment was formed.

But what of Megan's parentage? Should she tell him that part? Realising Tommy was their father-in-law would strike fear into any husband. Tommy had already indicated John was being considered for the trials, to see if he was worthy of his daughter's hand. It didn't matter that they had already married, that he had fathered her child. If he didn't perform well in the trials then he would be cast aside, probably sent to the Umbrans to become the plaything of the imps and the Lords. Oh, Liza knew those creatures.

In her younger days, Tommy had taken great delight in forcing her to accompany him off the shadow path and into the realm of Umbra. A sadistic reminder of her wedding. Its inhabitants had continued to terrify her, despite being courteous and respectful. She had seen beneath their mask.

Behind their civilities lurked cruelty and hunger. She'd been tolerated because of Tommy. But she was not of Tommy's blood and did not get any special treatment. Megan would be different. Through her, ran the blood of Hweol. That in and of itself would give her the safety her mother desired for her, but it was the change that worried Liza. As her true nature emerged and the Wheelborn of the Weald succumbed to the shadow of the Wheelborn of Umbra, she wondered what Megan would she become. Would she cast off her mother?

"Huh?" She realised John was speaking to her, had asked her a question.

"Do you know where they've gone?" asked John.

She nodded, unwilling to say.

"Will she come back?"

"Of course, she will," said Liza. "She's my daughter, your wife. Of course, she'll come back to us. Where else would she go?"

"And you're not worried?"

"No," she lied, patting his arm. "She's with her father. They'll both be fine." That part wasn't a lie. She just hadn't said who she meant.

"Probably a special feast of some kind," he muttered. "Something not for the likes of us."

There was jealousy in his voice and resentment. Oh, how she wished to erase all that, tell him the truth, but that would give way to pain and hurt. Best to leave him in envy's grip.

"It's tradition," said Liza. "Try not to dwell on it. You get used to it. Sometimes they bring back a gift."

"A gift?"

She lifted her arm to him, showed him the gold bangle on her wrist. "Over the years I've had necklaces and baubles. Filigree jewellery, pure gold."

"So they value you," he said. "I doubt they would pay me the same mind."

No. They wouldn't. The trinkets had come from Tommy, not from Simon. They were payment for services rendered. She wasn't going to say that either. In fact, she wouldn't even have worn the jewellery she sported that evening, but Tommy had insisted. It was his perverse delight. Something extra to torment Simon with. How her husband had stood it for so long, she couldn't understand. Sometimes she questioned whether he had any feelings at all for her. She raged inside. Years of resentment boiled below the surface. There was nothing she could do.

Somebody once had tried to fight back, to assert their independence from Tommy. She remembered her. Liza had been a child of only ten, but was summoned together with the rest of the village to witness the woman's punishment for speaking out.

Like Liza, she was forced into Tommy's bed, become his Wyve, but unlike Liza had never given him a child. That, in part, was why she was condemned. The trial's verdict, a foregone conclusion.

They had taken her to the Barren Field and bound her to the scarecrow which occupied its centre. A strange coupling and one that chilled those who watched. Fiddler had played his violin, sent not silver moths but ebony weevils, flying terrors out into the night. As he played, more and more carpeted the field, swirled around the woman's feet.

As she struggled against the straw man, holding her as close as a lover, the weevils had set to work, burrowed their way into her. Her screams had echoed round the field, sharp-edged, cutting. The villagers had remained unmoved at either the sight or the sound. What spell had Tommy cast that had prevented them from feeling revulsion, from coming to her aid? Why had they allowed her condemnation to go ahead? Because she had served her purpose.

The thought brought her back to Simon and Megan, had they served their purpose yet? They were back on the outskirts of Cropsoe. The village lay sleeping beyond them, waiting for their return.

Nothing appeared to have changed. A few ducks waddled across to the pond, an old cat stretched lazily, and a dog barked. The rural idyll awaited.

They took their leave of their travelling companions and headed back to the pub. The doors and windows were opened, tables covered with glasses and plates. All the leavings of the previous night's gathering remained. Yet nothing had been taken, nothing stolen. The Weald had thrown its protective blanket around the village.

"A lot to do," she said wearily, staring at the work ahead.

"The two of us'll make short work of it," said John.

"Are you—?"

"I'll be better off keeping busy. If I keep my mind occupied, I won't be worrying, will I?"

She smiled and patted his arm. "Come on, then. Let's get this lot cleared up, have it spotless before they get back. And they *will* get back," she said.

John knew she was lying but gave her a grateful look. It was the only way they could get through the day.

"Do you want any breakfast first?" she asked.

"No," he said. "Not much of an appetite, really. Maybe after." He swept his arm around the bar.

"Let's get going, then," she said.

Grabbing a bin bag, the first thing she cleared was the table where Tommy had cleaned the swords. The rags remained there, contaminating the pure morning air. She put on gloves, unable to bear to touch them, cast them into the bag. Around the room she went, picking up rubbish whilst John clinked the glasses as he gathered them. Soon there was a steady hum behind the bar as the glass washer swung into action. The water's temperature sterilising the pint pots.

She wished it was as easy to kill the virus that was the Weald. She stopped. She had forgotten to keep her thoughts in their protected corner. Left her mind open. And she had uttered treason. Others would know. Would Tommy come back and condemn her? She offered up an apology to the Mother. Tried to empty her mind of any dark thoughts, focus purely on the physical work in hand.

CHAPTER ELEVEN
THE SECOND TURN OF THE WHEEL

"The die has been cast," cried Tommy. "We plough the land at Scythington."

"Scythington!" called back the crowd surrounding the pub.

Liza had opened The Five Turns at midday, allowing herself only a few hours rest. She knew the villagers would drift in from that time; it was good custom. Most would be twitchy from the previous night, unable to sleep. The inhabitants of Cropsoe lived in a state of unsettled excitement during the visit of the Umbrans. Each day that passed allowed the sigh of relief that such an event was over, but then they would look ahead at what was to come. It always brought them back to the pub.

Liza knew the field to which they would walk that evening. First, they would travel the path of shadows which would take them quickly to their neighbour. Then all would troop out into the pastures. In the midst of this fertile land was one field. This was the Fallow Field and was always left for the Second Turn of the Wheel. By honouring the soil, the harvest in the whole of the Weald was assured. Blind eyes as well as the Wheel would be turned that evening.

She had still not seen Megan or Simon. John had tried to hide his worry, kept busy serving customers, supporting her as trade roared. Every time the door opened, she would raise her eyes hopefully, only to be disappointed. Eventually, there was the longed-for lull, and they were able to leave the pub in the hands of others and walk out to seek their family. They stood at the bounds between Cropsoe and Umbra, a mother and a husband, a wife and a father. They did not speak, each scared of revealing their fears.

Behind them, Liza and John could hear the gentle rise and fall of voices from The Five Turns, the occasional shout of laughter and a cheer. Someone sang, a maudlin song, the voice low and full of longing. She could feel the tears start to well, sought to push them back and think only of the return of her family. The shadow path stretched before them, leading away from the village and into the gloom. They could have walked its length, searched for those they awaited, but she did not trust either the air or soil of that place. Regardless of their claims, it was not a world of the Mother. She had felt its corruption and evil all those years ago and berated herself for not warning Megan sufficiently, not telling her the truth.

"Do you smell that?" asked John, as they both gazed in the same direction.

She sniffed, took in the air and its message, one she had sought to avoid. Who would return this way? Megan or Simon? Only one would return, that was what the air had told her. If she had inhaled deeper, she would have known who. She did not want to do that. Not yet. She wanted to put off the certainty of knowing for some time longer. It was the only way to keep Simon alive.

The offering Megan carried in her womb, would keep her safe for another two nights. She had known even before the message was carried on the breeze. John looked at her questioningly, waiting for her to explain. She said nothing, squeezed his hand and smiled, an action which said so much. Then she turned and walked back into the village.

She didn't return to the pub. Instead, she crossed the green and stepped across the threshold of the long-abandoned—in religious terms—village church of St. Catherine-by-the-Wheel. She had gone there as a child when services were allowed at Christmas and Easter, an opening of the doors to visiting ministers, part of the ploy to retain some appearance of contact with the outside world and prevent unwanted questions.

As a Wheelborn, she had sat in the first pew, able to look upon the face dying on the cross without hindrance. It had disconcerted her with its cruelty, the blood flowing from hands and feet, dripping as tears from his eyes. Only now did she see its true representation as the kindness of sacrifice, the taking on of pain so others would not suffer. This, a complete contrast to their own religion, the Wheel and its turning. So different to its yearly reliance on the feast of pain and suffering of the villagers of the Weald.

Those who administered its rites—Tommy, Fiddler, and Betty—knew it was cruel. Why else would they draw a veil across a child's eyes, prevent them seeing the rituals for what they truly were? By the time the veil was lifted, it was too late. You could say nothing, do nothing. Complicit in murder for years, why speak out now?

She pushed the heavy oak door and entered the old stone building, felt the cold air shift and then settle. Through broken slates she caught glimpses of the twilit sky, innocent stars peeping down at her, a golden respite to the dull gloom of her surroundings. Her footsteps on the cracked floor tiling echoed around her, sounding as if others followed her on this pilgrimage. Brushing away dead leaves and cobwebs from the pew, she took up her former position. The cross stood there, the stains on the body darker and deeper than she remembered but all was polished and clean as a result of Simon's weekly ministrations. Something else she would have to take over.

The painting to the left, a triptych showing the faces of St. Catherine in profile with the Virgin Mary in the middle, was cracked and showed water-damage, the onset of mildew. Even here the care appeared to be toward the male whilst the female was neglected. A Mother abandoned. She could not look at her any longer and rose to go when a small object protruding from beneath the pew caught her eye. It was the corner of a prayer cushion, one on which many would have knelt in times gone by.

Pulling it out, she expected it to be suffering the same decay as the rest of her surroundings but was surprised to find it was clean—and even carried the faint indentation of recent use. A thud from the same place caused her to look again. This time she pulled out a small Bible. Inside its cover was a name in washed-out ink but legible. Elizabeth Wheelborn. Her mother, the one for whom she had been named. The one who had vanished from her life with no explanation or discussion. When Simon came here, did he pray? Call upon their long-abandoned God? She knew the answer already. It fit with everything else that had changed on this turn of the Wheel. Another challenge and something already paid for. Umbra had already sent her its message, the smell of death on the breeze.

Curious, she opened the bible, found it automatically settled on a passage from Isaiah:

"So when you spread out your hands in prayer, I will hide My eyes from you; Yes,

even though you multiply prayers, I will not listen. Your hands are covered with blood. Wash yourselves, make yourselves clean; Remove the evil of your deeds from My sight. Cease to do evil, Learn to do good; Seek justice, Reprove the ruthless, Defend the orphan, Plead for the widow. Come now, and let us reason together," says the LORD. "Though your sins are as scarlet, They will be as white as snow; Though they are red like crimson, They will be like wool. If you consent and obey, You will eat the best of the land; But if you refuse and rebel, You will be devoured by the sword."

The sword. The turning of the Wheel was the time of the sword, and it drank freely. Simon had been reading this. With a certainty she knew it had been him, questioning the way of things, much as she had, but they had not spoken to each other. Oh, why had they not talked properly?

As they had followed Tommy on the night of the First Turn, Simon had started to open up. He had hinted at plans to help Megan and John leave. She in turn had mentioned the invitation she had sent to their friends from outside. Their time to talk had been cut short when they reached the village and after that, Simon had gone to Umbra with Megan.

Now it was too late. Guilt rose inside as she thought of how she had begun to despise him for his complicity. Looking back, there were so many small things he had done to protect her and Megan and she hadn't noticed. Her dismissiveness had made her blind. His latest rebellion, his agreement to the marriage, was not so little. Nor were the plans he had mentioned. He had finally had enough. As had she. It was too late for Simon. It would not be too late for their daughter.

Liza raised her eyes again to the crucified Christ. "You won't do anything for us," she said. "You didn't help me, or Simon. You left us on our own. If you were real, you would have done something, but you didn't. I, I *will* do something. I have to. Too much has been taken, and I will *not* allow Hweol to take anything more, in *anybody's* name." Anger rose up as her losses washed over her yet again.

"Have you *ever* existed? You said 'suffer the little children,' and they have suffered, even before they were born. How can that be right?" Religion and rite, worship and ritual, either to an invisible God or a bone-carved Son of Nature was a front for authority and control. "No!" She stood up and stared at the cross, the Bible falling unnoticed to the ground. "You don't exist, but Hweol does."

And then Fiddler began to play. The pub disgorged its occupants, and they combined with those waiting outside, becoming a moving singular mass. A black carpet rolling itself out across the countryside, infiltrating Liza's sanctuary in the church, pulling her outside to gather with the others. She pushed her way quickly through the crowds, eyes scanning rapidly for any sign of her daughter. She could see John opposite her. He was searching for Megan. For the moment, there was no sign of her, and they found themselves swept along with everybody else.

Fiddler's jewelled notes guided the villagers along the track and to the outskirts of Scythington. As they neared its boundaries, a shadow emerged from the side of the track. It was Megan. The young woman came over to her mother and took her arm so the two entered the village side by side. Liza went to ask her about her father, but a look from her daughter told her, *not yet*.

There was so much she wanted to ask her, but it would have to wait.

They were at the village's outskirts. The inhabitants walking out to meet them. In contrast to the bubbling excitement of those from Cropsoe, these people were subdued, casting anxious looks at each other and at Tommy. They had much to dread of the evening ahead of them. Representatives of the other villages attended as ritual demanded. It would be their duty to report back and spread the word of the night's events.

Fiddler made his way to the village green, the crowd parting before him like Moses through the Red Sea. Here was no bonfire. Here stood a scarecrow on a cross. Fiddler played another tune, a low deep melody, one of yearning, of summoning. This was not to gather the people; they were already there. This was calling to some other spirit, the one who was to share in the evening's gifts. Cropsoe and Scythington did not mingle. The two groups stood on opposite sides of the green.

Betty's dance this time was not wild but courtly, respectful. For the Second Turn, he wore a long gown, its colour that of the earth with an emerald trim. Vines of ivy circled his waist and his arms. A small circlet of wheat placed on his head. The music turned into a waltz. Liza could almost feel the world spin in time with the man. Then Betty walked over to her, took Megan's hand in his, and led her to the scarecrow.

Liza fought to keep hold of her, tried to pull her back, but the music made her weak. She was forced to loosen her grip, yield her daughter to the giant. All she could do was focus frightened eyes on her and watch as Megan, in contrast to her mother, moved away with easy confidence. Megan curtsied to the straw man, and then leaned in, whispered something into his ear before standing back.

The sackcloth head raised itself, its stitched eyes opening to reveal the darkest black orbs. The seam of its mouth broke into a torn grin. Arms and legs were wrenched away from the cross that bore it and at last it stood free, pausing to take in all who surrounded him. Its face returned to Megan's, rested on her awhile in assessment before he bowed and held out his hand.

Without hesitation, Megan took the straw paw, allowed herself to be whirled around the green as if it was an everyday occurrence. Neither looked anywhere else. Each looked only into the other's eyes. As the scarecrow seemed to tire, they turned toward Fiddler who lowered his violin. It was time.

"Greetings, people of Scythington. The Wheelborn thank you for your welcome on this the Second Turn of the Five Turns. You have reaped the harvest for centuries, your stomachs filled by Nature's abundance. It is your turn to feed the land, to return something of what was taken. Tell me, what is the Second Turn?" asked Tommy.

"The Second Turn is the Wheel that crushes. When the Son of the Soil is ploughed into the land. The Dance claims us all," came the response.

"Who will give up their son?"

"All will give up their sons."

At these words, young men stepped forward, one or two reluctantly. Liza could see some being forced forward by those behind.

"So many sons," cried Tommy. "But the Mother is a kind parent. She will only take one son. Let the man of straw choose who he will."

Like royalty processing, the scarecrow walked the circle of youth, Megan on his arm. They would stop at each one and the straw man would raise his stalked hand and stroke the face of the man in front of him. Most managed to remain impassive, but one or two flinched, looked revolted at his touch. If only they'd stood still. Didn't they know such movements singled them out?

Then the scarecrow walked the circle again before finally stopping and pulling the chosen one toward him. The youth stood between Megan and the scarecrow, and they all linked arms as if they were friends going for a stroll.

"The Son of the Soil has been chosen," cried Tommy. "To the field we dance!"

Fiddler's music once more became wild and untameable, driving unwilling feet to the Fallow Field where the golden light of dusk warmed the land, gave it a welcoming glow belying what was to happen that night.

A plough stood ready to be harnessed at the field's edge. But this plough was no horse-drawn implement. As the music continued, Betty gleefully pulled out four more youths from the crowd, dragged them to the machine where he and Tommy strapped them into place. The huge blades glinted in the dying light, catching the rays of the setting sun and flashing a strobe of silver across the field as if marking out its route. Curved and hooked, each blade was as big as the men who pulled the plough. Liza was already visualising what would happen but tried to push the image away. The truth was worse than any imagining, better not to think about it at all.

The Son of the Soil had been tied to the cross so recently vacated by the scarecrow. He was carried to the field by the villagers where he was laid down.

"Soon the Son will return to the land," said Tommy.

"The Son is the soil," responded the crowd.

"Nature reclaims that which was given," said Tommy.

"Nature takes back," said the villagers.

"Tonight is the Turn of the plough."

The group of four men moved forward, adjusting themselves to the weight of the machinery behind them. It moved surprisingly easily, blades sliding through the untended grass, churning it over, with amazing ease. The advance toward the crucified youth was almost reverential.

Liza tried not to look at him. She had known him quite well, one of Megan's early boyfriends. Was that why he had been chosen? Jack Duggan. An only child. Not so much a benevolent Mother Nature then. Couldn't the Mother have claimed another? There were families with an abundance of sons. He lay there, body rigid with fear, straining against his ties to try and free himself. Half-heartedly at first, as if he couldn't really believe what was happening, that this was some prank and at any minute someone would walk over and free him. The plough closed in on him, and his movements became more frantic.

The villagers held braziers aloft so the flames illuminated the circle which he occupied. His face was white. Liza thought for a moment she had never seen someone so pale. Then she remembered her own expression on the first night she had been sent to Tommy, and before, that other time with Hweol. When she had looked in the mirror upon her return, it was as if she had already become a ghost. Likewise Jack, who appeared to be struggling to escape his body. The strings at his wrists and ankles were bloodied as his useless efforts tore at his flesh. His head swung wildly from side to side, seeking out those who knew him. Calling to them to come and release him. Calling to his mother.

A plaintive cry which ripped through Liza who thought she could not bear it. An answering scream carried with it a terror she recognised. The horrific awareness of a mother knowing she was losing her child. It was a song she herself had once sung. Then Jack's words vanished and became one long howl of terror.

The scarecrow moved closer to the man and knelt down by his side, put his finger to his lips in a hushing movement. Jack continued to scream, mouth open in a wide O, but no sound came out anymore. Then the scarecrow moved back to Megan's side and took her hand. The pair waited. Liza looked on with even greater despair. Megan knew. Megan understood what was happening, what she was taking part in. *It was too late*, thought Liza. Umbra had her. Hweol had her. Would Liza be left with anything of her family?

The harnessed men were almost upon him, and she could see Jack mouth the names of those who approached. They would have known each other, grown up together. Possibly be close friends. That counted for nothing on the nights of the Wheel. All bonds were subordinate to the Wheelborn ritual.

And then they were walking over him as if he wasn't there, and Jack was given his voice again. Liza wanted to put her hands to her ears, to drown him out, but she daren't move. Tommy would often glance in her direction, and she had to show obedience, to hear the song of the Son of the Soil.

The men were beyond him, their machinery churning in their wake to take their place, then the arch of the ploughshare giving the youth a moment's grace as it curved through the air without touching him. It was the briefest of respites as the blades closed in and their edges sliced into Jack's body, curves hooking and releasing chunks of him up and turning him over into the soil. *Those* screams had lasted for a mercifully short time, the machine being so well maintained, oiled by so much blood.

"The plough is merciful," cried Tommy.

"The plough is merciful," repeated the audience. Without Fiddler's music to lift their spirits, theirs was a solemn response. That would soon change.

The harnessed team continued their journey to the far end of the field where they turned and came straight back again. Liza was able to bear this part. There were no more screams, no body. Jack had ceased to exist. There was little to focus on, just clods of dark soil being turned once more into the earth. When the team had completed their second run, they were released from their shackles and brought forward to join the others. None showed any real awareness of what they had done. Fiddler's music had taken their minds elsewhere as they'd pulled the plough. Its effects had not yet worn off. Later, their actions would be revealed, and this new self-knowledge would keep them tied to Hweol forever.

The rest of the crowd moved to where Jack had originally lain. The scarecrow stood directly over the spot. Around his padded feet, the torchlight showed crimson-coated earth. He dipped the wisps of his fingers into this before moving around the watchers, smearing his mark on their foreheads. Liza felt the slight scratch on her own skin, smelt the coppery notes of the soil.

Fiddler picked up his violin again. It was time to dance once more, to celebrate Nature's reaping. Food and drink appeared by magic, and small bonfires erupted into flame providing warmth and light. The mood lifted as the people allowed the alcohol and the music to deaden their senses, damp down their memories. Liza looked across and saw Joan Duggan, Jack's mother. She stood as a statue, ignoring those around her, rejecting the food and drink. Liza moved over to her side.

"You must eat, drink, dance," she whispered urgently. "If you don't, you might find yourself becoming an offering."

"Doesn't matter," said Joan, numbly. "That bastard has taken everything from me."

"You can't talk like that. If they hear you—"

"I don't care," said Joan.

Liza looked into the woman's deep brown eyes and saw all life gone. Her face, lined through work and worry, was stone. She took her hand. Cold to the touch, the grave was already upon her.

"Look, I know how you feel."

"How I feel? How can you?"

"Simon," said Liza.

Joan looked at her then. "Why don't you stop them then? Every year these murders are committed. By what? For what?"

"You know for what," said Liza. "For the Wheel, for Hweol."

"And if we didn't, if we put a stop to it, and Hweol was gone, we could join the rest of the world."

"No," said Liza. "The people of Umbra wouldn't allow it."

"Umbra? Sometimes I don't think that place exists. We only ever see it in shadow. I think they poison our drinks, our water, our minds."

Liza felt sick. She had shared similar thoughts at times but had witnessed more than Joan. Tommy had put her firmly in her place. If Joan continued to speak as she did then she would face as horrific a death as her son had. Tommy was not one for wasting a dramatic opportunity.

Joan took the matter out of Liza's hands. Without warning, she dashed forward and grabbed one of the flaming braziers from a villager and launched herself at the scarecrow, igniting its clothes with the fire. The scream from that creature was unlike anything Liza had ever heard, either in the Weald or in Umbra. It was a roar from another time, an agony deep and beyond measuring.

"See how you like it, you murdering bastard," screamed Joan, jabbing the scarecrow with another torch. The creature was an inferno, his stuffed limbs crackling into the night, his body disintegrating. There was a moment when nobody moved, Joan's actions being so unexpected. Then Betty was upon her. He grabbed the torches from her hands and cast them to the ground and then lifted the woman high above his head.

"What takes from Nature, we give to Nature," he roared. The surrounding fires flickered across Betty's body, turned him into a more monstrous giant than Liza had ever seen. He looked like the wild animal he really was, eyes ablaze and mouth open and hungry. He lifted the woman higher. She was silent, and as Betty brought her body down, breaking her back over his raised knee, Liza saw her eyes. They held the expression of one going to their death willingly. The snap of her spine rang out across the field, but she was not yet dead.

Betty dragged her broken form, as if she was a mere bag of rubbish, toward the smouldering remains of the scarecrow. He tossed her on top of the man of straw and stoked the flames. Still, she remained mute as the punishment she had meted out to the scarecrow was in turn delivered to her.

This time the villagers remained subdued, there was no cheer or ritual call and response. The people understood the woman's grief and were scared of what would happen to them, but they couldn't condemn her. This was something that had never happened before. It was a challenge to Tommy and his brethren. It was a challenge to Hweol.

Perhaps this is the start, thought Liza. *Perhaps I could do something.*

She looked across at Megan and saw her daughter and Tommy both staring directly back at her, as if reading her thoughts.

CHAPTER TWELVE
A NIGHT IN UMBRA

Twice Megan had accompanied Tommy to lead the ritual of the Turns.

"You have never Danced at this time before," had said Tommy on the night of the First Turn.

It was true; she hadn't. As a child and throughout her teenage years it was as if a curtain had hung over the truth of the ritual, something to be swept aside only when they came of age. She could remember bonfires and singing and dancing, merriment continuing late into the night as the villages came together to celebrate as they had done since time immemorial. She had skipped across the green with her friends, shrieking and laughing as flames shot into the sky. Then as a teen, she had walked more self-consciously with her friends, preferring to stay in their little huddle, too aloof to scamper as they had done once but enjoying the allowance of normally forbidden alcohol, savouring the autumnal barbecues.

Into her twenties she had continued to attend, becoming more and more aware there was something else behind the festivities of those six nights, something ancient and dark. This year, her twenty-fifth, was the year the scales finally fell from her eyes and she saw everything as it truly was. That was another part of tradition, this coming of age. With it came the realisation of complicity, the dreadful acceptance.

"As a Wheelborn, you will be my consort," said Tommy as they walked the path to Ashburn.

His tone brooked no refusal, and Megan accepted the honour, albeit reluctantly, not wanting to arouse his suspicions about her baby. Arm in arm, they walked, her hand resting on the rough cloth of his coat, his hand, leathered and clawed, placed on top of hers. His gesture could be mistaken as one of affection, but she was certain it implied ownership, possession. At first, she had recoiled from his touch, held herself tense as they walked between the trees of Umbra. Yet with each step together, she detected something changing inside her.

Thoughts of John, her parents, Cropsoe subsided. It was as if the world was raising a barrier to separate herself from everything she had known and taking her to a part of herself she had never met. It was both terrifying and exhilarating at the same time.

They paused at the turn on the path which led toward Hweol's home and bowed. Tommy turned to her then.

"The Wheelborn inside you is on the ascendant. It is not something to be fought or feared. Rather, it is to be embraced and celebrated. It is the true soul of you, and the Turns will allow you to recognise that, accept it."

She stared into his thundercloud eyes, saw the sparks leaping, the storm coming. The creatures of Umbra who surrounded them shared the same look. If there was a mirror, Megan knew her own would reflect theirs. Nor was the energy confined to the eyes, as his hand stroked her cheek in a parody of fatherly assurance. She could feel the power coursing through him. Up it came from deep in the soil of this world, feeding into the bodies of those who inhabited this realm. Like a lightning rod, his energy flowed into her, exciting her mind, thoughts fizzing. A natural high to be enjoyed and indulged. It felt as if every constraint lain upon her had been cast off.

She could not contain her laughter, heard her voice dance in delight through the branches bringing responses from those around her. Inside, the fluttering of her baby told her it was experiencing the same emotions. She was no longer daughter or wife; she was Wheelborn. It was that spirit which had guided her through the two Dances—despite its inherent darkness—and which came to the fore as each ritual progressed and the glitter dimmed slightly.

She thought back to the most recent event, her surprise at seeing Jack Duggan at the Second Turn. For some reason, he had slipped from her memory, an early love of hers, the boyfriend of her teenage years. How could she have forgotten him? They had wandered through meadows, swum in the river, danced during the Five Turns—not in the way they Danced now, but in that protected way that hid the truth. Stepping into adulthood, their participation had taken a different turn. Was it seeing his face that brought back that other part of her which the Wheelborn had overwhelmed and suppressed?

She had walked with the straw man along the perimeter of the crowd, enjoying the continuing sensation of excitement and expectation, looked upon familiar faces. Until it came to the choosing of the Son of the Soil. When the scarecrow reached in amongst those gathered before them and pulled out Jack, she felt something shift inside her, a seed of dread. The growing realisation that the Dances this year were intended as a message to her and her family.

Each time she had seen sacrifice, she suppressed the voice declaring it murder. That voice was locked away for the most part in the corner of her soul, defining her as a mother. This was the part even Tommy could not reach. Where she sought to send all her unbidden and fearful thoughts, all the hate growing inside her in case the Umbran read her mind and chose to punish her, or more importantly her baby. She did so reluctantly, felt such darkness of emotion was corrupting her womb, would mark the child and turn her into a monster.

Yet each step further into Umbra sloughed off all she had been, coated her in something else, dressed her in new colours. The small warning voice became no more than an unintelligible whisper, an irritation to be swiped away as if a mere insect. Another step and without realising it, she had become Wheelborn, the birth pains of her emergence fading as she moved on. Around her the colours of the forest deepened in their jewelled tones. The silvered imps flashed in and out of sight. Others moved closer to inspect the new arrival, and she returned their gaze without fear.

"Come," said Tommy. "Hweol wishes to sit with his daughter once more, to dine."

A hazy memory of another meal drifted through her consciousness. Was it yesterday, the day before? She had come here with someone. Who? A clench of her heart as she sought to remember, a coldness dampening her mood.

"Ease your mind, child," said Tommy, pausing in front of her, stroking her cheek, soothing away those growing worries.

The weight lifted, the thoughts vanished. Hweol. Yes, she would like to sit with him once more. To dine again in his presence was an honour.

"Nothing less than you deserve," said Tommy. "You are Daughter and

Mother."

Mother. Her slip-sliding consciousness drifted down to her womb and the child swimming in the dark. She would be a mother. Why had she kept it such a secret from Tommy? What would be done would be done in the Mother's honour.

"So like your mother," said Hweol, as she knelt before him.

She heard the approval in his voice and glowed with pride. She smiled up at him happily, noted how his eyes reflected the grey of her own.

"Come. We will sit together, you and I, and talk. Learn of each other as family should." He raised her up and led her by the hand to a small room in which a table was laid for the two of them. A tray was set by the fireside for Tommy. She noticed his grin when he saw the contents of his plate, not at all put out at his apparent demotion. A father looked after his family, and Hweol had provided for Tommy that night.

"Not many enter this small sanctuary of mine," said Hweol. "Only close family are allowed here. It is a place of tranquillity and calm."

And so it seemed to Megan. The sound of voices and laughter had fallen away. Nothing could be heard except the crackle of the fire, the occasional splutter of a spark. The aroma of whatever had been served up on their plates drifted temptingly around them, as did the warmth which wrapped her up in its arms and soothed her aches. On the walls hung soft animal pelts and spun tapestries whilst candles between them cast dancing shadows across the room. There was none of the weaponry associated with the hunter or the swords representing the Dance.

She felt no threat although her child quickened in her womb, seemed to be moving as if searching for a place to hide. Hide? Where had the thought come from. She put her hand on her belly and stroked it.

"The child is lively," said Hweol, observing her actions.

She could see a hint of a smile on the one uncovered part of the Hweol's face. He still wore the antlered skull of the Dance. "Must be the excitement of the past few days." She stifled a yawn as the fire exerted its effect on her and she became drowsy.

"Eat a little," said Hweol. "Then rest on my couch. A mother must take care."

Both Tommy and Hweol were smiling at her. She felt as if they had wrapped her in some protective cocoon. Barely registering what she ate, she almost sleepwalked to the bed. Unconsciousness swiftly claimed her, and she was drifting away into blissful sleep.

*****

Her slumber was so deep her child's agitation did not rouse her, Tommy noticed. He and Hweol both laid hands on Megan's belly. Their contact sent messages of ownership into the dark sea in which it swam. "A good offering," said Hweol. "The purest of blood can only bring us the Mother's favour."

"It would have been nice to have created a new generation," said Tommy, sighing.

"I share your regret," said Hweol. "If another could be found, then perhaps it would have been possible, but she is the only one at this time."

"There would have been another," said Tommy, "but she evaded us." The anger remained at Catherine's disobedience. It undermined his authority in the Weald. He had worried at Hweol's reaction.

"I know the one you mean," said Hweol. "I see all. Do not worry. She will be reclaimed."

Hweol returned to his meal. This time, Tommy joined him, finishing the contents of Megan's plate before extra dishes were brought in for them both. They continued to eat whilst Megan slept.

*****

Hours passed before she stirred, her eyes opening only as a soft dawn light probed at the room's threshold. She had slept there all night but felt more relaxed and refreshed than she had in a long time. Umbra had looked after her.

"It recognises its own," said Hweol, helping her sit up.

She did not shrink from his cold touch, did not notice the aged bone of his hand. Everything was as it should be. This was home, the certainty of it new and wonderful. She did not want to leave.

"You must return, I'm afraid," Hweol said. "Until the Dance is done. Then, if you wish, you may make your home here."

She was on her feet and was gazing out onto the forest, breathing in the cool, fresh air of the new day. Life was starting to re-emerge with flutterings amongst the undergrowth, the joyful song of birds above them. Yes, this was home. Did her child sense it? Megan searched inside herself, detected something, a hint of unhappiness. She dismissed it. A woman could imagine so much when pregnant. Hormones had a lot to answer for. She turned her thoughts away from the baby, exposed it further to the influence of Umbra and Hweol, sent it deeper into its own darkness.

The Third Turn awaited.

CHAPTER THIRTEEN
THE THIRD TURN OF THE WHEEL

The Wheel was turning easily now, its path inexorably pulling the people of the Weald into its wake. Sacrifice had been made, and it fed the life being reborn and renewed in the Umbra. Hweol could feel it fizzing through his limbs, the vibrancy which had died away as it always did at the end of the year was being rejuvenated. This was the third day of the Wheel, when not only the land but the sky would join.

*****

The Five Turns was even busier that night. Liza and John working flat out to fill the stomachs and drown the thirsts of their customers. Megan did not help. Stood and watched or sat at Tommy's side. The two shared many secret talks, and Liza itched to discover what they talked about, but Megan was unforthcoming. She was withdrawing from her mother. She would not reveal what had happened to Simon. That would be explained on the last night. The sixth night. For all the suffering of the other villages, nothing matched that which Cropsoe would face on this night. For now, they could focus on the Third Wheel.

As they left the village to tread yet again the path through the OtherWorld, Liza turned back and saw the pub, empty and abandoned. It was how she felt. She was not sure she could return to it. Perhaps tonight, being the night of the Crone, they might choose her. But it was not yet Cropsoe's time for the letting of blood. Tonight, they headed for Reaper's Hill. From this high point, they would see the Weald beneath them and the Crone would fly.

Despite the village's name, the path took them directly to its home on the hillside. The walkers noticed no incline, followed the same straight path, arrived full of energy, chatting and relaxed.

Fiddler moved to the front yet again, and the tune he played this time was scratchy. It was the irritated tone of an old woman. The bow complained across the strings which in turn protested the trials of their bones. The young did not understand the sufferings of the old. The complaints tore through the air, demanded the presence of those of Reaper's Hill who left their homes reluctantly. They had not gathered in readiness on the village green. They had preferred to remain hidden amongst their houses and woods. They would not come until they were formally summoned.

All knew the Third Turn of the Wheel was something to which none could dance. Even Betty walked ponderously, heavily. The weight of age hung heavy on them all.

"Greetings, people of Reaper's Hill. The Wheelborn thank you for your welcome on this, the Third Turn of the Five Turns. You have walked freely beneath Nature's canopy of blue. Gentle sun and soft rain have nurtured your harvest. It is your turn to feed the sky, to return something of what was taken. Tell me, what is the Third Turn?" asked Tommy.

"The Third Turn is the Wheel that flies. When the Crone rides the night and old bones are crumbled. The Dance claims us all," came the response.

"Who will give up their mother?"

Liza shuddered at these words, as did many. To even consider such a thing broke one of the most sacred of bonds of Nature herself. The veneration of the Mother was sacrosanct. This bastardisation of the tribute was one which never stood easily. Yet no one protested. All spoke up.

"All will give up their mothers," came the response.

Liza looked across at Megan. Did Megan even think this could apply to her? In the years to come, when her child grew, would it denounce her, give *her* up? Her daughter did not meet her eye.

This time no one was pushed forward. It was for the mothers to offer themselves. The old ones came first, frail and weak. They supported themselves on sticks or on each other's arms and stood in front of Tommy. At this point it was as if some extra energy had charged them, for they all straightened up, looked him defiantly in the eye, dared him to select them. He walked along their ranks as if inspecting his soldiers, examining each carefully until he had completed the first pass.

The village held its breath, this prolonging of the choice was mere stage play. He had already chosen. He walked back along the row until he came to Anne. Liza inhaled sharply. Another person close to her family. Was this all a threat? What was she supposed to be taking from its meaning?

Anne. No, she wouldn't think of her, but she couldn't help it. Old memories had a bad habit of demanding to be revisited, and they came back to her, vociferous, irksome. Once upon a time, they had regarded themselves as sisters. That was back in their infancy, when they had giggled together over the dressing up box, or sat and shared innocent picture books.

The friendship had continued through school and, at one point, they had almost become related when Anne and Liza's brother had become engaged. But the Wheel had turned and taken him, so the bond was never formed. As Anne was not as old as the Crones normally selected, it made Liza certain it was this old relationship which had brought her to Tommy's attention.

The man bowed to Anne and offered her his hand. She accepted it without a qualm, looked him straight in the eye and turned, defiant, toward the rest of the crowd. She had always been a brave woman. Liza doubted she could show such courage if put to the test.

"I have the Mother," said Tommy.

"You have the Mother," replied the villagers.

"The Mother is the protector," said Tommy. "She will die so her children live. She knows the Crone must make way for the Maid."

"The Crone must die," said the villagers. Few of them this time could look at Tommy or Anne.

Fiddler started to play, sending his notes out to bring back the spark that had accompanied them on the first two nights, but it only brought a little lift. Tonight would be a night of terror.

The music led them up the hill, along the path which zigzagged its way around the mound until they reached its summit, flattened by years of battering. Fiddler silenced his instrument which moaned and groaned before it finally settled with a drawn-out sigh. Nobody spoke, nobody moved. Everything remained in complete and total silence. The trees lower down had already stilled, and the clouds above no longer shifted. It was as if time had frozen. This was the Waiting.

Night was coming. She was a black hag, shaped by time immemorial. A wisp at first, her form becoming more substantial as she neared them. A swirling, roiling mass that threatened to suck up all below her into her vortex. Her roar was loud but soon softened to a cackle as she allowed herself the luxury of weaving in and out of the watchers, brushing their arms, pinching their cheeks, wallowing in the presence of those she was normally prohibited from taking.

Eventually, she condensed herself, drifted over to Tommy and Anne, swirling around them in her excited embrace. Gradually, she concentrated her efforts only on Anne. The woman stood stock still, eyes defiant, back proud, heart strong. Then the hag lifted her, sent her currents beneath Anne so she rose, gently at first, like those old paintings of the saints as they were transported to the heavens.

Liza watched her go. The dark cloud framing her, taking her up and up until she was high above them. At that point the hag began to spin, took her into her embrace, spinning faster and faster, tighter and tighter, until she was completely concealed by the cloud of her body. The rush of air smothered the sound of the woman as she was crushed and compressed. Yet, when the release came, she would not be dead. There would be enough life left in her for her to scream and protest her end. For the moment, they were spared.

The hag sent her through the sky as if she were a mere toy, something useless, ready to be cast aside. How many other women watching saw themselves in her, dreaded those later years?

But the ride was only one part of the ritual. She was the Mother who saw all. Old bones. They still had a part to play. Anne was hovering directly above them, and the crowd moved back so a space opened up beneath her. There was a pause as the winds dropped yet again; everything stopped and held its breath. They waited and waited. They waited until they could almost bear it no longer, as they knew they must.

And then it came. That driving force, that crashing energy. It drove her down, dropped her like a lift gone out of control, speeding toward the earth. They could all feel her coming, heard her screams on the currents that pulled them out of her.

The force of her fall pushed her into the ground, formed a pit beneath her, took her into the very earth itself. As Anne lay there, the hag wind worked at the sides of the pit, ripping out the soil and the stones, spinning them to the edges so they hovered on the rim. Then she disappeared briefly, a small respite allowing the villagers to gather their breath, to hope, but not to help the woman who lay suffering in the ground below them. Then the hag returned, and this time she carried not stones but boulders. Huge rocks to press and crush.

Liza's eyes followed as she took them as high as she could, up and up into the sky of the Weald kept her focus on the silent crowd, the solitary woman. The hag would cast the first stone, but the sons would follow. She was in position, arm poised, and then she hurled the boulder into the void below. Anne lay helpless as the rock sped toward her, braced ready for the impact, the pain. The next part was one of the worst betrayals in Liza's mind, when everyone the victim held dear, would pick up their stones and cast them at her. Even her own sons. They would give up their mother.

Liza could not watch, averted her eyes, only to find Tommy and Megan yet again watching her. Perhaps she should join Anne, finish it all. Not have to think about Simon or Megan again but her grandchild. Would she leave an innocent to be corrupted by the Umbrans? Perhaps, if she was weak. There must be a way to break the power of the Weald, of the Wheel.

Such thoughts were creeping more and more unbidden into her consciousness, a dangerous situation as she felt Tommy could read every part of her. Even now he was smiling at her. His usual sneering, possessive smile. There had never been anything there. She had been his mere plaything. A mortal. A human to humiliate and abuse. Her status as Wheelborn was less than Megan's through whom the lineage of Tommy and Hweol's flowed. Yet she was too weak to stand against them, and with every turn of the Wheel they would become stronger.

Tommy and Megan walked over to her. Megan gave her a stone and then both stood back. She knew what was expected. If she did not move, was not amongst the first, she would be marked. Wasn't she marked, anyway? Every way she turned she seemed to be controlled by the shadowy realm of Umbra, by Hweol, who would soon show his face in her world.

Yet his influence was confined to this little pocket of England. If he was as all powerful as they sought to imply then surely his power would extend further. But no. Beyond their world he was weak. Why? How? Tonight, was not the time.

The wall between worlds was thin. It was as if anybody could read her, reach into her heart and know her true feelings. Tonight, she would have to go along with things. She would have to cast her stone and then when all was over and the village slept, perhaps she could think more clearly. With an effort, she pushed such thoughts back into the darkness and felt the heft of the stone in her hand. It would be kinder to make an end of it sooner.

Liza walked to the edge of the pit, looked down at Anne. Their eyes met, and Liza understood what Anne was saying. Liza had already been forgiven. She raised her arm.

CHAPTER FOURTEEN
THE TRIAL

It never hurt to remind the people of the Weald, the consequences of forgetting where their loyalty, their obedience, was expected to lie. The Dance served much the same purpose, but that was a question of sacrifice and honour. A trial reinforced the laws of the land, reminded them of how life was supposed to be, and there hadn't been a trial for a long time. They had been lax, and perhaps that was why the modern world had encroached into their realm. They needed to buffer themselves against the tidal wave of signals lapping at their boundaries, block the messages transmitting through the skies. Never had the survival of those from Umbra been more under threat.

Once Tommy had thought man a simple beast, a domestic creature to be husbanded and tended like any farmyard animal. He had not thought they would have the imagination to jump beyond Nature's control, impose their will on their surroundings, and reinvent their place in the food chain. Yet they had. They had raised their eyes to the sky and into space, delved into the depths and the microcosmic. An extraordinary journey, although one which had no place here—unless they could manipulate it for themselves.

Perhaps that might be the next stage, the marriage of technology and Nature for the benefit of the Mother. Yet, he did not wish to travel that path. Tommy preferred the old ways, the *proper* ways, raw and real. They were in *his* church, adorned with the trappings of *his* religion. On the altar lay an antlered skull, wreathed in ivy and berries to represent Hweol and the Mother.

He had allowed the villagers to sleep after the previous night's exertions. He wanted them rested and observant. Their next lesson was to be carried out in the daylight hours. They would see what happened to those who allowed their children to stray. The parents of Amy, the Maid who'd died on the First Night, were to serve as the example. There was also the issue of Catherine. She had denied Hweol her baby. More than one trial, however, would mar the celebrations, destroy the mood. Justice had to be dealt with a light touch. He smiled to himself. She would not be forgotten, would be easily dealt with. Catherine would Dance with them on the final night with the rest of his Umbran brethren. He would send her an invitation. It wouldn't harm to have her attend the trial, sit at the front, learn the first part of the lesson.

A rise in the murmurs around him brought Tommy back to his surroundings. The old stone of the building sent a chill through those summoned, and the stained glass made shifting patterns in the flickering light. Braziers had been lit for all it was daylight. It was as if the sun had retreated from the village, unwilling to witness the events to come.

Hweol's court had already assembled in St. Catherine's. A curtain of shadow hanging around its edges, occasional flashes of ivory and silver, tooth and claw indicating the presence of the folk of Umbra. Those of the OtherWorld always attended such a trial for it was down to them to deliver the sentence, and they did this with gusto. It also added to the entertainment they enjoyed during the Dance, an unexpected bonus.

The jury was the traditional twelve of Albion, in this case six Lords and six Wyves facing each other in the choir. Tommy awaited the villagers from the altar steps, Betty and Fiddler sat at his feet, an unholy trinity. The fire of the braziers kept Betty occupied as the flames told him stories, created pictures in his head.

Occasionally, Betty would tell Tommy of what he had seen in the burning orange. Tales which would give those of the Weald nightmares but were mere fluff to an Umbran. It was an amusing entertainment on their many long journeys together. Perhaps after all this was done, they could sit at their own fire and share the stories, it would be a welcome relaxation.

In came the people of Ashburn, together with representatives from the remaining villages of the Weald. A solemn and steady troop of feet, eyes cast down, none willing to look at each other. Every face carried with it the same fearful expression. Old and young, they were all here for this was a lesson to be taught to all. Occasionally, a youth would glance up, defiance flickering briefly in their eye. Then they would see Tommy looking and the glimmer of bravery would be extinguished, their gaze once more returning to the ground.

An occasional cough, a few giggles—born of fear—disturbed this crowd, but on the whole they were silent. Those who were from the other villages would be required to relay the sights and decisions of the coming trial.

He waited for them to settle in the pews and then gave a signal. They knelt. He had put them in their place, and he would keep them there. This was part of the lesson. Unless otherwise indicated, they were to remain on their knees for as long as the proceedings continued. Pain and discomfort must be ignored. Any change in position would be frowned on—and dealt with.

Then came Nathaniel, Constance, and Catherine. Fiddler guided them in, playing a mournful air, but Betty did not dance. This was not his place, instead he sat at the feet of the judge, allowed his mind to be hypnotised by the dancing fires around him. He knew his place in the scheme of things.

Tommy regarded the Maid's parents, Nathaniel and Constance, carefully. It was always disappointing when both mother and father conspired against the claims of Hweol. Their daughter had never belonged to them in the way they imagined. All inhabitants of the Weald belonged only to the Mother, and Hweol had reclaimed Amy on the First Night. It was time to claim another. Perhaps he had grown lax in his administration of the Weald, been too kind, a benevolent tyrant. Yet it was more. The air in the world around him had changed.

Each time he returned to the Weald he could feel the buzzing and murmuring of signals sent invisibly through the ether. The wireless transmissions, the satellites, all sent their electricity into the atmosphere. It pushed and needled at him, lessened his power over others. It was taking more and more effort to resist and fight back, reassert his authority over *everything* around him in this world. One form of energy sapping another, as if the airborne electricity was feeding off *him*. It would not lessen, he realised. Not unless some disaster wiped out those little chips which defined the modern world.

How much longer would he and his kind be able to assert themselves as they did now? Soon, he thought, he would have to submit to the Renewal. The ultimate cleansing which would allow them to start again, with their powers once more at their peak. Would this Dance lead to such an event? He longed to feel the old energy, yet he had grown used to this little corner of the world, its people, the family he had built in the villages. It was here he, Betty, and Fiddler really came alive.

Perhaps they had got stuck in a rut and needed to climb out of it. The Wheel was turning, and they were moving with it as much as the villagers. Where would it take them? The arrivals had taken their seats in front of him. Thoughts of the future could wait. Only the present mattered.

He opened his mind and allowed his brethren from the OtherWorld to enter. They would be with him on this journey, know his mind. Even the jury, that emblem of justice. A false justice but one whose enactment was necessary.

Tommy stood and immediately the murmuring from beyond the veil stopped. He made his way to the pulpit, climbing its few steps in an almost reluctant manner. When he turned to face them all, he composed himself to convey sadness and disappointment, buried his excitement at what was to come.

The purpose of the trial was not mere admonishment and so reinforcing the laws of Hweol. It was also another chance to feed and nourish those from Umbra. Their shadows continued to glimmer around the building, taking a more solid shape before fading out again. Umbra had its viewing gallery and many of its inhabitants would weave themselves into the fabric of the building until it almost felt as if the church no longer sat in Cropsoe, but had lifted and transported to the OtherWorld, as indeed it had. Tommy stood for a moment, surveying his congregation. At last he removed his hat.

He leant forward, gnarled and dirt-crusted hands gripping the railing. Iron set in wood. He could feel the memories of those who had clasped this metal before him, had stood on this raised mahogany stage. Tommy remembered them all, preachers of flimsy faith, easily converted to the word of Nature, *his* word, *his* honesty—represented by the grime of his flesh. He had washed his hands in the soil of the Weald before entering, his sign of allegiance to the Mother.

In the front near the entrance, the people had washed their hands in the soil with which it had been filled. This was earth from his OtherWorld home. Sacred earth. Before him, in the front pew, sat Nathaniel and Constance, Catherine, flanked on either side by the Wheelborn of Cropsoe. Nathaniel stared at the floor, unable to look at Tommy. The women looked him directly in the eye. He could sense their challenge as much as he smelt their fear.

"Wheelborn and Weald born, welcome," he said.

There was no answering refrain. They did not know this song. It was one he would have to teach them.

"Children of Umbra, welcome," Tommy said.

A low murmur came from the shadows.

"The Laws of Hweol, founded in the love of the son for the Mother, have guided those of the Weald and of Umbra since time immemorial. It has allowed our worlds to flourish in tandem, deriving benefit and comfort from each other."

Tommy glossed over the true nature of things, that Umbra was a parasite, feeding on its host; a one-way relationship in reality. The older generations were blind to this, but the youngsters, they were seeing more beyond their borders via the all-pervasive internet, were itching to leave and experience the world. They needed to be brought to heel. If they wanted to travel the world, he would let them, except perhaps not the one they thought.

"This day however, is a sad occasion. It grieves me to discover the parent no longer teaches the child as they should, give freedoms they have not yet earned."

Tommy understood the need to hide in plain sight, maintain some form of contact with those beyond the borders of the Weald. It stopped awkward questions, allowed the area to remain one of apparently boring rural tranquillity. Why would any outsider wish to visit there? Locals who travelled the other way had to earn their privileges, and those who did would come back. Tommy always held something in reserve, binding them with invisible chains.

"On the First Night of our Dance, you witnessed the sacrifice of the Maid, for which we thank you. However, it has become known amongst us, the Maid, daughter of the Weald, has been spending time beyond our borders, was being sucked in by the lifestyle of those not us. Her experiences were discussed amongst our youth, encouraging them as well, to unwisely travel further. She has sown the seeds of dissatisfaction, and these must be pecked out as does the crow in the newly-sown field. The Maid has paid in full for her folly, so there is no taint in her sacrifice, but there are others who are ultimately responsible for this slide, this laxity in our community."

Tommy paused and looked at Nathaniel, Constance, and Catherine in turn. It was an interesting review. Nathaniel showed fear and uncertainty, cowered beneath his stare. The women continued to meet his gaze. Yes, they were scared. What woman, what person wouldn't be? But they were defiant. Both mothers who thought they'd done the best by their child regardless of the consequences.

Such mothers! He was proud of their strength. They would perform well in their coming ordeals. One sooner than the other.

"Parents are the guardians," he continued. "Of not just their children but also the laws of our world, and it is they who must answer for any deviation. The father is the one who must ensure obedience, oversee the natural order but the mother, the one who weaves the sacred bonds of family is the one who ultimately answers."

Again he looked at the three, saw the look of relief crawl across Nathaniel's face and then the guilt. Constance had seen his expression, snatched her hand away from her husband's as he attempted to comfort her. Turned her face forward whilst reaching her other hand out to Catherine, supporting the younger woman who had no one else to stand with her.

Tommy glanced at the congregation. Catherine's husband had raised his eyes, was looking at her, not with guilt or remorse, but frustration and anger. When he noticed Tommy looking, he shrugged his shoulders and bowed his head once more. Such a servile creature. He thought he had escaped, and he was right—for the moment. Catherine's baby, Emily, would be placed amongst the high born of Umbra to be raised amongst them. She deserved a good start. He hoped she would take after her mother. Her spirit and resourcefulness were to be admired. All he had to do was guide the child in the right way.

A Wyve had already stepped forward and taken the baby from her father, was cradling her in her arms at the back of the church. Occasionally, Emily would cry but was soon hushed. The Wyves had always proved good nursemaids. Catherine did not look around at these sounds. Her anguished expression showed him how it tore at her and still, she stood firm. For Emily to live, she would gladly pay the price.

"Constance Thorne. Will you stand?"

The woman rose, straight-backed, eyes fixed on him. He sensed the effort this cost her.

"You allowed Amy, your daughter, to visit towns and cities beyond our bounds. How do you plead?"

"Guilty," she said, her voice clear, strong.

"You allowed your daughter to carry out these visits beyond the permitted number of excursions and time limitations. How do you plead?"

"Guilty." No wavering.

A movement behind the front row. Her son had jumped up, was protesting. Nathaniel looked at his feet, his fear allowing his own son to slide toward danger. It was Constance who, with a slight bow to Tommy, turned and placed her hands on her son's shoulders, hushing him and pushing him back to his knees.

"All is well," she murmured. "It is to be. You can change nothing. Just serve the Mother."

For a moment, the youth appeared ready to argue with her, but there must have been something in her expression because he suddenly looked down once more. Tommy could see the boy's shoulders shaking, sobbing as he understood what his actions had cost her.

Tommy nodded in satisfaction at her words. A pity Hweol had not been invoked, but she had done enough and the boy would come to no harm. He nodded at Constance as she turned to face him once more, his gesture a reassurance. It was her turn to nod at him, the bargain struck. She would play her part without protest and her son would not be harmed.

"Do you have anything you wish to say?" he asked.

There was a slight hesitation. No doubt she had prepared a speech, exhorting others to challenge the status quo, but the intervention of her son had changed everything. She had to protect him.

"No."

Tommy acknowledged her response and then turned his focus back to the congregation. "You will all rise for our judgement."

The villagers rose. Catherine did not appear relieved at the apparent speed of proceedings, the overlooking of her 'crime' on this occasion. She looked resigned, fully aware her own ordeal was yet to come, had merely been delayed a while. Tommy descended the steps of the pulpit and stood in front of the Lords. Each of them raised a gloved left hand. Then he turned his attention to the Wyves. Each of the cowled Crones raised a withered left claw. Unanimous—as he had known it would be. Still, justice had to be seen to be done, and the jury heard.

Tommy stood before the antlered skull on the altar table. "The verdict is unanimous. Constance Thorne, you have been found guilty of treason against the Weald, the betrayal of Hweol. For this you will face the maximum penalty. As the seed in the field is sown, so shall it be scavenged."

"As the seed in the field is sown, so shall it be scavenged," came an echo from the shadows.

The villagers recognising what was demanded of them also repeated his words.

Constance swayed very slightly but then quickly recovered herself. "As the seed in the field is sown, so shall it be scavenged."

"Wyves."

The Crones stood and took their positions around the prisoner. Fiddler struck the note indicating the start of the procession. These were solemn, dark notes taking wing, becoming a flock and flying before them out into the open air. As usual, Tommy and Betty followed in his wake. He walked, constraining himself to the funereal pace of those behind him. His eyes, they followed those notes dancing before him, his longing to be amongst them evident.

Fiddler led them to a small field, no more than a paddock, one almost concealed from sight by the trees and hedges grown up around it. Nobody ever came here. Until recently, it was wild and overgrown. Now, other shadows had turned the soil so it lay bare and open. Tommy noticed how black the trees and fences looked, everything becoming dense and dark. A sombre cloud formed overhead, wearing clothes of mourning.

A flurry of expectation moved from branch to branch as the Wyves led Constance to the centre. They tied her to the pole normally reserved for a scarecrow. The villagers stood around the edge. Nobody looked at the ground anymore, all watched Constance, bearing witness. Tommy raised his hand, and Fiddler scraped his bow across in a raucous cawing to which the gathering darkness responded. Flashes of orange appeared as it moved closer, glittering eyes, amber darts hungry, feral, ready to feed on the bound figure beneath them.

Fiddler continued to bow, his movements wild and frenzied. Nobody moved, nobody danced. His music kept their feet frozen and their eyes focused ahead. They were not required to dance here, only to watch. A lesson to be learned.

Constance was only visible for a moment, the Wyves stepping back to Tommy's side. She was dressed in a black robe, the garb of both death and mourning, the contrast between its darkness and the pallor of her skin startling. Her hair was tied back so she could not hide her suffering behind its curtain. Tommy looked at her in sudden annoyance. The woman wore a slight smile, almost appeared contented. That would not do.

He beckoned the Wyve guarding her son over, indicated a place to Constance's side. The bound woman stopped smiling, understanding what he intended. She shook her head, her expression wild with fear. Tommy made another gesture, and the Wyve returned to the crowd, the boy going with her. Relief and obedience were etched across Constance's face. At last it was time.

The assault was led by two giants; crows who'd sat on Betty's shoulders as they walked to the field. They went straight for her eyes, each stabbing out an orb to leave empty sockets and blood streaming down her face.

Constance screamed, but soon her voice was drowned out by the crows as the rest of the flock attacked, became a murder.

As they cloaked the body, the sky reappeared once more, and light was allowed in. The crows were so highly packed it appeared as if a feathered scarecrow was doing a strange dance in the centre of the field. The caws, initially harsh and hungry, deepened and became softer, satisfied. Once sated, there was a huge up-rush and flapping of wings as the birds flew away and back to their roosts.

Nothing was left of Constance except for her clothing which although torn and shredded in parts remained surprisingly whole. The Wyves gathered them up. Nothing was ever wasted. The items would be used to dress other scarecrows, those at least would be already dead.

Tommy faced the villagers. "Sentence has been served and tonight, tonight we Dance."

His audience were cowed, not a hint of rebellion remained amongst them. The lesson was learned and reported across the Weald. His voice echoed across the field, drawing one or two crows back to the field, a sight at which some flinched. All was well once more.

Fiddler picked up on Tommy's change of mood, struck his bow again, played a melody which sent spirits soaring. Now Betty could play his part. He danced alongside Fiddler, leading the people back to their village before they departed in order to prepare themselves for the Fourth Turn. In the distance, a baby cried.

CHAPTER FIFTEEN
THE FOURTH TURN OF THE WHEEL

They were moving inexorably toward the end. The villagers had been summoned by whispered messages on the wind. They did not meet within their own bounds. For the Fourth Turn of the Wheel, the gathering was in the midst of Umbra. On this night, all humans would be allowed to step off the shadow highway and enter the forest of the OtherWorld. But only to bear witness. Not to interfere. From each end of the path, they came. Once more a procession, young and old, children clutching mother's arms, wives gripping husbands, husbands attempting to hold onto themselves.

The air was as subdued as the previous night, no doubt aided by the result of the trial. The Third Turn had taken a woman. The Fourth Turn took a man, another young man. Liza had come to regard it as Umbra's way of weeding out the undesirables from the gene pool. John walked at her side. Megan was again with Tommy. She seemed to have forgotten her husband.

Liza took his arm and squeezed it reassuringly. He gave her a faint smile. Under other circumstances Liza would have felt John was safe from selection, but the links to her and Megan from the previous nights undermined that. It would be a good way to rid oneself of a husband. Divorce did not happen in the Weald. Nobody sought it, nobody talked of it. Marriages continued until the cold of the grave came calling. And if the marriage was unhappy? All knew but everyone pretended nothing was amiss, including the couple. It was all part of the grand lie of the Weald. Another part of the idyll which everybody bought into.

"Has she said anything to you?" asked Liza.

John shook his head. "She barely comes near me. You see her in the pub. Sat next to Tommy, hanging onto his every word. She never comes to bed until I'm asleep. I tried to talk to her this morning, but she told me not to worry, everything would be all right."

"Perhaps whatever she's telling Tommy is keeping you safe," said Liza.

John looked at Tommy's back. "Somehow, I don't think so. I get the feeling I'm in the way."

Liza could say nothing in response, gave him another useless pat on the arm and they continued to walk on in silence. They were approaching the midpoint. Could see the other village not far ahead of them, gazes fixed firmly ahead, curiosity and anxiety hanging heavily over them. They reached the middle, and the gathering stopped.

"Tonight," said Tommy, "the people of Fleshing and the people of Cropsoe are joined as one. Tonight, they celebrate the Fourth Turn of the Wheel. They honour the people of Umbra with their presence and their sacrifice. They honour us with their blood. My friends, what is the Fourth Turn?"

There was a long silence and a cold, cold wind howled down the track behind them. Even as they spoke, a frost formed rapidly over the soil and on branches. Rime glinted in the darkness, breath on air turned to cold mist. The villagers pulled cloaks and coats tighter. They had come prepared.

As the temperature plunged in this shadow world, they gave Tommy his reply. "The Fourth Turn is the Wheel that freezes. When the Whelp walks in the forest. The Dance claims us all."

Soft flakes of snow drifted down, a gentle curtain of lace making everything beautiful. Some settled on Megan's hair, drifting down over her shoulders. It looked like a bridal veil. The snow did not settle in such a way on anyone else.

"I call to the Shadow King," cried Tommy. "To Hweol, the Keeper of the Wheel, the Master of Umbra and the Weald."

"We call to him," said the villagers.

"I call to the Lord of the Dance," said Tommy, as Fiddler once more played his violin. The music was as cold and sombre as the world around them. It made the blood pause and numbed the heart.

"The Dance claims us all," said the villagers.

Betty had moved to the centre. Was twirling around in a gown of bronze.

"Who will dance with the Maiden?" asked Tommy.

No one answered.

"Who will dance with the Fool?" he tried

No one answered. It had always been scripted thus.

"I am a Maid alone," said Betty, pretending to sob into his hands, but they could see him grinning between his splayed fingers. "Will no one take pity and dance with me? The King demands I have a partner."

Still the silence. All looked at the ground. They could not even look at those closest to them. It was as if they were trying to make themselves invisible, sink into themselves. Betty was looking at them. His mournful expression gone. His general good humour returned.

He simpered his way around the circle, wove in and out of the rows until he had assessed every young man in the Fleshing crowd. He reached in between the rows, as he had done on the Second Turn, and took the hand of a youth. He hung back and at first Liza could not make out the chosen until he was suddenly forced out from amongst his kin. Nobody looked at him. He cried out at Betty's touch, but already where the giant's skin had made contact with him, his flesh was turning blue. She knew him. David.

"The Whelp becomes the Man of Ice. His way is through the forest," said Tommy, and he stood aside, bowing to the couple as they passed him by.

Behind Tommy and the Whelp all walked. The branches and foliage parted as if pulled by an unseen hand, allowing the people to enter into the world which was normally denied to them.

Liza watched their backs as they strolled on ahead. He was another she had known well. He was known also to John who struggled to retain his composure. It was his younger brother. A lad who had become a bit of a ne'er-do-well, had built an unfortunate reputation once upon a time, but who had recently begun to turn his life around.

John stepped up his pace, and Liza stayed with him. The gap between them and the party at the head of the procession narrowed. Soon, they were almost within touching distance. John went to reach out, but Liza prevented him, pulling him back from taking a fatal stretch.

"Touch ice and you will freeze," she said. "It's too late. You can't save him."

Their voices carried on the cold clear air but no one paid any attention.

She had stated the truth of the matter. Reluctantly, he dropped back a little.

Liza relaxed, taking in her surroundings. She had always attempted to imprint this route onto her mind. Umbra was a hidden world, and she wanted to know how to get back home should she ever get lost. But the routes and images refused to remain in her memory, slipped away as easily as a wisp of smoke. It was as if the land had no intention of letting a true picture of itself leave the land of the path. Umbra had many ways of protecting itself, of hiding in plain sight. It was a living entity and the Wheel was its heart. If only she could stop it beating.

"No," said a voice, a whisper from the trees. "The Wheel will always turn, the heart will beat. You have no say."

Tommy turned and smiled at her, gave a slight bow of his head. Whatever she thought, whatever she felt, was of no consequence. They were all secondary to the desires of the Wheel, but a seed had taken root. She buried it for now, pretended not to acknowledge it. When she was safe back in Cropsoe, perhaps then she could do *something*. In the meantime, she would follow the Dance and burn the images she knew were coming into her own heart. Whatever she did, she would carry the faces of Anne, Jack, and David with her. Of Megan. The image was something she could not yet face, yet something was coming.

The troupe had entered into a clearing which widened to a dirt path that ran in a circular direction, edging a silver-coated lake that disappeared into the distance. The water here was of a kind she had never seen, never touched or drunk from. To sup unbidden, uninvited, from the lake was to take poison into oneself. They were all strung out, a human necklace, a choker around the edge. Betty stepped onto the ice and led David across to its centre.

Liza heard the groaning protest of the ice as it felt Betty's weight. Hairline fissures appeared, and it seemed as if it would break at any moment. Such a thing would not happen. Not whilst Betty was on the ice. Only when he returned to the shore would it be possible.

In the centre of the ice was a huge pillar, a solid block of frozen water. Betty led his partner toward it, pushed him against its smooth cold surface. Already blue, his body turned white as the column of ice claimed him, marched over his skin. It didn't absorb him completely. His face was unmasked. The purity of emotion displayed would be his ultimate gift. There would be nowhere to hide.

"I can't watch," said John.

"You have to," said Liza. "They're watching us, and there are two nights left. Who do you think they will choose?"

Both knew. Out of everyone around them, both felt the cold presence of Umbra upon their souls.

"We will talk when we return," said Liza, fixing John with a meaningful look.

Something must've registered with him as he nodded in reply and then turned his face defiantly toward his brother.

"I will watch," he said, "and I will remember."

"We will never forget," said Liza.

"No," said John.

Megan chose that moment to approach her mother and husband. She looked strangely elated, her eyes sparkled. Liza had never seen her more beautiful. Her secret pregnancy was already brushing her with its touch. Liza decided then and there if Megan said nothing about it to John that evening, she would tell John herself. He had a right to know.

"Mother," said Megan, strangely formal.

Liza did not respond. She had nothing to say. There was only one question on her lips. So far, Megan had refused to tell her, had refused to give any clue as to Simon's whereabouts.

"I don't need to tell you," said Megan before she even said anything. "Can't you feel him? Sense his spirit around you? He has been given to remain in Umbra as its servant. He does not need, nor wish to return home."

"But he is *my* husband, *your* father," said Liza, angry at Megan's flippant tone.

"No," said Megan, "he is no longer either, and he was never my father anyway, was he?"

John looked shocked.

"Didn't know, did you?" said Megan. "Nor did I until recently. Then I found out what Tommy and my mum got up to. Amazing what you can buy in a pub."

The cruelty of her words shocked Liza. Without thinking, she lashed out, slapping Megan across her cheek, leaving a red sting on the side of her face. The sound crashed through the wintered forest. Everyone turned to look them, distracted from their role as witness. Tommy joined them, anger flashing in his eyes.

"To strike one's daughter is against the Wheel," he said.

"To abuse one's mother is likewise against the code," said Liza, digging inside her for some remnant of strength.

Tommy looked hard at her for a moment and then burst out laughing. "I'll give you that."

"You cannot let her treat me like that," cried Megan. "She sold herself."

"No," said Tommy. "Your mother served the Wheel. She did what was required. Perfect obedience. You should venerate such a one as she. Learn from her. It would aid your survival in this place."

The implied threat seemed to shock Megan as much as her mother's slap had done.

"See daughter," said Liza, "it doesn't do to become proud in a place such as this, with a man such as he. Nobody is sacred."

"Except the child," said Tommy.

John looked bewildered.

Tommy grinned. Liza could see the malice warming his face. "You're to be a father," he said to John, "perhaps."

John reached out to Megan, but she shrank back from his touch. "A child, you're pregnant? Why didn't you tell me? You've been pretending as if I don't exist, as if I have no part in your life these past few days, and then I find out you're having a baby." He stopped. Looked at Tommy, then at Megan. "It is mine, isn't it? It's not *his*?"

Tommy laughed even harder.

Liza knew his game, sowing the seeds of discontent and mistrust.

The scream from the centre of the lake drew their attention back to the sacrifice about to be made. All elements were honoured during the Dance. The fire of the First Turn, the air of the Third Turn, now it was water.

Small holes appeared in the ice around David, but the trapped youth did not sink. He remained suspended in full view of the watchers. Up through these holes arced water forming a piercing stream which directed itself at its victim. As the water touched his exposed skin, he screamed in pain, his mouth opening wide, allowing the water to force its way down his throat. A continuing and unrelenting pressure which refused to allow him time to take a breath, to gag or reject it. On and on it came, a continual fountain drowning him above water. The parts of his body encased in ice appeared to convulse, but there was nowhere for the body to go, its movements contained so the pressure from within grew.

The icy tomb turned a faint pink as the water could no longer gain entry, having filled the man as a tap would fill a tank. The cold froze the liquid before it touched the surface of the lake, froze it all the way back up to the source of the fountain so all knew the inside of the body itself had turned to ice. The screaming had stopped as his voice was taken from him, but there was some slight movement in his face. A slight flicker of his eyes, unless that was the water invading another part of his body, triggering another responsive impulse. The pink deepened and diffused further throughout the column.

Liza understood what was happening, vessels and organs exploding and rupturing inside, corrupted by one of the purest elements on the planet. A life-giver in the Weald, its twin was a corrupting poison in Umbra as was so much else birthed in that realm. The mask of his face was frozen in contorted agony. The whole of his body turning crimson as it imploded, froze as it became liquid until he was a smudged scarlet shadow drifting momentarily in ice, until that little movement was frozen. He was gone. Another offering to this cruellest of Mothers. Nature red in tooth and claw had never appeared more apt.

CHAPTER SIXTEEN
THE END OF SECRETS

"When did you send the invitation out?" asked John, the following day.

"A few weeks back," said Liza.

"And you are sure they will come?" John's face wore a look of desperation as they both stared out the window. "This will work?"

"The Wheel demands blood. Sometimes I think it doesn't care where it comes from."

How could she be so callous and cold hearted as to lead a friend, a stranger to the Weald, into its dark heart. She could not give up those from the Weald, they were well known. It had to be someone else if she hoped to convince Tommy. Yet another sacrifice must be made. When would it ever stop? When she had originally sent the invitation, it had been purely as one friend to another with no ulterior motive. She needed her friend's expertise, possibly her husband's blood.

"But it is…"

Murder.

The word hung unspoken in the air between them. What had happened over the past few days was murder, but they had absorbed it. Years of witnessing and the inevitability of the ceremony had conditioned them. Tonight was something else. Liza herself had suffered the turn of the Fifth Wheel. That night had been the claiming of the unborn, and it had taken her son. Simon's son. That child, Tommy had had no claim on, but he always took what wasn't his. No second of the night had ever been forgotten, those hours relived every day of her life. They had all stood beneath the scarlet moon waiting until the crimson orb had finally shed its blood, leaving the Earth scabbed and crusted beneath its pallid gaze.

Silence had played out across the recently ploughed field, empty and devoid of life—almost. She could still herself see, how in the centre of the field she knelt, head bowed to the earth as if in prayer. If she moved closer to her memory, she would see her lips moving soundlessly, but it had been no prayer, just her mouth stretching repeatedly as if screaming. Her eyes wild and unfocused had darted back and forth although they saw nothing.

Her eyes, as she clutched at her belly, and her legs, bare to the night air, had turned black, painted—not in night's colours—but in shades of magenta and scarlet.

It wasn't just the moon that bled. Slowly, she had uncurled herself, pulled her hands out of the soil through which her fingers scrabbled as if seeking something, *perhaps*, she thought, searching in her madness for some fragment of the child she had lost. Liza remembered looking across the field to the village. The lights had been on in Cropsoe, its inhabitants celebrating through the remaining hours of night, toasting their good luck, conveniently ignoring the price she had paid—for *them*.

Liza had thought of her father-in-law. He would have been doing good business that night. At such times, the pub remained open all hours. She had wondered if Simon was in The Five Turns, drowning his sorrows in Richard Wheelborn's famous beer. The child had been his, too.

And then she recalled more. The crack of a twig had drawn her eyes toward the small copse at the edge of the field where a vague shape moved and swayed. It had come toward her, slowly at first, then running, stumbling before it collapsed at her side and pulled her close. Her husband had sobbed uncontrollably as he clung to her. Yet she had drawn no comfort from his presence, remained rigid, unbending, in his arms. Her eyes had remained dry, unresponsive. Eventually, Simon had calmed and eased away from her, a puzzled look on his face. He had raised his hand to stroke her cheek, but she jerked away from him.

"I've done nothing," he had said.

Exactly. He had done nothing. When the Wheel had turned and chosen her, he had done nothing. When the Five Turns ended, he had done nothing. When the blood had been summoned, he had done nothing.

Since then she had attended the ceremony as required but never raised her eyes from the ground. The victim's screams were beyond anything she could ever bear. Simon had done nothing to protect her. He stood and watched, unable to even meet her eyes. Like all the other husbands, fathers and brothers of the Weald. Until that point, she'd had very little to do with Tommy. But that night she had been given to both Hweol *and* to Tommy, before her body had healed completely—and Simon had done nothing.

She had turned against her husband, forgetting it was Hweol who had gifted her to Tommy in the first place. Simon had no power against the Lord of Umbra.

Whilst she was concerned as to his fate, there was also a degree of indifference and —she had to admit—a feeling of relief. Regardless that Tommy would continue to demand her presence in his bed. It would no longer be adultery or betrayal. Not that she ever really considered she was betraying her husband. It was he who had instigated it; he had no claim on her. What her future would be, she had very little idea. The steps, admittedly cruel, she had taken to try and protect her unborn grandchild, were in place. The Wheel was turning. Simon was gone, but she sensed, more and more, he *had* done something. The husband she had dismissed as weak, had been defying Hweol in his own unspoken way. Again, if only they'd talked.

A child would still be lost to the world, but it would not be *her* grandchild. She had to keep that thought upmost in her mind for what was to come. She had formed her plan but kept most of it from her son-in-law. She was not sure how much she could tell him. In Cropsoe, secrets had a way of coming out into the open, whilst the land read the minds of the unguarded.

The door to the pub opened, the draught, rather than the noise, catching Liza's notice. Her daughter stood framed in oak. John rushed over to greet her but paused, hesitant, apparently unsure of her reaction. She looked pale, undernourished, was swaying slightly. She stood there but for a moment and then fell forward. John, being so close, was able to catch her. Liza stepped forward to her other side, and they both supported her over to the small fire. The stones still held the warmth from the earlier fire and radiated a strong welcome.

"Meg, Megan," Liza reached a hand out, pushed the hair out of her daughter's face, stroked the pallid skin beneath. Her lips were an unnatural shade, her eyes bright but unfocused. It had only been a few days since she had taken to being Tommy's constant companion, but already her body felt frail, weak beneath her touch. It was not a good sign.

"Where have you been?" Liza asked.

Megan turned her face away, gazed into the fire, appeared to be struggling to gather her thoughts together. "He knows," she said.

"He knows? You mean, John?" asked Liza, puzzled. "Tommy told him, in the forest. Have you forgotten?"

"No. I don't mean him. I mean Hweol. He knows about the baby."

"You've been to Hweol?"

It came as no surprise. In fact, she had anticipated it, but she needed to know how far Megan had been sucked into the monster's plans, how much of the human remained.

"Yes. Tommy took me and Dad. We ate..."

"Your father, love," said Liza. "Where is he?" She needed to hear it from her daughter, without Tommy or Hweol to weave her words.

Megan shook her head. Her lower lip trembled slightly and then she appeared to pull herself together. She took a deep breath. "He's gone."

Her tone was one of final admittance, acceptance of what had been done. Liza understood the words thrown at her on the night of the Fourth Turn where her daughter had earned such a stinging rebuke had not been her own. They were another mark of Hweol's cruelty as he took over her mind. Here, in his absence, his influence was lessened, and all could feel at last the weight of truth.

Liza had foreseen this, steeled herself for the confirmation, but when it came it was still a blow. Much as she had come to feel mostly contempt for her weak husband, he had still been a form of a safety barrier between her and Umbra. His service prevented Hweol from making greater demands of her and her daughter, although her own duties with regard to Tommy were bad enough.

"I thought he was welcome in the forest. I mean, they invited us to dine. They offered him food and drink. They laughed and joked with him. They treated him like a brother."

"And you?"

She glanced around momentarily. "They treated me well. They did not harm me. Respected me. Tommy told me things." Here her strength appeared to fail her. "He told me he was my real father."

Liza looked into her eyes, expected to see anger there, saw only worry and pity.

"I know," said Megan. "I've known for a long time and all those hints he kept tossing out over the past few nights, how could I not guess? I didn't want to have it confirmed, that's all. When Tommy started telling me his stories, how he controlled everyone in the Weald, I had to stay with him. To find out. I needed to know if my baby was safe. If there was any chance of escape."

"And?" This from John.

She turned toward him and shook her head. "It doesn't matter. It doesn't matter if we're related, if the child is his grandchild. It is the blood of the unborn Hweol wants. And do you know something?" A desperate look swept across her face. "At one point I would have gladly given the child up. I don't know what tricks he uses or how Umbra hypnotises you, but it had me. Until…"

"Until what?"

"The Fourth Turn. Your slap and the cold did something to me, woke me up from whatever dream state they put me into. I don't think they realise. When I saw what had been done, when I heard them talking about the Fifth Turn and how I would be given to Betty, I… Well, I just ran. I'm surprised they didn't follow me here."

"No need," said John. "Where else would you go? They'll know where to find you."

There was silence for a while and then Megan voiced the thoughts Liza had long been harbouring, "We need to stop him. Get out of the Weald."

It was traitorous talk, and their words were probably being carried on the breeze and through the ground to Hweol in Umbra. He heard everything.

"Don't worry," said Liza, "I'll get you both out, and I'll finish this."

Her tone made Megan look even more worried. "You sound as if you won't come with us."

"It's possible. Don't worry. I will try to come with you if I can. If not, promise me, you won't wait. You'll go—for the baby." This was what it boiled down to, the future, the next generation, something which she would probably not survive to witness.

Megan nodded, and John took her hand.

"First thing, is to get some food into you and let you rest a while." The mundane acts of staying alive. It all seemed so trite and irrelevant.

"But we don't have long!"

Megan was right, yet the human body demanded certain requirements be satisfied in order for it to continue functioning. "We have enough time. If we try anything in the state you're in, we won't get very far. Besides we have guests arriving in the pub soon. Ava and Adrian. Remember Ava, Megan? She's a doctor."

"Someone from outside the Weald! Will they be allowed in at this time?"

Liza smiled. "They've been here before and never come to any harm. The Weald knows we need proper medical care."

"Why don't you call the doctor?" asked John.

"Because I don't trust him with either Megan or the baby. We've been in contact for a while. Ava said she needed a few days in the countryside to recharge her batteries. I told her we had plenty of room. I'm sure she won't mind giving you the once over. She also said she had some good news."

"And you say they're arriving today?" said Megan.

"Any time," said Liza. "I don't think they'll come to any harm. If anything happened to them, others might come looking." Hweol and Tommy wouldn't want that. She hoped she was right.

All heads turned in the direction of the still open door.

Megan was the first to break the silence. "Mum, all those years. I'm sorry for what I said at the Fourth Turn. I don't... Everything's been confused... Tommy."

Liza said nothing. What could she say? She knew the spells which Tommy wove, his distortions and lies, the corrupting influence of Umbra. None of it had been Megan's fault. All she could do was pull her daughter into a tight hug. She had her child back.

"Why did Dad let it happen? Why didn't he stop it, protect you?" asked Megan, when at last they broke apart.

"Because the Weald owns him. He, we, are Wheelborn. As are you.

Remember how it took you over."

"But it doesn't have a complete hold over us, the women," she said. "Why not?"

Liza could not answer. Blind obedience, ritual obeisance. That had never been her. Was there some taint of resistance in her blood? She had never been the purest of the pure.

Or was it the Fifth Turn, her own loss which caused the growing discontent, the determination to change things. Was it the Mother? Perhaps.

"Come on," said John, taking his wife's arm. "I'll run you a warm bath, ease the aches."

"Aches?" Liza looked at her daughter with concern.

"It's nothing, Mum. A few twinges, that's all."

Megan's expression gave little away, and that worried Liza all the more. "Go up. I'll bring you some soup up in a minute. Chicken soup for the soul!"

The joke fell a little flat, but Megan gave her mother another brief hug before heading up the stairs.

"John," she said, once Megan was out of sight, "you'd better pack as quickly as you can and get ready to move. Take the money from the till. There's plenty there to see you through. The car is in the garage. It's got a full tank of petrol. If you don't leave with Ava, at least that should get you out."

"We need to start moving before the three arrive," said John, his worried expression matching her own.

"They won't be here until dusk," said Liza. "We have plenty of time."

"And you," said John. "What do you intend to do?"

Liza allowed herself a faint smile and shrugged. "At the moment I'm not sure, but I'm certain something will come to me. Go."

She wanted them out of there. Wanted time to think. For Megan to have come back like this, to have come back at all was a complete surprise. It was possible Tommy had sent her in as a spy, but she seemed genuine in her thoughts about him. What had happened in the forest?

No, there was not time to think about that. She had only a few hours to hatch her plan regardless of the confidence with which she had expressed herself to John.

Tonight, the ritual would take place in the Souling Field of Lower Soulsbury. There would be no gathering in the pub to wait for Fiddler to play his music and lead them out. This was a walk no one wanted to make because of the suffering of the innocent it involved.

Her hand went instinctively to her womb as she remembered her first child. She had felt the first flutterings the night Tommy arrived. It had been as if the baby had realised the danger to itself and was communicating its fear to her. By that time, she had been frozen with terror. Unable to think of flight, she had been forced to walk the penitent's way on behalf of the village. She had carried all their sins for them. For them, she gave her child.

The walk had been horrific enough, the growing dread at what lay ahead of her. The silent watching of those she considered family and friends. None had looked her in the eye as she walked the path, barefoot, dressed only in a white shift. Her husband had led her there. He had given her to Tommy as if she was a commodity to be traded. She remembered the cold numbness creeping up through the soil and into her feet. Sharp stones and frozen ridges had dug in, cut flesh so grit rubbed into open wounds, made them larger. A stinging prelude to greater pain.

Part of her had never wanted the walk to end, knowing that ahead of her lay the opening to the dreaded space one woman entered at the turn of the Fifth Wheel. It had been a small field, but its path was on an incline. The gradient allowed the villagers remaining outside to see over the hedge and witness events without contaminating the hallowed ground. Admittance to the field was for Tommy, Betty, Fiddler, and herself alone. Simon had stood at the gate, apart.

Liza couldn't imagine that for Megan. She would not let her daughter go in there on her own. Even if everything went wrong, she would remain at her side. They would have to kill her first. An all too real possibility.

It was something which occupied her mind more and more. Could she face such a threat? For her family? The thought of an end to it all, of a permanent blackness wrapping her up and keeping her safe, had become strangely attractive. Yes, she could face it. It would stop everything, stop her suffering. First, she had to know Megan was safe and then, that the Dance was done. More than Five Turns had to end. There was another, the Sixth Night. All of Umbra attended on that occasion. Vultures come to pick the village clean. No more, she decided. No more.

CHAPTER SEVENTEEN
HOPE

The pub continued in a silence broken only by the steady ticking of the clock. The solemnity of the sky cast a gloom which permeated the bar. Liza sat frowning at the dying embers of the range fire. She should be stoking it up, preparing it for their prospective guests, providing the right ambience, as they said. She stared at the glowing coals, watched the ash form as each received a coating of death, much like she felt. The minutes ticked by as her mind remained empty of any plan other than one which would betray a friend.

Confident when talking to Megan and John, she had felt so certain she could come up with something to thwart Tommy. Instead, all she'd experienced was an overwhelming tiredness and dispiriting sense of failure. The sound of a car engine woke her from her reverie, and she was shocked to realise her expected visitors had arrived. She had lost hours to thought with nothing to show for it. The Wheel was still turning and Megan was at its centre.

Unwillingly, Liza walked to the door. She was torn. She was no longer sure she wanted her friend here, even though she could examine Megan and put their minds at rest. By not changing Ava's mind when she'd called, she had endangered her.

The Range Rover crunched across the gravel, coming to a halt as Liza stepped out to greet her guests.

Dr. Ava Taylor had changed little in the few years Liza had grown to know her. The woman first appeared in the Weald four years ago, an accidental visit which had turned into a regular occurrence. Two or three times a year she came to stay in the village, normally spring and summer, times when she said she needed to recharge her batteries. As far as Liza knew, she had never met Tommy or his Umbran friends, never been present on the nights of ritual. It was as if she had slipped in unnoticed, when the Weald's guard was down. Yet nothing was done without purpose.

Liza inspected her carefully, in case she revealed herself to be someone from the shadow world sent to spy on them, but there was nothing about her to arouse suspicion. Slim and efficient, early thirties, soft chestnut hair held loosely back from her face—which looked a little on the tired side. She came forward with the same frank and open smile she always showed to Liza.

Liza looked round for Adrian. Her husband was usually with her, but on this occasion, Liza noticed she was on her own.

Ava was a guest, but Liza regarded her as a friend. One of her few contacts from the world outside. Simon had never paid her much attention beyond warning Liza to guard her tongue and leaving the two women to talk.

They even shared many walks around the local countryside, yet, in all this time, Liza remained true to her word and never discussed Tommy or any of the Weald's strange rituals. It was as if such thoughts vanished from her mind when they were together, possibly the Weald infiltrating her innermost thoughts, protecting itself in this way. She wanted to tell her everything. There was an air about Ava, however, which indicated she had her own problems and such a talk would have to wait.

"You look well," said Liza, taking Ava's hands in hers.

Feeling the tension running through her body, she tried to push back her guilt at the escape plan reforming in her mind, the one to which Ava, *her friend*, was becoming central. A different plan to the original one of a simple flight and escape. Liza began to regard herself as much a monster as Tommy. A lesser evil, perhaps, but still evil. If only she hadn't hinted at good news when they'd last spoken.

"All the better for escaping that bloody cesspit of a city. I couldn't stand it for another minute."

"Then you've come to the right place," said Liza. "A few days rest and relaxation and you'll be able to cope with anything life throws at you." The lies were scarily easy to voice.

"I hope so. It came right out of the blue," said Ava. "It's making me evaluate what I really want."

"That bad, eh?"

"Yeah," said Ava. "Although I do have a bit of good news." There was a delighted look in Ava's eyes, and Liza's heart sank.

"What?" she asked, knowing the answer, dreading it.

"I'm having a baby," said Ava, her eyes sparkling with delight. "Never thought I could have a child. Remember I told you about all that when I first came here? When I fell apart?"

Liza remembered. They had walked most of the day, chatting about all sorts of mundane things. Then, as dusk fell and they walked the meadows back to The Five Turns, Ava had stopped, just stood there shaking and crying. Liza had held and soothed her until she could talk. Ava told her any hope of motherhood had been dashed and of the disappointment of her husband.

"That's wonderful news," cried Liza, hugging her with false enthusiasm. "You must be so pleased. And Adrian?"

Ava's face took on its earlier sorrowful look. "Once perhaps, but all these years he's been living a lie, deceiving me. We've separated."

She looked exhausted, almost haunted.

"We'll talk later, after you've rested," said Liza, guiding her inside.

She needed to get Ava away from her, allow herself to process the news, try and come up with an alternative to the plan which had finally, horrifically, taken root. Her arrival, her condition, was too much of a coincidence. Perhaps the Weald had been watching her these past few years and had decided to give Liza a helping hand. The price, however, the death of another unborn innocent, the torture of another woman, was too high.

"I've put you in the same room as always. Go on up. I'll bring you some food in an hour or so, but for now, you should sleep."

Ava nodded, a grateful look washing over her face as she allowed Liza to lead her toward the stairs.

After she'd helped Ava with her luggage and settled her in, Liza once more sat in the pub on her own. Her head was filled with one idea only, and it was an abomination. The Fifth Turn of the Wheel demanded the blood of the innocent. Whose child would be sacrificed, Megan's or Ava's? Try as she might, she could not dislodge the thought of the escape route the Weald had permitted.

Part of her wanted to run up to Ava's room right away, pull her up from the bed and grab her luggage, force her into her car and away from the Weald. The other part, the one thinking of Megan and of the other women to come, prevented her from moving.

A glint of metal on a nearby table caught her eye. Ava's car keys. Liza picked them up and went out to the car, inserted them into the lock. Climbing in, she settled herself in the driver's seat and stared at the control panel for a moment, before powering the ignition. Ava let her drive it on her last visit when Liza revealed how rarely she was allowed to drive Simon's car. The visits became tiny acts of rebellion against controlling and distant husbands. Even when Ava's husband accompanied her, Adrian remained in the bar, knocking back the spirits whilst Simon and the locals told him stories of Weald—the edited version tourist guides would call 'quaint.'

Liza carefully put the car into gear and drove it to the back of the pub, away from anybody's sight. Of course, there was no Simon there to worry about, but she needed to prevent Tommy from catching a glimpse of it. He would guess she intended to use such a car for some wild escape. Mothers protected their children and what else could they do except try and run away?

None of the three were in the pub at the moment, so it gave her time to position it well away from the line of sight of their bedroom windows. It was her backup plan. If Simon's car stalled for some reason, if the reach of the Weald went as far as that part of her embryonic idea, then they could still get John and Megan out. Perhaps they should forget about Simon's car completely and head for Ava's car first.

And what would Ava say? By then Liza knew Ava would not be saying anything, would be in the world of madness Liza herself had experienced.

But she could not think of that extreme, to acknowledge to herself the extent of the possibilities of her plan and its truly horrific nature. It was as if someone outside of herself was writing the script, guiding her through the ghastly play, allocating roles to actors as they appeared on scene.

A creak on the stair alerted her back to the present. She turned to see

Megan and John descending toward her, John clutching a suitcase in one hand as he sought to support his wife in the other. They looked anxiously at her. Liza took a deep breath. She was embarking on a path that would condemn her forever, but it was for her daughter and grandchild.

"Here," Liza said, giving John the car keys.

He looked puzzled.

"Ava's here," she said. "She's resting upstairs at the moment. Go and put your stuff in there."

"They've agreed to help us get away?" he asked.

Liza could not meet his eye. "Adrian didn't come. Only Ava. She'll help. We just need to finalise our plans a little more."

Megan looked at her sharply but said nothing. They did not speak until John returned, sitting on either side of the cold hearth, both absorbed in thoughts which could not be spoken in the Weald. The land listened closely on days such as these.

"Right," said John, as he came over to them. "Tell us what's going on. From the way you spoke earlier, I'd say you haven't discussed anything with Ava yet."

"No," Liza admitted. "She has her own problems. That's why she's here. To get away and to think."

"Problems?"

Liza looked into her daughter's questioning eyes. God forgive her for what she was about to say. "She and Adrian have been having difficulties and then, to cap it all, she found out she's pregnant."

"She's going to have a baby! But that's wonderful. I mean, she always thought she couldn't." And then Liza's face must've told them something of what she was thinking, of the possibility of an escape—for them. "No," said Megan, paling a little more if that was at all possible. "No, you can't do that to her."

"It's sick," said John in disgust, as he caught on. "You're sick to even think such a thing."

Liza shrugged helplessly. "It's all I have. Can you come up with anything better?"

He stared at her and then dropped his head in shame. "No," he said.

"But how can you condemn a woman to that? Do you have any idea of the suffering she'll go through?"

"Yes," said Liza.

"Oh, I know you've witnessed it," said John. "But I mean the real suffering. How can you possibly have any idea?"

Liza never told either John or Megan of her own experience of the Fifth Turn. Now, perhaps. But it seemed Megan already knew.

"You've been through it, haven't you?" whispered Megan, taking her mother's hand. "They took a child from you."

Liza held her daughter's gaze, despite feeling the tears that always came at the reminder of her loss, of the pain and torment of that night. She wanted no woman to go through that, least of all her own daughter.

"Yes," she said, at last. "I was expecting a son. Simon's son. Tommy took him away from me." She turned to look fiercely at John. "Yes, I know what that sort of pain is like. I can remember how it felt, as if I was being ripped apart. I saw the blood, my blood, my child's blood, dripping out onto the soil, sinking into the earth whilst the village looked on. I remember every minute, every second of that night. I remember a husband who stood by and did nothing, I remember how the Wheel turns on the Fifth Night all right. Do you know something else? If I could take a woman's place tonight and put a stop to it, then I would gladly do so."

As she spoke, yet another thought came to her. One in which two innocents survived but which held no future for her. Could she do it? It would take all of their care and subterfuge to survive the night. Even if the women were found out after the event, they would be safe. Another such turn of the Wheel was not permitted for another year. That part of the escape would have to be led by John if she was not around. The thought made her pause, swallow, as she realised it was the only way.

"We can save you and Ava," she said. "But it will be up to John to get you both away from this place."

"I don't understand," said Megan.

"What if... What if we introduce Tommy to Ava? He will know she is carrying. He always does. The only reason you would be chosen tonight is because you are the only pregnant woman in the Weald. If he saw a chance to save his own grandchild, a Wheelborn, he would, wouldn't he?"

Megan and John nodded.

"And then, as we go into the field, it is dark, isn't it? I would dress like Ava, substitute myself in her place. That's when you have to be ready, John. Get Ava and Megan back to the car, get out of the village."

He nodded again, a degree of reluctance on his face but counterbalanced by hope. "It sounds simple," he said.

"Simple is usually best," said Liza.

"How do we persuade Ava to come with us?"

"We tell her it's a village gathering, an old tradition to celebrate the onset of winter. When we all gather and feast and light a fire."

"Which is the truth," said John.

"Once there, you know how the evening pans out. It will be when Fiddler plays, and Ava will be led into the field and then left. When that happens, I will sneak in from the downside. Nobody can see me there, and I'll take her place, send her back the way I came. John, you must make sure you're waiting for her. Then get them away. Get them out of the village."

"Won't anyone notice?" asked Megan.

"They won't notice until it's too late. When only my blood touches the soil, then the Weald will know and the old promise will be broken. When promises are broken it weakens the bond between the people and the land. It loosens the chains."

"It's such a huge risk," said Megan. "And if it works it means, it means…"

Already the tears were falling. Liza pulled her daughter into her arms, held tightly, oh so tightly.

"I do it gladly," said Liza. "This land has always depended on sacrifice and suffering to survive. Well, I am continuing this tradition of my own free will, but for a different purpose. I will do whatever it takes and gladly. It is what I want. What I have to do. You know that, don't you? There is no other way."

As she spoke and felt her love for her daughter flow through her, all thought of the pain ahead vanished. It would be bearable because this was what would carry her through it. This would take her to the world beyond and give her peace. A sense of calm, almost tranquillity, settled over her. Fear had gone, and she was glad. It would allow her to play her part to the full that evening.

The only part she still disliked was the knowledge her friend would experience the terror she had felt, although she would escape before it became physical. She could not warn her, could not prepare her. To do so was to risk her plans. Risk them all.

"I said I'd get her something to eat," said Liza, rising with a smile. "I'll take her up some soup. Let her know about the gathering. While I'm gone, do you two think you can ready yourselves? When you see me in the field, you have to turn your backs, you have to run. Promise me that you *will* run."

This time they both hugged her, the three of them clinging tightly to each other for the last time. Hope and despair, love and terror all intermingled. Liza extricated herself and set off to play her part. When she turned to look down at the bar, she saw John sitting with his arms around Megan. She was leaning her head on his shoulder. Neither spoke. They sat, listening to the silence as she had done earlier. Their lives were changing, and the future was becoming strange and uncertain.

CHAPTER EIGHTEEN
THE FIFTH TURN OF THE WHEEL

"We can't let her do it," said Megan, after her mother had gone upstairs.

"If I knew of any other way, I'd try and stop it, believe me," said John. "But if you really think about it, it's a plan that might work."

"It might," said Megan, "or it might end up with both Ava and Mum dead, with us stuck here and Tommy…"

"It's the only way," said John. "It's our only chance."

"Our baby's only chance," agreed Megan. "And perhaps if it goes wrong, it's better to lose our child than to allow it to grow up in a place as twisted as this."

That drew a shocked response from him.

Megan had tried not to think such a thing, but the more she remembered how her father, how Simon, a faithful servant of the Weald, had been hunted down, how they destroyed others close to her, she could bear it no longer. Despite the heartbreak, anything would be better than putting their child at the risk of such a future event.

If she was going to have a baby, better to raise it in freedom than in the dark corruptness of the Weald. She did not want this child to be Wheelborn. Like her mother, she knew the Wheel had to stop turning.

"We should eat something," said Megan, although it was the last thing she wanted to do. "We'll need our strength this evening. I'll get some more of the soup Mum made up. You'd better check our room. Make sure we've got everything, that nothing's left behind to call us back or give a clue so someone can follow us."

"I've already checked," protested John.

"We have to be sure," insisted Megan.

There was nothing left up there—she already knew that—but she needed to keep John busy before he started to dwell on events. Out of the two of them, she was the stronger. It was how she had survived the pull of the Weald, how she had not been absorbed into Hweol's world. He had sensed something of her strength but not gauged how she kept a part of herself detached from their influence. He didn't know she had some protection from the Mother, now she was to become a mother herself. As for Tommy. She'd given the appearance of being completely under his spell.

The sights she'd seen sickened her, but she held on to that little bit of herself buried deep inside, nurtured and protected it, protected the mother she was becoming as much as the child growing inside her. Both Hweol and Tommy appeared to have forgotten the power of the Mother in Nature, and something told her Nature herself wanted to right this wrong.

The smugness of the power of the male had become too much for the Mother to bear. *Mother Nature was the ultimate feminist*, thought Megan. It was an idea that made her smile, gave her comfort and strength. She was not fighting the land. She was fighting the corrupt beings who made their home there. Perhaps she should have tried to explain that idea to her own mother. It might have given her strength, more confidence to face the night ahead. With the Mother on their side, they would have nothing to fear.

By the time John returned, she'd almost finished her first bowl of soup and was pouring another one, ripping off a crust of bread from the loaf as she did so. Her appetite was sharp, stirred by renewed hope. She had never felt so hungry. Its warmth spread easily through her, and her body relaxed a little more. She was able to think more clearly. First, she needed to reassure her mother. She remembered the looks she had been given when she'd walked with Tommy. Her mother had thought her lost to Umbra, become a traitor. Before they left tonight, she needed to explain to Liza how she'd remained with Tommy in order to protect them all. That she had come to the conclusion that the Weald needed to be destroyed. Would her mum believe her? Both knew how Tommy wove his spells, how the power of Hweol reached out through him into hearts and minds of others. They would have to trust each other.

John ate his food in silence.

She could see the pressure already furrowing his brow. Megan reached her hand across to him and squeezed it. "We're going to be fine. It's going to work."

"And your mum?"

Megan nodded. "We can't change that. It's what she wants. We can honour that best by getting away from here and making sure our baby grows up untainted."

"Even though…"

John didn't continue, but Megan understood he was going to say 'even though she was part Wheelborn.' It meant she carried the blood of Tommy and Hweol inside her. This had worried her until she knew her baby was a girl. Some instinct told her so, and that gave her the strength and determination to continue. The female was more kin to the Mother than to Hweol. She had that on her side.

When they'd finished eating, Megan cleared the plates and tidied up.

"Don't know why you're bothering," said John. "After tonight there'll be no one here to take care of this place."

True, none of her family, anyway. Suddenly she hated the building. It sheltered those monsters when they returned each year to take away what was special to their people. It harboured their evil weapons and their thoughts. It *colluded* in the terrorising of the Weald, if you could believe a building capable of such scheming. In some ways it was as alive as the land. Could it read her thoughts as she touched its timber, as she trod its floorboards? She hoped not, for if such was the case then all was lost.

"Perhaps it's time for this place to have a rest," said Megan.

"I know what I'd like to do," said John.

Megan put a finger to his lips and hushed him. Best not to speak such thoughts aloud. She slipped a box of matches into her jacket pocket. Just in case.

"Ready?" she asked him.

"Ready," he said, and they clung to each other, as they felt themselves cast adrift from everything they had ever known, each the only anchor the other had.

"Megan!" The cheerful cry made her jump.

It was Ava. The doctor was making her way swiftly down the stairs. "I believe congratulations are in order!"

"Mum told you then," said Megan, allowing herself a smile, to be enveloped, albeit briefly, into an air of normality.

"Couldn't keep it to herself," grinned Ava. "You know what prospective grandparents are like. Wait until it's born. She'll be spoiling it rotten."

That hurt and it was hard to keep the smile on her face. Nor did she look at Liza. She couldn't bear it. This child would never know its grandmother.

"Are you coming to the Turning?" John asked. It brought the point of the evening sharply back into the focus.

"The Turning? Oh, the little get together Liza was telling me about, cider around the bonfire and all that. Sounds lovely, actually."

"Good," said Liza. "A bit of fresh air is something we all need, and it looks like a perfect night."

They were at the door by that time. John opened it to reveal a cloudless sky. A soft moon washed over the village, and stars sparkled above them.

"You don't see such sights in the city," said Ava. "It's beautiful. I could stand here and look at the stars forever."

"And then we'd all freeze to death," said Liza, laughing. "Come on, we'd best get going. Don't want to miss all the fun."

They stepped out into the night, and Liza shut the door behind them.

"You don't lock the doors?" asked Ava.

"No," said Megan, "nobody steals anything round here." *Not anything inanimate*, she added in her head. What was stolen was something she could not talk about.

Ava linked her arm through Liza's, and Megan and John followed behind. They strolled along the village lane already carrying shadows. Many had made their way to the meeting place already. There were polite '*Good Evenings*' between the groups, but most kept to their own little families. Talk was subdued. Ava did not appear to notice, which Megan was thankful for. That would change soon enough. The atmosphere was charged. One could sense it, almost touch the sense of waiting, of wanting, of hunger seeping out of Umbra.

After a little while, she heard heavy steps behind her and turned, knowing who it was before she even caught sight of him.

"Tommy," she said.

In front of her, Ava and Liza continued to walk on ahead, the gap between the two couples widening.

"Megan," he said. "A good night for the offering, is it not?"

She smiled, squeezed John's hand tightly. "So it seems."

Then he sniffed, there was something else. Was this the moment that would start their whole desperate scheme?

"I sense," he said, "I sense a stranger and not one, but two. Perhaps," he looked at her thoughtfully, "perhaps my grandchild will live. Hweol would be happy if that were possible."

"What do you mean?" she asked, pretending innocence.

"There is another here who carries what is needed." Tommy was smiling broadly, his usual expression when he scented blood. "I will investigate."

He strode on ahead and Megan felt her body relax as the tension flooded out of her. She felt the same response in John.

"Should we catch them up?" he asked.

"No, best play as little a part in this as possible," she said. "Mum knows what to do."

And she didn't want to catch up with them for another reason. She didn't want to be in the presence of a woman she was exposing to danger, and she couldn't bear to be near her mother, knowing what would happen later. If she did, she knew she would breakdown and ruin everything. Safer for all of them if they hung back, remained separate.

By now, Tommy was in animated conversation with the women. Ava threw back her head in laughter. What jokes had he been telling her? What charms was he casting over the woman? The crowds were growing, stretched out alongside the hedge, all capable of seeing what was to happen beneath. She and John pushed their way through the throng until they were at the farthest end of the hedge, where Liza told them to wait. That was all they could do—wait. The rest was in Liza's hands.

They waited for the summoning. Megan glanced to her left, saw Sarah Duggan, aunt of Jack. The woman stared back, fury radiating from her even in the darkness. The flickering braziers cast shadows across the faces of the crowd. Sarah looked demonic.

She walked toward Megan, who backed away.

John, paying little attention to those near them, saw her.

"Come to watch someone else die for you?" sneered Sarah.

Megan could barely respond. She and John both knew the answer to that, but they could not tell Sarah. They had to put up with whatever she threw at them.

"I never asked for that," said Megan. "It is Hweol who chooses, you *know* that."

"But you are Wheelborn. You can influence him. You've done it tonight, haven't you?"

"What do you mean?"

"Hah, a stranger so conveniently arrives from outside, stays at The Five Turns. I bet she has what is needed, like you."

"What do you mean?"

"I know you're expecting," hissed Sarah. "I can tell. Women can, you know. Women who have been mothers themselves."

Here Megan choked, had to steady herself. Recalled the story of Mary walking out of Cropsoe, never to be seen again. Woman after woman had lost a child to Hweol. Sarah was simply one more in a long line, albeit the most recent.

"Why should you know the joy of parenthood when you steal it from others?" Sarah said.

"I did not steal it," said Megan.

Sarah grabbed her arm, started pulling her toward the crowd. "Why don't we ask the people? Put it to the vote?"

Her grip was tight and painful, and Megan felt panic rise in her. This stupid woman would ruin everything. If she carried on causing a disturbance, Tommy would see them, would spend the rest of the evening watching.

"You little bitch," snarled Sarah. "Our Jack was always too good for you, and you murdered him."

"No," said Megan, trying to pull away.

Then John came between them. He put a firm arm around Sarah, said in a loud voice, "Why don't you come and stand with us? It's not good to be on your own this evening."

And she was on her own, no child, no nephew, a husband long since disappeared in Umbra. Very few associated with her these days. She was regarded as unlucky, but they pitied her, so they would listen if she spoke out.

"Sarah," John said firmly. Megan had never heard that tone before. There was a strength there she'd never suspected. "Come this way a little. Let us talk."

"John," warned Megan.

He looked at her and shook his head. "No, I think this'll be okay. She's like your mum. Thinks this should all end."

Sarah looked at him sharply but released her grip on Megan, allowed herself to be guided away from the edge of the crowd so they were again in the relative safety of their own solitude. Once they were a reasonable distance, John began to talk.

"You know Liza lost a son here. On a night like this. You must remember that?"

Sarah nodded.

"Then how can you say this family desires such bloodshed, that they sacrifice others when they themselves are at risk of the same suffering?"

Sarah remained quiet, but there was an expectant look in her eyes.

"We'll let you into a secret, but you must promise you won't tell anyone. Promise."

"I don't..."

"If you don't then I'll have to take you back to the village. Oh, don't look like that. I won't harm you, but I will make sure you can do no harm to *us*."

Sarah nodded her acquiescence. Her reluctance apparent.

"Yes, Megan is expecting a baby. Until Ava turned up, our baby was at risk tonight. When Ava came, Liza hadn't known she was pregnant. Once Ava told her, it was then Liza came up with the plan."

"So Liza will sacrifice another woman's child for her own grandchild?" Sarah's eyes once more blazed with injustice.

"No. There is a point in the ceremony when the woman is left alone, when the fires die down and the darkness claims her. That is when Liza will switch places with Ava, and I will get them both away. No child will die tonight."

"But Liza will," said Sarah, horrified understanding dawning on her face. "She is sacrificing herself for you."

"For our baby," said John, sadly. "If there was any other way, we'd have taken it, believe me. With Simon gone…"

"Simon's gone?"

"In Umbra," said Megan. "He was hunted."

"I didn't know," said Sarah, "I am so sorry." The woman's mood had changed completely, her contempt and anger replaced by awareness of their common bond.

"Thank you," said John. "Do you think you can keep all of this to yourself."

This time Sarah smiled at them. "Yes. And I'll do whatever is needed to help. Both Liza and I have suffered, and it is time to stop the Wheel."

The woman took both their hands and squeezed. For the first time that evening, Megan felt certain everything would turn out as her mother had planned. It would be all right—almost.

"How do you feel?" asked Sarah, as they stood and waited. The waiting was deliberate, a ploy to heighten tension so when the woman was taken, the relief would outweigh the outrage. That would come later but by then it would be too late.

"It's that old saying, isn't it?" she replied. "Caught between the Devil and the deep blue sea. And the Devil is here."

"Do you know when I go to sleep, all I ever see is Jack's face. That look of terror. I don't sleep much these days. I can't bear to shut my eyes."

"I feel like that," said Megan, "I see Dad running through the forest, the imps after him, hear them tearing at him, ripping him apart. When … when I found him, there was nothing left, a scrap of his jacket," she paused to pull something from her pocket, "only this. Tommy laughed and Fiddler played and Betty danced, like they always do."

"Then we stop the Dance and get rid of the devils," said Sarah."

There was nothing else to say. The three of them turned their faces to the field, focused on the goings-on around them. If they got distracted, they might miss their cue, might end up risking everything.

The field, small and square, was lit by bonfires burning at each of its corners. Tonight, was the last turn of the Wheel, but tomorrow would come the Dance. She did not want to be here for that. The murmur of the crowds died away, stilled by the silvery notes of Fiddler's instrument, sparking glitter into the night sky. A pretty sight masking an ugly performance.

Tommy stood at the gate, a solitary man, shrouded in shadow but outlined by the flames. They could not see his face. He spoke the traditional greeting, the last time it would be heard this year, and hopefully the last time anybody would ever hear it again.

"Greetings, blood of the Weald, people of Fleshing, of Scythington, of Ashburn, of Reaper's Hill, of Soulsbury. The Wheelborn thank you for your gifts on this, the Fifth Turn of the Five Turns. You have sustained the land for centuries with your devotion and your sacrifice, and tonight, you continue with that tradition. Tell me, what are the Turns?"

"The First Turn is the Wheel that burns, the Maid who is wed to the land of the dead. The Dance claims us all."

"We bow to the Maid who will show her love," said Tommy.

"We bow to the Maid," came the response.

"What is the Second Turn?"

"The Second Turn is the Wheel that crushes. When the son of the soil is ploughed into the land. The Dance claims us all."

"What is the Third Turn?"

"The Third Turn is the Wheel that flies. When the crone rides the night, and old bones are crumbled. The Dance claims us all."

The chant and response floated clear across the night sky to Umbra, to where Hweol was listening. He would come when the darkness crept across the fields. That was when Liza had to switch with Ava. That was the time of danger.

"What is the Fourth Turn?"

"The Fourth Turn is the Wheel that freezes. When the Whelp walks in the forest. The Dance claims us all."

"My friends, tell me. What is the Fifth Turn?"

"The Fifth Turn is the Wheel that bleeds. When the unborn are taken into the womb of Nature, their blood the right of the OtherWorld. The Fifth Night is the night of the Wheelborn. The Dance claims us all."

The night of the Wheelborn. In so many ways.

Megan felt sick, not through any pregnancy-induced nausea, but the imaginings of what was to come. "I don't think I can do this," she whispered.

Sarah took her hand, and John slipped his arm around her shoulders. "You can. You're strong, like your mum. You can do this. You will do this."

"We can do this together," said Sarah.

They kept their faces forward as they talked. Betty and Fiddler were walking the length of the hedgerows, ostensibly to perform to all those watching but in reality making sure all were focused on Tommy.

The music stopped, and Tommy bowed to Ava who, still clueless about what was to happen. She took the hand he offered and allowed herself to be walked into the centre of the field.

"Why is no one else coming?" Megan heard her ask, her voice clear in the silence.

"This Dance is only for one, for she who is chosen," said Tommy and then dropped her hand, walking back to the field's entrance where the gate was pulled shut. Only Betty and Fiddler remained in the field with her. Fiddler struck up the music once more, a wild, manic tune that tore through every cell in Megan's body, discordant and jarring, adding to her feeling of nausea.

Betty danced around Ava, a lunatic flailing of arms and legs, bizarre and upsetting. Ava looked distressed. Megan could see her head turning, searching for a familiar, friendly face. The fires died down as Ava screamed out. Soon Hweol would come, after she had been bound with the ropes. It was almost time.

As the last of the fires died out, the darkness was complete. Six villagers entered the field, guided only by some instinct sent from Hweol. No lights were allowed at this time. They walked across the field, singing a strange song Hweol sent to their lips. Later, they would say they did not know what they sang, could remember nothing. From the corner of her eye, Megan saw a shape, crouched low, running into the darkness, toward Ava.

"Get ready," said John.

"When you go," said Sarah, "if they see you or suspect anything, I will distract them."

"But they could kill you," said Megan.

"Your mother has accepted her fate. She is a true Wheelborn, not the bastardised version Hweol has turned us all into. If she can do this, then so can I. For the people, for my son, my nephew."

As they talked, they kept their gaze fixed on the field, noticed another shape move toward them, closer and closer. Megan could see Betty returning to their end of the hedgerow.

Ava got to them not a moment too soon. John pulled her through a gap, pushed her to the ground where she lay too shocked to protest.

Betty had reached them. He paused for a moment, staring at Megan, then he smiled. For one horrible moment she thought he was going to pull her into the field, force her to dance with him, but no, not yet. He turned and skipped back toward Tommy.

"Now," said Sarah, helping Ava to her feet. "Run. All of you. The wheel will turn soon."

But Megan remained frozen to the spot, looking back toward her mother who was facing again an ordeal she had suffered so long ago, who, because she did not have the offering needed, would be condemned to an agonising death.

"Megan," said John, pulling at her arm. "We have to go. It's what she wants. If we stay any longer, it's all over—for all of us. Do you want that?"

Reluctantly, Megan allowed her husband to guide her away from the field. His arm was around her, his other hand out and guiding the stunned Ava to whom he uttered soothing words, explaining as much as he could in the time they had. Ava said very little as they stumbled and tripped over ploughed furrows and overgrown tracks through a nearby copse. Soon they were back on the lane to Cropsoe, and John forced them into a run.

Megan was soon breathless, gasping as her muscles protested and the fear and nausea rose up in her again.

Ava appeared unable to continue much further. "Couldn't you go and get the car? Come back for us?" she asked.

"No," said John. "They might get to you. I'm keeping you both with me. We're nearly there. A little farther."

The women were staggering, but Cropsoe was in front of them, The Five Turns straight ahead. Then they were in the car park, climbing into the Range Rover, John turning on the ignition. Ava didn't even comment that they had taken over her car. She sat there, pale and stunned.

Megan wondered at her thoughts. Had she made any sense as to the evening's events? Did she comprehend how close to danger she still was?

John put the car in gear and drove away, keeping the lights off so they were unnoticed. He was taking the road past Reaper's Hill, far from the current celebrations. There was a carriageway nearby which nobody ever used, the diversion sign having been in place for decades. He put his foot down, and they headed into the long dark night.

Only when he could discern the sign did he turn the lights on. He drove straight at the sign and onto the carriageway, almost into the path of a lorry. It was as if Hweol was going to stop them at the very last minute. Somehow their luck held, and John spun the car the correct way. They had escaped the Weald and in the land of the living, carrying their children with them.

"We'll put a bit more mileage between us and that place and then we'll stop," said John. "Then we'll explain everything properly, Ava."

The woman in the back seat nodded miserably.

Megan gazed out the window. It reflected back her shockingly pale face, a ghost. She was back in the field by her mother's side. There was a bond there allowing Wheelborn to communicate with Wheelborn, and Megan was travelling it to be with her mother in those final moments. She would stay with her mother for as long as she could. Mother and daughter against Hweol. When life left the mother, then Megan would return. Hweol could not corrupt that bond. This was something the Mother gifted.

Megan let out a small cry of anguish. She felt John take her hand. Liza was gone.

A service station loomed ahead, busy with continual traffic. A safe place to stop at last.

CHAPTER NINETEEN
HWEOL WILL NOT BE DENIED

Liza stood silent in the field, waiting. She was glad Ava had obeyed her without question. She hoped the woman would forgive her, and Megan, for those few moments of subterfuge. It was a dangerous plan. One she wasn't sure would work, but it had. It had been so simple, so straightforward. Perhaps that was why Tommy sensed nothing awry in their behaviour that evening. Normally so astute, he would pick up on the slightest thing. Perhaps because he was sated, lulled, by the previous four days' offerings.

Well, she would be the last. Although there was still the Dance tomorrow. She thought of the swords, sharpened and hungry, back in The Five Turns. If only they'd had a chance to destroy that place, that would have put a complete end to everything. Life was full of *if onlys*, and she had no time to dwell on that anymore.

The air around her shifted slightly. She saw the shapes approach her, heard the songs sung in that strange tongue, words of Umbra filtering out into her world. She did not understand them, but sensed their meaning. She straightened herself up. Summoned all her remaining courage, focused only on Megan, the baby, John. Could see them in her mind's eye driving along that road to freedom, Megan's ghostly face looking back at her.

Six women walked toward her, each carrying a heavy rope. Sending women to do this task was the ultimate in horror.

Liza pulled her hood up to conceal her face. She'd taken Ava's jacket and luckily, the two women were much the same build. The subterfuge would last a little while longer.

Then they were upon her. They lifted her wrists and bound them separately. Then she was forced down, onto her back on the cold, icy soil. Her legs were tied. The final ropes were fastened around her waist. The women walked back the way they had come, pulling the rope tight behind them.

Liza felt the pull on her limbs as they were tugged away from her, spreadeagling her in the silent night. Yet this was not the worst moment.

The ropes were no longer tearing at her. She could almost describe her body as undergoing a gentle stretch. Soon, they would bring the Wheel and she would be mounted on that, turned and turned again until the blood poured out of her. But this time she was an empty vessel. How would Hweol take that? How would the land react to not having what was promised? To the breaking of the bond between village and Umbra?

She turned her head, first toward the area where her family had stood. She wanted to be quite sure they'd gone. She already knew they had, could sense Megan's distance in her head, but she needed the confirmation of her eyes, now fully adjusted to night vision. Their place was empty. How long before anyone noticed? She prayed they would be so busy dealing with her that it would be too late to go hunting for Megan or Ava.

Fiddler resumed playing, skimming his bow across the strings. Red notes this time showering into the sky and onto the ground, blood spattering the charcoal canvas, pre-empting what was to come. Betty danced around him, catching the red confetti, smearing it across his face and along his bare arms and legs so he looked more like a monster than ever. At least Megan escaped that fate. Then the gate opened, and the wheel was brought in. Upright, they steered it across the field, long wooden poles guiding it, each held by one of the imps from Umbra. They needed no light to traverse the ground, headed straight toward Liza, steadily, surely. Then, just before they reached her, it was laid on the ground, ready to receive her.

They came for her then, those little imps, scratchy claws grabbing hold of her, lifting her up onto the steel monster. The ropes slackened as she was fitted into place. Then the bonds were tightened, cutting into flesh, preventing any slipping anyway. Her heart pounded, a steady rhythm defiant and strong. *Not yet*, she thought, *not yet*. The fear would come, returning in force with the pain she remembered from that former time, but not yet. She could hold it together for a little while longer, pretend for a little while longer. Although, if she were Ava, a stranger to the village, wouldn't she have been crying out, demanding to be freed, asking what were they doing to her?

But Liza daren't risk her voice. She was well known, would be recognised as soon as the first word was out of her mouth. She couldn't disguise it, either. No. She would remain dumb. Hope they interpreted that as frozen terror. Then another figure entered the field. A man—no, a giant—antlers atop his head. The Horned One had come for that which was his. On either side of him rode his Lords. These were the hunters who had chased her husband down and murdered him. Would they condemn her to the same fate? Rip her to pieces? Oh God.

She closed her eyes, felt Megan's presence. Heard her voice whisper that she was safe, that they were all safe and away from here. It gave her strength, and she lifted her head up once more.

I'll stay with you, said Megan. *For as long as possible.*

Liza did not want her daughter to witness this, but she needed her strength, understood this last contact was a gift from the Mother. She was not alone. *My grandchild lives*, she thought grimly. That is enough. He stood in front of her. The Horned One. The monster who destroyed so many lives with his demand for blood.

Still he did not see her properly, her hood well down over her face, but he sensed something, was sniffing the air. A step nearer, his nostrils flaring as he breathed her in. Then the sudden shock of recognition, and the hood was torn from her head. She was forced to confront him then, this desecration of nature, this beast from the shadows of Umbra.

She smiled.

Eyes blazed. The deep red of the Fifth Turn raged at her. Long and hard, he stared, reading her, searching her. She could feel him probing her mind, stalking the corridors he had laid claim to all these years. But she fought him. From somewhere she managed to summon the strength to build walls, to deny him entry, so he had to retreat thwarted and furious.

He threw back his head and roared his anger to the night sky, his voice scattering Fiddler's accompanying music so his notes rained down in a shower of blood. The music slowed, became hesitant, something that had never happened before. Tommy, Fiddler, and Betty came closer, stood alongside Hweol. The crowd, watching in silence, stirred at this unexpected turn of events. A low murmur reached across the field.

She held herself tightly, her defiance holding her together. Stared into the animal not of this world, the monstrosity that had taken her own son, forced her to send her remaining child away.

"You deny me? Your Master? On the Fifth Turn?"

"Yes." Her voice was unwavering, clear across the night.

The murmur from the watching villagers grew louder, and she saw someone to her right clamber through the hedge. The figure waved an arm and others, at first hesitant, but then more surely, followed. The mass of darkness approached like a tidal wave, creeping up on those gathered in the field's centre, surrounding them.

Tommy noticed but paid no attention. To acknowledge their unwanted presence was to create another weakening of their hold. She understood that. At the front of the crowd she could see Sarah Duggan. Was the woman going to help? After everything she had gone through? Liza doubted anything much would change, that she would be spectacularly rescued in any way, but her presence did much to add to her strength, fortify her in the presence of Hweol. She returned her gaze to him.

CHAPTER TWENTY
SABOTAGE OF THE FIFTH TURN

"You owe me blood," growled Hweol.

"No," she said. "I gave that many years ago, and I have been giving it time and again as have the others here tonight. I will not give you what you want on this night. I take back any promises to you. You have no hold over me. Only Mother Nature has the right to take."

"And am I not the offspring of Nature? The Son of the Mother?" There was fury in his voice unlike any she had heard before. It was not born of fire but of ice. It was cold, so cold it misted his breath and sent the temperature plummeting, dowsing the remaining embers of the fires, smothering the lighted torches the villagers carried with them. "These lands belong to me. They are part of Umbra, and you challenge it? Perhaps you should spend a while in *my* lands."

"And be reunited with my husband, perhaps?"

Hweol smiled thinly. "We had great sport with that man. You have spirit. I think we would have even greater fun with you."

The imps surrounding him giggled, their silvery laughter sending icy tentacles out onto the soil and edging the empty branches, glittering hair and clothes. The winter of Umbra was reaching out to them. The horses of the Lords, stamped their hooves and snickered impatiently as if sensing the opportunity of an unexpected hunt.

"Tonight demands blood," he said finally, "and I *will* take it." He turned to the crowds of Umbran and Weald alike. "The Wheel will still turn for the Fifth time. The sacrifice will be made. Soil needs to be fed. Your sons and daughters, your harvest and families, all need to be fed. Defy me and you will starve. Your communities will die, and you will sink into the earth with no one to mourn you."

"Better that than more years of slavery," said a voice.

Liza recognised the voice. It was Sarah. The woman was going to get herself killed.

Hweol turned toward Sarah. "You speak unwisely, but because you have already suffered sacrifice this year, I will allow you to remain. Out of pity and my compassion. Speak again, and you must suffer the consequences."

"Only the Mother can silence me," said Sarah and walked past Hweol to stand at Liza's side. She reached out and took Liza's hand.

"Another Crone who wishes to take the turn of the Wheel," sneered Tommy.

Fiddler looked worried. "I have no music for this."

"Because this music has not yet been written," said Sarah.

"Tonight, we make our own," said Liza.

"Then it will be filled with the song of your pain and your agony," said Hweol to them both.

He clicked his bony fingers, and the imps swarmed toward Sarah. Then they were on her and Liza, moving the already bound woman over so room could be made for both of them.

"Fiddler," said Hweol. "Play."

The man ran his bow across uncertain strings, but as the ropes were tightened once more and Hweol drew himself up to his full height, the music became more certain.

"Tonight," said Hweol, "the turn of the Wheel shall not take place in this world. It will be consecrated in Umbra, and you will all witness. You will all take heed. You will see what happens to those who choose to break their vows to Hweol."

The crowd fell back, and the imps took their place alongside the huge wheel, now placed between long poles which they supported on their backs. Hweol let out one more mighty roar at the moon which fled behind a passing cloud. Then he turned and led the people of the Weald onto the shadow path. He walked at its front with the Lords behind him. After them came Tommy, Betty, and Fiddler. The music was still playing and Betty was dancing, become a whirling dervish, swirling his skirts which crackled in the biting cold. Then came the imps, hauling over the wheel. As it turned so the women were rotated with it, one minute upright, the next grazing at the ground. Mud and stones flicked up from feet, hitting their faces causing numerous cuts and grazes, a swarm of tiny stings. Then they were back upright.

"I can bear this," said Sarah.

"Don't talk," said Liza. "Save your strength. There is more, and it is much, much worse."

"I remember," said Sarah. "We face it together."

Liza was thankful she was not alone. She drew comfort from the other woman's shared suffering.

Behind the wheel walked the villagers, those Liza had fed and drawn pints for over the years. She'd listened to their sorrows, comforted them in times of need, been the friend they'd all demanded. But now, it was as if they were strangers. They did not look at her or Sarah, kept their eyes to the ground, shamed at their behaviour. She needed to rouse them from their stupor, get them to react, to start the challenge to Hweol that would at last destroy him.

"Sing," she called out to them, when she was once more upright. "Sing and let them know you are people of the Weald, not cowards crawling into Umbra."

The world turned upside down. "Think of those nights when we all sang together," she said, when upright again. "When we celebrated life and passing. We were all friends then. I still regard you as friends. Will you sing one song for me to mark my passing? Help me face this with strength?"

"Fiddler makes the music," snapped Tommy.

"We make our own," said Liza, and she started to sing. It was an old folk song, a lullaby she had often sung to Megan as a baby. A traditional lullaby of the Weald:

Hush, my child, your Mother's here
In the dark, there is naught to fear
I'll hold you close until the break of day
Keep the monsters of the night at bay…

Sarah sang too, and soon one or two more hesitant voices joined in. The women. It was the mothers of the Weald who were singing, and their voices were soft and gently breaking through the ice of Umbra, dissolving the ice on the branches so the water dripped as tears, sobbed onto the ground.

As the sound reached the ears of Hweol and the hardened ground softened into mud, the Lords whipped their horses around and rode amongst the crowd, beating them into silence. The throng left bodies prone behind them. Nobody looked back. Nobody saw the hands of others reach out and pull those on the ground into the trees. Only Liza and Sarah saw.

"I hope they are friends," said Liza, as she watched the fallen vanish.

"There are such here?" asked Sarah.

"Some," said Liza. "But they never show themselves. They're too weak."

"And we're not?"

"No," said Liza. "Something is already changing. Don't you feel it?" She didn't say that she doubted either of them would live to see it through—they were only the catalyst, after all.

Hweol lead them off the track and down into a part of Umbra none of them had ever set foot in before. They were in a flat open space at the bottom of a valley. Mountains soared over them on either side. Liza had only ever experienced woods and trees in Umbra, not this.

In the centre of this space was an old stone floor made out of huge rocks. As they neared it, the wheel rotated smoothly. She could see strange carvings amidst rusted stains. Rust. Blood. A groove ran around it, its width a perfect fit for the wheel on which they were travelling. She had got used to the topsy-turvy motion of the wheel, and its rhythm had dispelled her fear for the time being. Seeing where the wheel was to come to rest brought the terror rushing back.

Megan was still with her, murmuring memories, talking to her, keeping her away from it all.

The imps hauled the wheel up onto the stone base, removed the shafts, and then allowed it to crash to the ground so it slotted into place. The fall was jarring, jolted every bone in her body. Both women let out an involuntary cry at the pain, at the suddenness of their fall. Liza could barely move her neck. Fire burned up through her bones.

Sarah whimpered slightly beside her.

Liza tried moving fingers and toes, felt a faint response in each. Not broken then. Her back was in agony.

"Sarah," she whispered. Liza felt a slight touch of her hand as the woman reached out to her.

"I'm fine," came the response. "A bit winded but otherwise okay."

Nobody seemed to be paying any attention to them. Liza turned her head to try and see what was happening. The villagers were forced to their knees, facing a huge stone throne on which Hweol sat. He looked down at them all, seemed to grow in size so he towered over everyone. The Lords dismounted and imps took the horses away to graze. The assembly was ready.

Other creatures moved around the wheel, fixing it to chains and rods, building a mechanism of some sort that would not be good for either woman. These creatures she had never seen before, small like the imps, only they were not silver but black, clawed and leathery. Their song was not silver but steel, chains weaving across the air, cruel and heavy. Tongues lolled; snide grins leered across their faces. Demons? She considered Hweol might be the Devil. If that was the case, how could they fight against him? What use was her pathetic little sacrifice going to be?

A gentle breeze caressed her cheek and stilled her thoughts. The air was not any she had breathed in Umbra. This was the air of the Weald. It had entered with them, permeated the chinks in the barrier between Umbra and the world. A beautiful contaminant which gave her strength.

"It's changing," she whispered to Sarah. "It's changing already."

A nearby demon heard her comments and let out a cackle. "No, lady. No power can change this. The Wheel will turn as it always has, and tonight you will turn as they turned at the beginning of time. When we are finished with you, those you have left behind will wish they kept to the traditions of the Wheel. Much less messy." And then the last chain was in place.

Hweol rose from his throne. "Today is the Fifth Turn of the Wheel," he roared. "Nothing will stop it turning. Tell me. What is the Fifth Turn?"

The crowd responded in a subdued tone, and Liza could sense the fear beneath it. "The Fifth Turn is the Wheel that bleeds. When the unborn are taken into the womb of Nature, their blood the right of the OtherWorld. The Fifth Night is the night of the Wheelborn. The dance claims us all."

"Tonight, we have lost the unborn. Still, we take life into the womb of

Nature. We give one mother to another. The Fifth Night is the night of the Wheelborn, as it always has been, as it always will be. The Dance claims us all. Tomorrow you *will* dance."

The crowd bowed its obedience.

"No," cried Liza, seeing Hweol continuing to rule for years to come. "No. The soil needs the unborn. If it is not gifted that, the old oaths have been broken. Hweol will have broken his promise."

"You dare continue to challenge me, knowing what you will soon be facing?" he demanded.

"We may be broken on the Wheel," said Liza, "but so will you."

Blood and darkness cracked across her vision as Hweol lashed her with a whip snatched from one of his Lords. Copper filled her mouth, and for a brief moment she felt as if she were drowning before it cleared. She spat out the vile taste, gasped for precious breath. It was starting and there would be worse to come. A crimson streak also ran across Sarah's face.

Sarah smiled faintly. "Don't worry. He missed me. It's just your blood."

"But next time it'll be yours," sniggered one of the demons.

Her smile slipped.

"You will give your blood," said Hweol, "and we will all drink of it."

Liza felt Megan shudder at this. She could not allow her to remain. Down through that invisible link she sent her the words to send her away. At first Megan resisted, until her child made its presence felt, and mother withdrew from mother.

Liza felt relief then. She stretched her fingers out to Sarah, fingertip to fingertip, they could barely touch. "Ready?"

"Ready," said Sarah.

"I wish you didn't have to go through this."

"I wish neither of us did, but hopefully we will be the last."

"The land takes blood," said Hweol, overhearing them. "It does not matter who from."

"There I think you will find you are wrong," said Liza. "You have taken too much. You have corrupted Nature and her land. The Mother is angry, and she will turn against you. She is preparing."

He laughed then. A prideful sound, echoing around the valley. "How little you know," he said, and gave a signal.

Four demons stepped forward. Each clasped a lever, pushed down, and the wheel turned. Slowly they rotated, the wheel being lowered down into the ground, away from the sky, away from the villagers. As they sank lower into the depths, Liza saw only the antlers of the Horned One as he stared down at them. Then light became but a speck, and the rotation paused.

Other creatures came out of the darkness, slippery things, hissing and weaving between the spokes. Scaled hands, shapes to which her mind could give no form. They worked on different parts of the wheel, inner rings within rings before they withdrew. Once more Liza heard the crunch of the levers. The wheel, or wheels as they had become—wheels within wheels—began to turn.

Liza felt her head turn one way, her neck another, her trunk, arms, and legs, all working against each other. The gentle tug turned to unbearable agony as sockets were pulled and bones dislocated, grinding and grinding as the wheel turned, twisting her body so it fought against itself. At first, she screamed. Then she heard its echo in the chambers and realised it was Sarah. Neither woman could have comforted the other; it was not physically possible. More turns, and she could feel the dislocation stretching, pulling. Felt skin tearing, ripping apart, the container of her body opening. Still she lived, how?

Her heart hammered, blood roared in her ears, filled her eyes, drowned her. She was being drained, opened up and poured out over the floor of this subterranean world. Occasionally, the blackness claimed her, and she sank into its oblivion with relief. Then she would be jerked back to her surroundings, forced to endure even more, even worse. Her screams had stopped, as had Sarah's. Their dislocated jaws, torn nerves, muscle damage, all combined to prevent them from uttering a sound. It didn't stop them feeling the pain. Not yet.

Whoever designed this wheel timed it so the senses felt the suffering right up until the last possible minute. They had adjusted the wheel, made the turns last longer. An exquisite agony, horrific and unbearable. Liza felt as if her head had become detached from the rest of her body, although she knew that was not possible if she still felt alive. And she did. If she'd been able to look down at herself, she would have seen she was not far off from that point. Her spinal column was only just in contact with her neck. The slightest movement would soon end that connection completely, and the wheel was getting slower. Soon, soon.

Eyes gleamed with excitement around them. Around the rim of the wheel they lurked. On edges above, they stared down. So much hunger could be read in those eyes. Agony. More and more. Slower still. Pain…beyond…beyond…oh God. This was more than she had experienced that night, more than she could ever have envisaged. Her last thoughts as the wheel made one more slight, final, fatal move was, *Was it worth it?*

*****

At the bottom of the shaft, all was silent apart from a steady lapping as the creatures drank from what was given. Others collected their offerings in buckets to be returned to the surface. The bodies were picked, bit by bit, from the wheel and cast into a nearby pit which descended even further than the one into which Simon had looked. Soon the wheel had been picked clean. One could even say it gleamed in the darkness. Then it turned again. Rose back up into the light toward Hweol and the waiting villagers.

There were low groans when they saw its empty state, accompanied as always, by relief that it was over, the women's suffering done. The imps filled goblets with the blood of the women and Hweol took one. He raised it to the greying sky. The sun that was threatening to rise, already pushing aside the curtain of night.

"One mother gives to another," he cried. "This is the blood of the Fifth Turn. The Dance claims us all, and tomorrow we Dance."

He took a sip and then scattered the contents on the ground. The imps worked their way through the crowd, anointing the forehead of each with the blood before forcing them to sip from the cup. By being blooded in Umbra, the bond between the people was strengthened. Hweol felt as if order was restored. But something felt wrong. The soil had accepted his offering and still…

He shook it off, the challenge to his authority had marred the evening, but now all was as it should be. Tomorrow the swords would be drawn and all would Dance. Umbra would be able to rest for the winter. He gestured to the people to stand and wearily they got to their feet, turned them in the direction of home.

"Go," he said. "Tomorrow we will Dance. Prepare yourselves."

*****

After the crowds had gone, Tommy, Betty, and Fiddler followed.

"The swords are ready?" asked Betty.

"Have been for a long time," said Tommy.

"The pub will be empty when we get back," said Betty. "Always fancied being a landlord."

"Well, it's yours if you want it," said Tommy.

"Really," said Betty, surprised at the immediate agreement.

"All I need is my room. I prefer a nomad's life."

"And when Megan comes back.," said Betty.

"You think she will come back?" asked Fiddler.

"I know she will," said Betty.

Tommy looked at them and said nothing.

CHAPTER TWENTY-ONE
LOSS

They pulled up in a corner of the car park, sat in silence as each tried to come to terms with what they had escaped.

"Is it over?" asked John.

"Yes," said Megan. "Mum's gone."

There was only a void in place of the bond she had always shared with her mother. She had been cast adrift. A sudden ache in her womb made her start, brought her back to the present. Another pulse, a cramp reminiscent of those which occurred with so much regularity, month in, month out.

"What is it?" John flicked on the interior light, was looking at her with even greater concern.

"I … It's …" Fear took hold, growing in certainty as the ache increased. *No, no, no*, not after everything, not after all she sacrificed, her mother had sacrificed. "*No.*" Her voice came out strangled, a whimper, causing Ava to stir and look over the back of her chair.

Megan understood it then. Leaving Cropsoe broke not just the bond with her mother but that with her baby. Hweol was taking his revenge, taking her child from her. She felt the blood trickle down her leg, soak into her jeans.

"It's the baby," she whispered, the awful realisation claiming her completely.

"Hospital," said Ava, her professional training kicking in. "Now."

Thankfully, the city wasn't far, and the hospital was clearly sign-posted, but that brought no relief. By the time they drew up at A&E, the blood was pouring from her. It was not gentle, gradual, but a violent flood, a torrent that left her sick and shaking, disoriented and detached from everyone around her.

"Can you walk?" asked a nurse.

A stupid question. Couldn't she see? Megan looked at her blankly, saw the bright lights and began to sway. A porter rushed over with a wheelchair and soon they were hurrying down stark corridors, clinical and harsh, toward the gynaecological ward. John held her hand all this time and tried to comfort her, but she did not hear him, could not make out his words. She had turned her mind inwards. She did not notice when they separated, and she was taken into a darkened room, a sharp contrast to those she had passed.

They laid her on a bed and proceeded to clean her up, supplying a heavy gauze to absorb the blood that would not stop coming, not speaking or asking questions, not comforting. She was left alone. Nobody came to her. Nobody told her what was happening. She was left to stare into the darkness, feeling strangely detached from her own suffering, from the child which rejected her. She put that down to Tommy and Hweol. They had spoken to the child in the OtherWorld, crooned songs in a strange tongue, branded the child as theirs even before it was born. She might have escaped but they would take her baby.

She stared at the clock, watched the hands drag themselves round. Another hour passed and then a doctor finally appeared, looking flustered but unapologetic. The examination was rough, cursory. Her words diffident, a muttered something about haemorrhaging, an annoyed tone at having to set up a drip.

Megan couldn't believe the dismissiveness of what she was going through, could say nothing to get a response from either the doctor or the nurse who attached a tube to her hand. Her eyes fought to stay awake. She wanted to see John, but they'd given her something to knock her out. That or the loss of blood had finally taken its toll because she fell asleep, dreamlessly, deeply.

When she woke it was to more darkness. She was in a different room, a small ward with other women.

"We'll be moving you in a bit," said a nurse, noticing she was awake. "Nothing to worry about. It's just we didn't have anywhere else to put you tonight."

Megan stared at her, wondered what on earth she meant. Then when the porters came and moved her bed, she caught sight of the sign on the wall. Hysterectomy. They had put her here, a woman losing her child, amongst a group of women voluntarily giving up their rights to motherhood. Unfair perhaps, she knew not all were necessarily there through choice, but that didn't matter. Overwhelmed, it had become a nightmare from which she had desperately wanted to escape and even as she thought that, the pain spasmed into life, and she felt the force of her loss.

Eventually, she was put into yet another ward. This one with only two other women in it. One was asleep. The other sat up, wide awake, staring into the distance. It was not yet dawn.

The nurse left her, a cursory request made that should she go to the toilet and take the small dish with her so they could monitor the blood loss. Monitor blood loss? She would be monitoring *the death of her child*. Did they not understand that, or care? John and Ava, she was told were outside, but they could not see her yet. They said it was best she got some rest. But sleep did not come this time. Only memories of nightmares, of bodies crushed and bloodied, of flesh torn apart. The ache grew worse.

The first trip to the toilet filled the dish with blood which she obediently handed over to the nurse, who took it without a word. Another hour passed, another dish filled. That final cramp, the sheer agony told her it was the end. Again, the dish, and this time she could see the shape of what would have been, swimming beneath the blood. A dish to delight both Hweol and Tommy. The nurse took it without speaking, but soon returned with the doctor. They drew the curtains around her bed, and she tried to listen as he talked at her in a high-pitched voice she could neither understand nor follow.

The nurse thrust a leaflet into her hand and that was it.

It was all over. She could go home once a scan confirmed everything was indeed 'gone.' They wheeled her swiftly out of the ward as if desperate to get rid of her. John rushed over and held her before the nurse pushed her rapidly on. John and Ava following behind, unable to talk to her. The light shining in from a nearby window showed it was now day. More people were moving about the corridors. A clock indicated it was 9 a.m.

There was a pause in her ordeal whilst they stationed her between two heavily pregnant women, each awaiting their own more cheerful scan. Then she was back on a table, looking at an ultrasound showing an empty womb.

"All gone," said the doctor. "There's nothing left."

If he said anything else, she didn't hear it as she exited the room and was handed back to her husband. They were free to go home.

Home? Anger rose in her then. Yes, she wanted to go back. She wanted to destroy Hweol and everything he stood for. He had taken too much from her.

"Don't," said Ava, when they reached her flat. "Stay with me a while. You should rest. You shouldn't exert yourself. You've been through so much."

But Megan wouldn't listen. "I'm going back today whether you like it or not," she said, looking at John.

He didn't like it. She knew that, but he would go with her.

"I can't come with you," said Ava, "you understand."

Megan smiled. This woman would keep her baby and having explained how the Wheelborn worked, she needed to be kept free from its contamination.

"I'm so sorry you got caught up in all this," said Megan. "This is not your problem, your ordeal. There is no shame in remaining here. You have a child and a future to think about."

"I'll go to the police," said Ava, her eyes bright with tears.

"No," said Megan. "They wouldn't believe you. Even if they did send somebody, Hweol and Tommy would only show them what he wanted them to see."

"I have to do something," said Ava.

"No," repeated Megan. "You still have your child. Do nothing that will endanger either of you. Forget us. It's what I would do if I was in your position, if I was still a mother."

Her voice trailed off as her loss came back with full force. She ached with emptiness, but there was also rage, such rage and fury as she had never known.

Ava looked relieved as Megan absolved her of any further involvement, although she still appeared anxious.

"We will come back when it's all over," said Megan. "If we can."

"Can't you wait? Please. You must give yourself time to rest after what you've been through."

Megan shook her head. "There have been Five Turns of the Wheel. The sixth day is the day of the Dance. To stop it, to stop it all, we have to go back."

At that, Ava finally gave up and hugged them both. She pressed the car keys into Megan's hand. "Bring it back when you're done." Both knew that would probably never happen.

As they drove away, Megan turned and saw Ava watching them from her window.

"You're sure about this?" said John.

"They took my baby, our baby," said Megan.

She looked at his profile. His face was stern, set hard. He'd said little since they left the hospital, barely acknowledged their loss. Did he feel it as much as her? She had kept the truth of her pregnancy from him.

He nodded. Swallowed. "Why didn't you tell me when you first found out?"

She shrugged. She still wasn't completely sure herself. "I don't know. I didn't want to tell anyone, not until Tommy had gone. I felt it was dangerous for him to know. I was right." She shifted uncomfortably in the passenger seat. The chair was covered in old blankets to hide the dark stain that continued to send its coppery tang into the air around them. She opened the window wider. "Do you hate me?"

He reached across and squeezed her hand, keeping his eyes fixed firmly on the road ahead. "No. Never. Part of me always hoped we would escape Cropsoe one day. I knew things were wrong underneath. I think we all did, but no one was ever strong enough to do anything about it, to try, until your mother. All I know is that people—creatures—such as Tommy, Betty, and Fiddler have no part in the modern world. Wherever they go, they leave suffering in their wake. Too many have been sacrificed. My brother…"

David. He had been given to the Dance, but he would not be forgotten. What they would be doing on their return would not just be for their own child, or her mother, but also his brother, and all the others sacrificed over the years. The roads became horribly familiar, the fields and hills rolling out before them, a welcoming carpet of the rural idyll. Part of her wanted to stop the car and turn around, go back to Ava's, never return to this godforsaken land, but she knew she would be haunted by the Wheelborn until it was stopped, until the Wheel stopped turning.

"Where do we go?" asked John.

"Home," she said. Where else was there except The Five Turns? They would know. They would be waiting. Better to confront them directly. "But I don't want you with me. I want you to hide. Down in our cellar is best. You can get in there from the back car park. Tommy promised me to Betty. If he sees you, he might be tempted to…"

She couldn't bring herself to say the words. The three would kill her husband, of that she was sure. If not them, then Hweol would intervene. No, she had to go in as the grieving mother, the distraught daughter, the abandoned wife, the penitent.

"How do we stop the Dance?"

"I don't know, yet. My mother disrupted the balance of things when she took Ava's place. Promises have already been broken. If the promise of the Dance is also destroyed then Hweol will be weakened. The Mother is already unhappy with him. You can almost see it in the light over the hills. Look!"

John eased off the accelerator, stopped. Signs directed them to Cropsoe, Ashburn, Scything, but he ignored that. He followed the direction of Megan's finger. They stared at the grey shroud gathering over everything. It was midday and already the surrounding countryside was closing down. It wasn't even the grey of threatening rain or a coming storm. There was something else up there, a cloak of misery being cast across the landscape. It reflected her mood, to have lost so much in such a short time should have destroyed her but instead, it made her angry. Cautiously, they drove on.

The fury and determination to stop Hweol and his people kept the exhaustion at bay, allowed her to go on despite her weakness. She still ached, felt slightly disoriented, numbed, and that was all she desired. Grief was something to be delayed until she'd time to mourn.

They came to the crossroads that would send them back into the village. John stopped the car again. "Are you absolutely certain?"

"Yes, you know you don't have to come," she said.

Whatever happened needed to be a result of free will, not coercion. She did not want to feel guilt for what might happen to another human being.

He cupped her face in his hands, strong, firm, the expression in his eyes equally resolute. He kissed her gently. "I have a family to fight for."

She almost broke at that, could barely let him go. Somehow, she loosened her grip on her husband and allowed him to start the car and continue their return to Hweol.

CHAPTER TWENTY-TWO
THE RETURN

Not even a day had passed and they were back here, reeled in like fish on a hook, to be reclaimed by Hweol. *No*, thought Megan, *that was not going to happen*. The night to come belonged to the Wheelborn, and she would take it away from them, continue what her mother began with her subversion of the Fifth Turn of the Wheel.

Already the air was charged with expectation. Preparations for this day were a ritual in themselves. Unless you were Wheelborn, you stayed inside. To walk the streets was not safe even in daylight. The cries reached Megan's ears. The Ravaging had begun. Across the fields around the village she glimpsed flashes of silver, sometimes only a solitary spark, others a more substantial thread. The OtherWorld had freed the imps it bred, allowed its children to hunt in Nature's open canopy. They pursued and caught any living thing, fox or bird, ant or cow. All could be taken.

Megan was safe—in theory. It was possible Hweol had condemned her, but something told her any punishment would be in front of the whole village, public and spectacular. John, however, was in more immediate danger. The scent of him would already be dispersing across the village and out into the land. The imps needed only the tiniest of particles to latch onto their prey.

The distance between the car and the back entrance to the pub was short. Still, he could've parked closer. She glanced across the nearest fields, the stray specks combining into silver ribbons, a stream that flowed toward them, mercury rising.

Megan grabbed his hand and they sprinted across the car park. She held the key ready, prayed Tommy and the others had returned to Hweol and not the pub. Not yet, anyway. She had the key in the door, was turning, trying to turn it.

"I can't," she said, jiggling the key in frustration.

"Hey, steady," said John, taking the key from her. "You could jam it."

Megan stared past him, saw the poison lapping up against the hedge, threatening to spill over at any moment, heard the jingling and the howls of delight.

"Come and play, Wheelborn," cried the imps.

"Come and hunt."

"Let's play hunt the husband." Shrieks of laughter accompanied this last one.

"John," Megan urged.

A welcome click and John was through the door, pulling Megan with him, slamming the wood in the face of those who bore down on them. Howls of disappointment and annoyance accompanied this. The door trembled at the onslaught but it did not give. They would have to accept defeat. Hweol's silver children were not permitted to cross the threshold of any human dwelling unless invited. The noise subsided, yet Megan sensed their continued presence. There would be one left on guard.

Their sighting was a blow to their plans. Megan had hoped to present herself returning as a penitent child, broken by recent events, whilst John hid in the cellar, awaiting the moment they could use the element of surprise against Tommy. They should've known, the Weald always knew. Hweol, Tommy, they all knew. Knew the two of them were hiding in the dark, planning the Wheel's end. Nor would they come for them. All they had to do was wait for the couple to crawl to them. No, she would never crawl and never beg, no matter what they threatened.

"What now?" asked John.

She shrugged her shoulders. "We go up."

"Do you think they're there?"

Megan cast her senses around the pub, touched nothing, no other presence except an image from beyond, sent no doubt by Tommy. She could see the three running with the imps, a riot of blood as they slashed and hacked at whatever crossed their path. Fiddler was playing, his notes turning to black, poisonous darts shooting at the sky to slaughter the flocks startled from their roosts. Betty was roaring across stubbled fields, his dress swirling, ribboned hair flying. There was nothing remotely funny in this; it merely added to the horror. This dress was only ever worn for the rites of the Wheel, for those six days when life became a torment.

In other parts of the country, similar troupes would be visiting villages and hamlets as they had done for hundreds of years. Their function was to entertain, to mark the season; *their* Bettys were not monsters. Here in the Weald tradition had become distorted and bastardised as Hweol claimed it for his own, turned it to his own purpose, turned the Wheel. The three were intent on blood. Tommy's message was clear.

"You shouldn't have come back with me," she said, catching hold of John's arm as he headed toward the stairs. "They'll use you against me, hurt you, threaten."

John gave her a small smile, pulled her tightly into his arms. She buried herself against his chest, allowed the hand stroking her hair to soothe her, to enjoy, for a minute—the feeling of being safe and loved. "I know. But it's my decision. There is no life beyond here without you. I have no one, nothing else, except you and the memory of our child. If it all ends here, then I accept it. If what we do stops the Wheel, stops the slaughter, allows others to live a normal life, even at the cost of our own deaths, then so be it."

Megan drew back slightly then, looked him full in the face. "I used to think you were weak," she admitted, "that you were as enslaved to Hweol as the others. I was wrong. You have been my rock without me realising it. I've been so blinkered, so stupid."

He stopped her with a kiss. There was no more need of words.

As they parted once more, Megan felt herself blinking back tears. "I wish we had more time," she whispered.

John traced his finger along the damp track on her cheek. "Whichever way it goes," he said, "we'll be together. So you could say we've got all the time in the world."

Megan smiled, straightened herself up. "Right. Let's go and see what we can do."

They moved cautiously up the stairs, halting briefly at the cellar door to hear if anyone was on the other side, but there was nothing, only silence.

Stepping out into the bar, Megan saw nothing had changed. There was an emptiness, gaps left by her mother and father--she refused to regard Tommy in this light, still claimed Simon as her parent.

Grey light filtered in, broken sporadically by flashes of silver as the imps brought their hunt into the village. The howls and frantic cries of terrified animals pierced the walls. Family pets left forgotten outside by their owners as they barricaded themselves against the Ravaging were swooped on and torn apart. Larger creatures were claimed likewise, horses from nearby stables, the donkey from the paddock across the road, all were taken.

Megan didn't look out the window. She knew what she would see. Teeth and claws ripping and shredding with orgiastic delight, feeding on viscera, flaying flesh. All in the Weald, in Wheelborn, had witnessed it once they came of age.

"They will be preparing the green soon," she said. "Readying it for the Dance."

"And Tommy will come for his swords."

"His swords."

"He's cleaned them," said John. "They're ready for tonight."

"And if they're not? If they're contaminated in some way? What then? The swords might turn against their owner."

They sat in silence, considered the blades that stopped the Wheel turning for a year but always by claiming its price in blood.

There were five swords. Megan remembered the first evening when Tommy laid them out on the table and proceeded with the cleansing of the blades—as much a part of the tradition as anything else. Underneath that air of expectancy hanging over the village, she had sensed another layer, a layer of hunger. Not just of Hweol and the Wheelborn for its offering, but the hunger of the blades. Steel had not fed for a year, its edge blunted, starved of sustenance. It demanded its offering.

The swords had come alive under Tommy's caress, responding to the stroke of his hand as he burnished and oiled them as one would a lover. When he played their edges against the whetting stone, they purred in delight. Glowing, they had rested on that velvet cloth, content with their rebirth, alive once more, ready to play their part. At that point it was forbidden for anyone to touch them except for Tommy, Betty, or Fiddler—until the Dancers were chosen.

"Come on," said Megan, "let's get them. We might get an idea when they're in front of us."

"Couldn't we hide them?" asked John.

"No, they have a voice. They will be found."

Up to Tommy's room they went, the one he used to rest on that first night, to store the swords, to… She thought of her mother and pushed the image away. Now was not time. The bag, a thick, green canvas, lay on the centre of the bed waiting. *Not waiting for us*, thought Megan as she undid the ties that held the roll together.

Carefully, she pulled the heavy material apart until it was flat on the bed, its contents lying innocently before them. Immediately, a low hum filled the room.

"Do you hear that?" she asked.

He shook his head. "Hear what?"

She folded the cloth over again and the hum stopped. Then she exposed them once more, and it restarted. As she listened, the hum became more tangible, turned into words—a song. They were singing a song to her, and it was in the language of the Wheelborn.

"What," said John.

She raised her hand to hush him. Tried to focus on the swords, translating the old tongue, trying to understand. Whatever it was, she felt it compelling her to reach out and touch them, pick them up. The words became clearer as they spoke to the Wheelborn in her. Her arm was out in front of her, hand reaching forward, fingers stretching to the blade that was calling.

John tried to stop her. "What if they make you turn on me, turn against yourself?"

She understood his concern. So many spells were woven in this land that it was possible contact might turn her from wife to enemy. Hadn't she succumbed to the voice of Hweol once before? She had broken that enchantment with the part of her the Mother had allowed to keep for herself. She knew the Mother would do the same again, would guide and protect her.

"It's okay," she said, suddenly certain. "Everything will be okay." It didn't mean it would be painless. There was no certainty they would not suffer, only that the Mother was with them and things were about to change.

One hand curled around the walnut handle, melded to its curve. The wood felt warm, inviting, fitting her hand like a glove. Her other hand grasped the flattened handle at the opposite end of the blade, then she raised the metal in front of her. It shimmered and glowed, reflected her own face before others appeared, villagers she'd known who had died at its touch. Their death cries vibrated along the steel, travelled its distance and into her, humming their torture, screaming it louder as it reached her brain where the souls gathered and cried out for vengeance. It was overwhelming, their terror and despair, but she could not shut the voices down. Would not even if she could. They were here to help her.

Megan looked again at the blade. It was empty, reflected only her face. It no longer spoke. She placed it back on the cloth and did the same with the remaining swords until the air stopped humming and she carried the victims of the Dance in her head and her heart. The load was almost beyond bearing.

"Megan?" John was looking at her anxiously.

Again, she reassured him. "It's fine. Those swords are empty at last. Everyone who has suffered is here." She tapped her head. "I will hold them for now but tonight at the Dance…" She shrugged, unsure exactly what the next stage involved.

"That's it? That's our plan? To go to the Dance?" He was incredulous.

Megan wrapped the swords back in their cloth so the bag looked untouched.

"Tommy will not take the swords out until he's on the green"

"And?" John was puzzled.

"Steel demands blood and when it has been emptied, it needs that of the sons of Hweol, or of Hweol himself, to give it life again."

"I don't understand."

"When they sang, I learned how they were created. Tonight, we take them back to the beginning and then destroy the swords."

"Why not destroy them now? The furnace in the old forge is always going. The fire never goes out."

"The swords are the only way to get rid of Tommy, Betty, and Fiddler. We need to get rid of them first."

The way she said it sounded simple and straightforward, but there would be others there, even if they destroyed the three, who would try and stop the destruction of the swords. Tonight was for the Wheelborn, when Hweol brought the imps, the Lords and his Hunters, the Wyves to celebrate the Final Turn of the Wheel, the Dance. She looked at her husband. "I will be able to hold out against them more than you because we are kin. I will distract them, do what I can whilst you get the swords to the forge."

"But..."

"No," she said, more firmly. "Being Wheelborn gives me more time and strength than you would have against their spells. The Mother is with me, as are the lost."

John nodded reluctant acceptance. He reached out to her once more, but this time she backed away.

"I can't," she said in response to his hurt look. "In case I...contaminate you. I carry the souls of the swords. They would leave a mark on you, and I don't want to risk Tommy or the others detecting that."

He dropped his hand but moved as close to her as he could. They reached out to each other but did not touch. In their distance, they were as close as they'd ever been.

"So what do we do?"

"Go and pour ourselves a drink," said Megan. "I think some of Dad's special brandy would fit the bill."

John laughed. "Yeah, that's pretty powerful stuff. Why not? Eat, drink, and be merry."

He stopped as they caught each other's eye, full awareness and understanding of their possible deaths crashing in on them as it moved from the abstract to reality.

"I think I really need that drink," said Megan.

Together, in silence, they went back downstairs, took their seats at their usual table. There, they drank a toast to Liza and Simon, their child, and each other.

CHAPTER TWENTY-THREE
THE SIXTH TURN

Tommy ran. No, he didn't run, he hurled himself amongst the imps, delighting in the slaughter around him, the blood frenzy which would reach its climax that night. He didn't normally take part in The Ravaging, preferring to spectate, a benevolent observer. This time, however, he descended into its midst. The corruption of the Turn of the Fifth Wheel had enraged him, although Hweol absolved him of fault, said the women's sacrifice was enough. The Five Turns were for the villagers and the Sixth Turn belonged to the Umbrans. He would make sure they taught the villagers a lesson they would never forget. The Ravaging was a mere prelude.

The women betrayed him, his own daughter betrayed him, yet already he had wreaked some small revenge in that area. Her child. Did she really think a child of the Wheelborn would be allowed to breathe the air of the free world? He laughed aloud as he continued to sprint across fields plucking crows from the sky and wringing their necks, crushing rabbits and lambs beneath heavy spiked boots.

He'd spoken to that child in the darkness of its womb, instilled it with such terror, its heart had stilled and the blood flown. His own grandchild, yes, but there would be other children. After the Wheel finished its turn, he would choose another wife…or two. He thought of Catherine and smiled. He still had time, so much time, to reclaim what he'd lost in the past few days. For the moment, he wanted to cast off his worries, his plans, his future. He wanted to rediscover the essence of himself, to wallow in the bloodthirst of the Wheelborn, to delight in its traditions and rituals, to become as one with his family.

Silver streaks darted past him, gleeful in their slaughter.

"Come, brother," they cried, as he ran amongst them, "come and play."

And as he ran, Betty roared alongside him, eyes crazed with the wildness of destruction. His feet left craters into which imps fell and tumbled, but this only seemed to delight them. They whooped and hollered at his parting. They cheered him on as he cast himself amongst a herd of cows, wrestling the bull, their protector, to the ground. A flick of the wrist, and he snapped its neck. A small tug and the bloodied horns were in his hand. Then he turned upon the herd, used the horns to attack and eviscerate, stab and carve.

Imps hovered at the edge of his madness awaiting their turn to flay flesh, extract skull and bone. Hides and ivory all to be taken to adorn the site of the Sixth Turn of the Dance. Others collected the ravens, plucked their wings to be woven into ceremonial cloaks. All around him, he witnessed the industry of slaughter. In the distance, he saw Fiddler, sat on a gate, busy with his bow. The wildness of his music only added to the momentum all around them.

The song fired their blood, those who had any, stoked the flames of their deadly lust so the slaughter became more intense, ever wilder in its tribute to Hweol. He ran as the grey clouds gathered, ready to spread their smothering pall across this corner of their world. Darkness always came early on the sixth day, hiding them from the world, almost hiding them from themselves.

As darkness grew, so the veil would thin, and those of the OtherWorld not already there would soon step across and join them. The Sixth Turn was for the Wheelborn, for family. He could smell them on the air, his brothers, his sisters, his daughter. He gave a victorious cry. She had come back. She would not be forgiven. No betrayal would ever be forgiven. She would be invited to the Dance, her and that fool of a husband of hers. The only thing he regretted was having to break his promise to Betty.

The light dimmed, a sign to begin the gathering. He waved his hat at Fiddler who'd been watching his progress expectantly. On cue, the man played a different tune. One slower and more mournful. The pace of slaughter lessened and the imps gathered what they could and headed to Cropsoe. Behind them came the Wyves, hefting earlier remains into wagons brought by a few farmers, whilst old Fairbrother's ploughshare was set to work across the desecrated fields. Into the soil went blood and bone, fleece and hide, turned and turned again into the soil of the Weald. Nothing was overlooked, nothing forgotten.

The silver crowd milled around Tommy as they waited for Betty and

Fiddler to join them. The two appeared swiftly, blooded in the usual fashion, and took their places at Tommy's side.

"Welcome, family to the free skies of the Weald, the home of the Wheelborn. Tonight is the Sixth Turn, and to whom does it belong?" he asked.

"To the Wheelborn," came the reply.

"And what do the Wheelborn do on this night?"

"We feast," they cried.

"We drink," they shouted.

"We Dance," they howled.

At this the skies went black. As before a storm, the branches stilled and leaves ceased their whispering, the few birds remaining from the slaughter stopped their calls, the air around them fell away. The OtherWorld and the Weald had combined. Time had ceased.

Tommy turned and surveyed those around him. They had done well. Hweol would be pleased with their industry. They had a Dance to prepare.

"Family of the Wheelborn," he said. "Brothers and sisters, the hub awaits. The Wheel is ready for its final turn. Tonight is the turn that protects us all, that holds the Weald in serfdom to Hweol, that ensures our survival. Let us start the Sixth Dance. Fiddler?"

Fiddler plucked the strings and yet another song drifted across the valley. The notes twirled around the crowd, nudging them forward, nipping at their heels so the imps cavorted and jigged along the lane. Even the horses on which the Hunters and Lords sat pranced in time to its rhythm. Laughter and excited chatter accompanied Fiddler as the group made its way to Cropsoe.

Along the winding lanes they skipped, their voices rising to a cheer at the sight of the village as it appeared before them. Fiddler played them on to the green and continued to bow the strings as the imps prepared the site. Wooden stakes marked out the perimeter and silver creatures flitted in and out of these, weaving strands of willow to form the rim of the wheel, their work lit by braziers placed atop each stake.

In the centre of the wheel, the hub, a much thicker trunk, a monstrous trunk, was being raised with Betty's help. The colour of its wood was deep and dark, stained by the blood of the many who had Danced here over the years. The imps added to this, smearing it with clots of bloodied flesh, unreeling and hanging viscera from its peak to form a strange type of maypole. These ribbons when pulled out straight formed the spokes of the wheel.

Everything was almost ready. The spit fired up for roasting, barrels rolled into the circle but not to drink from. At present they were empty.

Tommy strolled around, allowed himself to feel the satisfaction of a job well done. The Wyves were weaving bone, creating Hweol's throne. It was almost ready. It was time for the Sixth Gathering.

Tommy signalled to Fiddler who bowed in return. The small man walked up to one side of the empty throne whilst Tommy took the other. Betty remained in the middle.

"Wheelborn, our time of renewal is at hand," cried Tommy, as imps and Wyves, Hunters and OtherWorld folk gathered around him. He could see the glitter in their eyes, almost taste the thirst that still sat upon them despite their earlier frenzy. They had not yet been sated. Neither had he. "We have served Hweol and the Mother, done our duty to the Weald, maintained the traditions demanded of us. You have all played your part and for that, I thank you."

"And Hweol thanks you." The deep lyrical voice wove its way across the green as its owner passed between the waves of silver, a clear parting of the seas opening up in front of him. The skull-crowned Lord of the Wheelborn took his place on the throne. Tommy kneeled before him. Fiddler stopped playing and bowed.

"This is the Sixth Turn of the Wheel," proclaimed Hweol. "It is the night of the Wheelborn and those who are our kin. It is *our* turn to Dance, and it is time for the swords to sing. Dance, while the blades are gathered. Dance for the Mother, and Dance for me," he cried.

The crowd cheered, some of its members taking up the ribbons from the totem in the middle as the others moved to the rim to form a wheel within a wheel. Fiddler struck up once more. Tonight would be the last time he picked up the instrument until another year passed. It would be a long rest, but rest Tommy knew his brother sorely needed after these six days.

The imps paced around the totem until they completed five turns, then they all faced the centre and bowed. Turned about to face the crowd and bowed again. Stood still as statues. Waiting, waiting, waiting as the stars shone softly on sleeping villages where the curtains were pulled against the dark and doors bolted against strangers. Even the soil beneath Tommy's feet seemed to be holding its breath. He grinned as he thought of what was to come, let them free themselves, let them have their release. A nod of his head and music erupted, a frantic rhythm forcing everyone to the dance.

All had a hand on tendrils, the shrivelling cordage of beast and man. Around and around, in and out they wove, pulled outwards, the strain showing as they tugged at the ribboned viscera. Chunks of the totem broke away and the central pole opened like the petals on a flower, the sides coming down and down. A song was filling the air, one of anguish and pain as the tendrils tied to the captive entombed in the trunk also peeled away at the body. Tommy recognised him. Old Fairbrother. The man whose dog he'd killed. He'd been found wandering near the border. That was dangerous. He was howling, much like that dog of his had done.

The pace of the music increased in time to his guttural agonies, the crowds joining in with his chorus of pain. Harder they pulled, began to peel him apart, stretching and stretching, dislocating, disjointing, releasing the blood which flowed into waiting vessels. As the body gave, the imps resumed dancing. Spinning around the hub until the man was ripped apart and his song ended. The Wyves gathered him up, draped his remnants at Hweol's feet whilst their children hung the ribbons around the willow weave. Woodsmen moved forward and gathered the peeled strips of the trunk, these would be rejoined and pressed ready for the next year.

The centre of the green was empty once more. The stained grass hidden by night's shadow. It almost looked perfectly normal. The Wheelborn drank and chatted in the interval. The night's entertainment would continue soon enough when Betty returned with the swords.

CHAPTER TWENTY-FOUR
THE MOTHER SPEAKS

Megan and John sat in the stillness of the pub, the only sound that of the *tick tock* of an old clock. They heard the music across the green, shuddered at the sound of the dying man, but they had not intervened. There was nothing they could do. Megan wondered what her husband might be thinking but closed her mind to that train of thought as guilt sought to immobilise her, deflect her from the path she'd chosen.

It couldn't be long. Someone would come soon and sure enough, she heard the sound of heavy footsteps crunching across the gravel, a stomping which could only signify Betty. Her heart sank.

The door slammed open and the monster appeared, still bloodied from the afternoon's exertions, smelling of sweat, reeking of death. He did not see them as they sat there, his mind focused purely on collecting the swords. The building seemed to shake as he marched to its upper floor. It was almost as if it couldn't take his weight anymore, was sinking beneath the mass of the mountainous Wheelborn. She watched his face as he reached the bottom of the stairs, recognised that strange light in his eye as the one she witnessed that night of her last meal with her father at Hweol's table. It did not offer hope.

Then he was at the door. "Come," he said, without looking or turning around. "You are expected."

Neither moved. "I know you're both there. I can smell you as surely as you can smell me. Noticed you as soon as I came in. Tommy's promised you'll Dance with me tonight."

"If you touch my wife…" John rose from his chair.

"No," whispered Megan. "There's nothing you can do."

"That's right, little man," sneered Betty. "There's nothing you can do except watch—provided you can still see anything after we're done with you."

Megan gave her husband another sharp look, and she saw the effort it cost him to push his anger down. "Hweol is waiting. He'll be angry if you delay."

Betty opened the door but stood aside. They were to go ahead of him.

Across the green, she saw the flames dance against the night, tongues and fingers of fire reaching up and reaching out. Megan had observed them from her window year upon year but had never seen beyond the shadows they threw. This would be the first time she had ever entered the circle.

The smell of burning wood tinged the air, added memories of bygone bonfire nights, but beneath that she sensed something more—a metallic bouquet, meaty, earthy, raw. Death had already visited the Wheel, and she wondered whose would come next. She glanced anxiously at John, but he kept his face set determinedly forward. False bravado that only served to deepen her fear for him.

Behind them, Betty crooned to the bundle in his arms, a mother singing a lullaby to her child. Occasionally, a little giggle would interrupt his song only heightening her imagined horrors even more.

They were at the rim of the Wheel, the willow branches patched with something she couldn't quite make out. Automatically, she and John reached for each other's hand, but they didn't quite touch. They didn't dare. The humming began. As they broke through into the wheel, the song she had absorbed from the swords started again, voices groaning in terror even as they cried out for vengeance.

Why are you afraid? she asked them, *when Hweol can do nothing more to hurt you?*

You think we only suffer in the flesh? Oh, there is another plane of existence, and the agonies there are inescapable. Destroy the swords tonight and you release us all. We will guide you but that doesn't mean we are any less afraid.

The voices dropped to a murmur as she took in the scene around her. The centre was clear but everything else was like an outdoor abattoir. Offal and flayed skin hung like bunting around the sides, the gathered crowd, the grotesques of the OtherWorld wore aprons of blood. All eyes turned on them. Giggles broke out from their ranks. Silver chimes of laughter and sly jokes. She was glad John could not understand their language.

Betty nudged them forward. "Time to pay your respects." He nodded in the direction of Hweol.

She heard John's sharp intake of breath. He had never seen Hweol properly before.

The antlered skull rose up on the dais, his cloak of freshly-flayed skin crimson in the firelight. The ivory mask covered most of his face, only the cruel mouth with razor teeth left revealed. As he stood, he seemed to grow above them, expand to blot out the stars. She could not take her eyes from his masked face. Only when a voice screamed behind her eyes was the spell broken, and he shrank back to the size she remembered. Glancing across at John, she was in no doubt he still saw him as a giant. She could not warn him.

Megan looked to Hweol's left, to where Tommy stood.

"Daughter," he said.

She offered him no acknowledgement.

"Perhaps I deserve such cold treatment," he said. "But, tonight we bring people together to re-establish the bonds of family and as we two *are* family. We will Dance tonight. He," he jerked his head dismissively in John's direction, "he is not family."

Small hands flicked out, imps grabbed John's arms, and they took him to the centre of the green where Betty was laying the swords out in a dazzling star. He made no sound of protest. An effort she knew was costing him dear.

"Seems you are the star attraction," said Tommy maliciously.

Walk with him, urged the voices. *Let Tommy sense our presence. He will think the steel still holds us. If you hang back, our voice will be fainter.*

Obediently, Megan followed, making it appear she was willingly participating.

John stood at the centre of the pentangle, his face white and tense, but he stood straight and proud, kept his gaze fixed on her.

"This is the time of the Three," announced Hweol. "My sons will dance and the swords will drink, and their strength will be renewed."

The air shifted slightly, and Megan felt as if she'd been transported to the OtherWorld. Then it shifted again, and she remained in Cropsoe. The veil was almost transparent tonight.

Ask him, said one of the voices she carried. *Ask about Her.*

"And what of the Mother?" said Megan. "Is this not Her time?"

"Of course, it is," said Hweol smoothly. "It is known, it does not need to be said." But he looked annoyed at this reminder of another's hold on the land and one greater than his own.

One of the Wyves stepped forward, plucked at the strings of Fiddler's violin, and a new song filled the air. Voices of the watchers rose up in repeated chorus.

"Kill Winter, Kill Dark, Kill Death."

To which the three responded, "We kill, we kill, we kill."

"Kill the Dark, Kill Night, Kill the Void."

"We kill, we kill, we kill." The triumvirate seemed almost hypnotised, their eyes glazed in a distant trance.

Megan found she was holding her breath as they reached for the handles of the rapper swords…close…fingers reaching out…almost there…would soon touch—provided they did not look into the blade's surface beforehand. Fiddler grasped his first, reached to hold the free handle of Betty's. Betty was picking his sword up, taking Tommy's, and then it was Tommy's turn.

A puzzled look flicked across his face as he lifted the knife, reached for Fiddler's to close the circle.

He feels the emptiness, said the voices. *Doesn't realise yet, soon.*

She watched Tommy's other hand, so painfully slow, stretching for Fiddler's knife, there, almost there, a fingertip touch. The hand curled and the circle was fixed, just as Tommy realised what had happened. He opened his mouth to speak but nothing came out.

Time for us to sing, said the voices, *let us be heard, release us.*

Megan opened her mouth and watched her breath curl away, wrap itself around the transfixed trio, spread to form spectral shapes, wraiths who wove in and out of the group. They drifted over John, murmured something she could not make out, guided him outside the circle, and no one stopped him.

"We danced for Hweol
And quenched his thirst
We danced for the blades
Were forever cursed

We danced for the Mother
As loving sons
We danced for the Weald
Gave our lives and blood"

As her song died out, others spoke from the air around them. "The swords are empty," cried one of the wraiths. "They need to drink. They need the blood of the Wheelborn or the Mother will be angry."

The swords twitched in the hands of the men, the handles forcing them to move, to turn and turnabout.

Hweol finally broke from his own trance. "No," he commanded, "they will not Dance. They do not Dance."

"Wrong," cried a woman's voice, and Megan realised it was her own, but it was not her speaking. "All Wheelborn are my children and all will Dance for me when I demand. Even you, Hweol. This celebration has become dark and cruel over the years, and tonight it will be Danced for the last time."

Hunters and Wyves, Imps and Lords murmured angrily, surged forward. They had forgotten the rule of the Mother, obeyed only that of Hweol. She did not command them—but they were wrong, needed reminding of the true nature of things, and She stopped them with Her breath. Sent whispers into their mind, showed them a life exiled from the OtherWorld, forced to live in the Weald as mere mortals—should She allow them to survive. Then She reminded them of Her power in Umbra and cast them images of it dying before them.

"Hweol tried to usurp me," she murmured, "and now my son, and you Umbrans, must learn and change." They stepped back, retreated further and further until the veil lifted and absorbed them once more, but they had not gone completely, would still witness what was to come. The Mother would deal with them later. Only Tommy, Fiddler, and Betty remained with John and Megan watching and Hweol transfixed by the power of the Mother.

"Take your place," said the Mother, "and sing for me."

Obediently, Hweol entered the circle, stood in its midst.

"The land needs your blood to kill Winter. What will you do?" sang

Hweol.

"We kill," sang his sons.

"The land needs your blood to kill Dark. What will you do?"

"We kill."

"The land needs your blood to kill Death," sang Hweol.

"We kill, we kill, we kill."

The swords twitched in their hands and the three moved. Spinning around, twisting and turning, circling Hweol, cat and mouse, steel teasing flesh. Hweol turned, trying to seek an escape route and failing every time. His sons tried to pull back whenever they closed in on him, but they were powerless.

Movement became faster, a blur of silver flashing faster than the sea of imps Megan had witnessed earlier. It was no longer silver alone; it was silver and crimson. Just a nick or two at first until the knives cut deeper, sliced into Hweol. As Megan watched, she remembered her mother and father, her unborn child. All those whose deaths had gone before demanded she witness this justice. John stared on, his face impassive. She could feel the emotion coursing through him as his hand gripped hers, safe to touch each other.

Hweol fell to the ground, and the Dance stilled. Tommy, Fiddler, and Betty stood, breathing heavily.

John and Megan stepped forward, pulled the knives from their grasp. The three yielded their weapons surprisingly easily. None appeared to register what was happening, their gaze fixed on the torn flesh and shredded bone heaped between them. The crowds in the shadow of the OtherWorld stood shocked and uncertain.

Carrying the swords in their arms, they wove their way between imps and Lords, Hunters and Wyves. One of these Crones caught Megan's eye as they retreated. A look that expressed no thanks, only pure hatred.

"They won't let us get away," said Megan, feeling a chill run through her. The sword hummed in her hand. It was one of those which had carved Hweol with its steel. Megan did not want to look but her eyes were dragged toward the blade. She saw mists shift to reveal red eyes, unmistakable eyes. She heard the voice she had hoped would be silenced forever. It started to speak, as the others had done, to drift up and into her.

"I am the Dance," said Hweol. "I can never die, can never be destroyed. The Mother will not kill Her only Son."

"No," said Megan, "but She will sacrifice him."

She pushed his presence away from her, forced it back into the metal which misted over once more. The Mother remained with her, was giving her the strength to withstand Hweol's final efforts. They ran along the lane toward the Forge, ignoring the doors which had opened, the villagers who came out to see the disturbance, who glanced uncertainly back to the green.

"The Dance," called out one. "Is it done?"

Megan didn't answer him. She couldn't answer him. Not until she saw the fire claim the knives would she know it was all over. It wasn't far.

"Megan!"

She glanced at John who jerked his head back to the green behind them. The Lords and Wyves, the imps and the Hunters had gathered and were following them, the horde radiating anger, its malevolence reaching toward them. Those villagers who ventured out, retreated back behind their doors.

Megan and John were at the Forge. What could they do? They entered and stood in front of the furnace where the fire continued to roar.

"What are you waiting for?" asked John as she paused before the flames and the mob continued to gather at their back.

She said nothing, stared at the metal in her hands. It was starting to sing again. This time it was no plea for freedom, no threat, just a simple lullaby. One sung to her by her mother all those years ago. Her mind flipped back to the time as she conjured up Liza's image. The woman so much younger and more vibrant then. It was an image she wanted to cling on to and never let go. The verses subsided but she remained in her trance-like state, buried in the past with her mother.

"Megan, for God's sake!" John grabbed at the knife, but she evaded him, stepped away from the fire. He looked at her and then at the knives he carried. Without another word he threw them into the flames and then made a lunge for the remaining sword. This time he was able to take it from her.

"No," said Megan, on full alert, aware of Hweol's trick and the time she'd given him, the *freedom* she'd given him to allow his spirit to enter her. "No, don't." She needed the knife to imprison Hweol once more, to get him out of her head. John moved closer to the fire. "No!" This time she screamed at him, but it had no effect. She rushed forward, felt the heat from the furnace blasting through the door. A wide door, big enough for someone to fall through should they trip. "No."

Hweol's voice was whispering to her again. Words in the old language, a ritual chant. *Daughter*, he murmured, *I told you, you would not be able to rid yourself of me. We are kin. We are family. And I will always be with you.*

She felt his presence probing her mind, rifling through her memories, seeking out the soul of her. Moving closer, ever closer to that darkness which belonged only to the Mother. Except the Mother wasn't there, only Megan and Hweol. Her arms were reaching out. Hweol didn't control her yet, she thought, relief flooding through her as her arms stretched out, the wooden handles close to her fingertips.

Reaching further, passing the wood, closing in on the metal which reflected the heat of the fire. If she had to, she would take the knife by its blade. Megan steeled herself for the cut but saw her hands. Both hands move beyond the knife. Up, up toward John as if to embrace him.

"John," her voice choked, and she suddenly couldn't say anything, felt only her body rebelling against her, taking commands from someone, something else. "John, I'm sorry, I've…"

"Megan?" Finally, he was listening to her. She had time.

The Umbrans were with them. Blocking out their escape from the forge, the coldness of their presence a stark contrast to the volcanic environment. They did not come closer. They kept their distance as if an audience at a play. Simply watched as if what would be would be.

Other words were whispered around her. The whisper grew to a roar, and Hweol's voice was called again and again, the noise pounding through her, naming her, claiming her. She tried again to speak to John but no words came out. This time he came toward her. He was bringing the knife back to her. Hweol was coursing through her, his essence pushing Megan's own spirit back into the darkness, burying it in a place, away from everyone, away from John. So that gradually the person who looked out at the man was not his wife.

Does he see the change? she wondered as she sank away from the world, becoming a defeated prisoner in her own body.

She could see him looking, trying to read her and then, yes, there was something. An understanding, a realisation. It froze him. That was enough for Hweol. The body that had been Megan's moved toward her husband, once more raised her hands to him but this time it was to push, a gentle nudge at first so he stumbled back toward the furnace. Then another push and another until he was up against the opening into the Hell blazing behind him. He dropped the knife and grasped either side of the brick cavity in a vain attempt to prevent himself from being pushed through. His screams ricocheted around the small workspace, the imps responding to his howl, who once more sang their poisonous silver.

Fiddler pulled out his violin, plucked at the strings. Sparks danced around them, fireflies zooming straight toward John. Pinching him with their sting, irritating gnats he had to swat away, had to lift his hands from the frame to fight them off.

One final push.

His screams did not last long as the flames devoured him, melting him, melding him with the metal offerings of the knives.

Betty took iron pincers and reached for the metal, pulling out their distorted and disfigured forms.

"We'll take them to our smiths," said Tommy. "They will be reclaimed."

As Betty walked past Megan, the buried part of her heard John's voice, his song of agony buried in the steel. Hweol had retreated for the moment, knowing she would follow her husband freely to the OtherWorld. Perhaps she had hopes of reclaiming him, and there were ways. It depended on how obedient she would be as a daughter.

The crowd parted. Imps danced around her as she followed Betty. By her side, one of the Wyves carried Hweol's bones.

"We will have a Dance in Umbra," cried Tommy behind them. "Hweol will be reborn, and Betty will be given a Wyve, a Wheelborn. Wedding and rebirth, the Wheel turns again!"

The Umbrans cheered.

Betty turned and grinned at Megan, dancing and skipping around her, skillfully avoiding the imps who imitated him.

Hweol remained silent. She sensed him conserving his energy. He'd shown her how he would be reborn, re-boned, and there was nothing she could do about it. She was a mere vessel until that end was achieved. It had all gone so wrong.

"Mother!" she cried aloud as she followed Betty. The Wyves cackled at the weakness of her voice, the pain it conveyed. That cackle grew into a torment as they walked through Cropsoe, taking the path which would lead them back into the shadows. They stopped.

The fires which had been left to burn themselves out and turned to smouldering ash, erupted again, becoming a wall of flame whose reach stretched out from Cropsoe, claiming the hedges lining the road they would take. To return to Umbra they had to walk through its blaze. The Crones eyed the fires nervously. The excited chatter of the imps hushed.

All backed away. All except Megan. She looked back at The Five Turns, saw the villagers gathered at its front, their numbers swelling as dark figures crossed fields and filled the lanes, villagers from the other parts of the Weald. Hweol remained silent inside her. The Mother was giving her this moment. She understood what was to happen. It was for her to take these interlopers away, back to their own world, and for her to create new rituals, kinder dances for the Umbrans to celebrate.

The Mother had not killed her son, but it was a chastisement, a reminder. Even the Mother would not break the bonds that tied her to her child. Would she be strong enough? Megan sensed Hweol, felt disgust, felt unclean at his presence. She would rid herself of him as soon as she could. John needed her. His spirit was trapped and must be freed. Yes, she could do this. She was a wife who would walk through the flames for her husband.

Betty? She looked up at the monster. She would think of something. The Mother would help her, she knew that now.

She was Wheelborn and could not stay in the Weald, not if she wanted to stop the Wheel from turning. She looked once more at the wall of flame and walked through it.

ABOUT THE AUTHOR

Stephanie Ellis' poetry has been published in the *HWA Poetry Showcase Volumes VI, VII and VII,* Black Spot Books *Under Her Skin* and online at Visual Verse. She has also co-written a collection of found poetry, *Foundlings,* with Cindy O'Quinn based on the work of Alessandro Manzetti and Linda D. Addison. A gathering of her dark twists on traditional nursery rhymes can be found in the collection, *One, Two, I See You.*

Stephanie Ellis writes dark speculative prose and poetry and has been published in a variety of magazines and anthologies, the most recent being Scott J. Moses' *What One Wouldn't Do,* Demain Publishing's *A Silent Dystopia* and Brigids Gate Press' *Were Tales.* Her longer work includes the novel, *The Five Turns of the Wheel,* and the novellas, *Bottled* and *Paused.* Her short stories can be found in the collections, *The Reckoning,* and *As the Wheel Turns.* She is co-editor of Trembling With Fear, HorrorTree.com's online magazine, and also co-edited the *Daughters of Darkness* anthologies. She is an active member of the HWA and can be found at https://stephanieellis.org and on twitter at @el_stevie.

CONTENT WARNINGS

Human sacrifice
Miscarriage
Implied rape

MORE FROM BRIGIDS GATE PRESS

Visit our website at: www.brigidsgatepress.com

Coming July 2022

Arthur, whose life was devastated by the brutal murder of his wife, must come to terms with his diagnosis of dementia. He moves into a new home at a retirement community, and shortly after, has his life turned upside down again when his wife's ghost visits him and sends him on a quest to find her killer so her spirit can move on. With his family and his doctor concerned that his dementia is advancing, will he be able to solve the murder before his independence is permanently restricted?

A Man in Winter examines the horrors of isolation, dementia, loss, and the ghosts that come back to haunt us.

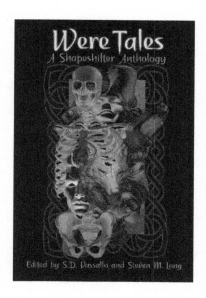

Available on Amazon

Werewolves. Berserkers. Kitsune. From the most ancient times, tales have been told of people who transform into beasts. Sometimes they're friendly and helpful. Sometimes they're tricksters, playing jokes on their hapless victims. And sometimes, they're terrifying.

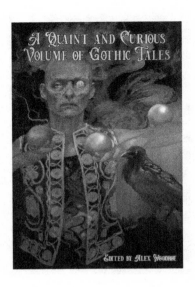

Available where books are sold

A Quaint and Curious Volume of Gothic Tales; 23 stories of madness, pain, ghosts, curses, unspoken secrets, greed, murder, and one of the creepiest collections of dolls ever. Ranging from traditional gothic themes to more modern tropes, this anthology is sure to please the reader…and send a cold shiver or two down their spine.

So, come on in; enter the parlor, find a place by the fire, and experience the beautiful, dark, and occasionally heartbreaking stories told by the authors. The editor, Alex Woodroe, has passionately and carefully curated a powerful volume of stories, written by an amazing and diverse group of contemporary women writers.

Available on Amazon

Sing O Muse, of the rage of Medusa, cursed by gods and feared by men...

From the mists of time, and ages past,
The muses have gathered; hear now their songs.

A web of revenge spun 'neath the moon;
A poet's wife who breaks her bonds;
A warrior woman on a quest of honor;
A painful lesson for a treacherous heart;
A goddess and a mortal, bound together by the travails of motherhood.
And more.

Listen to the muses, as they sing aloud...HER story.

Musings of the Muses is an anthology of 65 stories and poems based on Greek myths. The stories and poems, like the myths themselves, cast long shadows of horror, fantasy, love, betrayal, vengeance, and redemption. This anthology revisits those old tales and presents them anew, from her point of view.

Made in the USA
Coppell, TX
21 May 2022

78032954R10125